Wichita Payback

Wichita Detective
Book One

Patrick Andrews

ROUGH
EDGES
PRESS

Wichita Payback
Paperback Edition
Copyright © 2022 Patrick Andrews

Rough Edges Press
An Imprint of Wolfpack Publishing
5130 S. Fort Apache Rd. 215-380
Las Vegas, NV 89148

roughedgespress.com

This book is a work of fiction. Any references to historical events, real people or real places are used fictitiously. Other names, characters, places and events are products of the author's imagination, and any resemblance to actual events, places or persons, living or dead, is entirely coincidental.

All rights reserved. No part of this book may be reproduced by any means without the prior written consent of the publisher, other than brief quotes for reviews.

Paperback ISBN 978-1-68549-144-4
eBook ISBN 978-1-68549-143-7
LCCN 2022942378

*Dedicated to
Wichita, Kansas*

WICHITA PAYBACK

*I'm Wichita born and Wichita bred;
and when I die, I'll be Wichita dead.*

– Schoolboy chant of yesteryear

Wichita, Kansas 1947...

Before World War II, the city was a quiet center of commerce and a hub of American civil aviation. However, after the attack on Pearl Harbor by the Japanese, the city became a major manufacturing center for warplanes. People from all over the country flocked to Wichita for the jobs offered by Boeing and other aircraft manufacturers. The influx of workers was so great that it created a need for an entire new town. This mass produced community was dubbed Planeview and was built to house those workers unable to find homes within Wichita proper.

The wage-earners who toiled in the defense industry put in long hours. When their shifts and overtime ended they needed to blow off steam. Many of them played as hard as they worked, flocking to a plethora of night spots that sprang up in Sedgwick County during those heady days.

After the war Wichita continued to prosper and the healthy economy provided good lives for the city's citizens. Another aspect of those days were the "blue laws" that were on the books in Kansas. The state was dry, which provided a large and profitable market for bootleggers. Gambling was illegal, but bookies abounded in various locations in the less respectable areas of the city. Call girls found opportunities in certain hotels where visiting businessmen came to conduct commercial dealings with local industries.

Bail bondsmen operated within this underground vice trade. Some of these individuals were barely more respectable than their clients. Local cops performed arrests and interrogations without the hindrance of the Miranda Law or any other particular observance of civil rights. Wichitans living in this subculture had the same attitudes as the wild cowboys, gunfighters, and saloon gals in the old days of cattle drives. It was not unusual that many times local disputes among the lawbreakers ended in murder.

Enter Dwayne Wheeler, a slightly felonious private detective, who plies his trade on both sides of the law. Dwayne is on familiar terms with a variety of reprobates, leading him into extra-legal and risky capers, yet he has connections within polite society and law enforcement as well.

Chapter 1

It was seven o'clock on a warm spring Monday morning, and Dwayne Wheeler was beginning the work week in one of his frequent circumstances of financial distress. A series of unwise bets on the ponies were at the root of the problem.

However, to Dwayne's way of thinking, such predicaments were the spice of life. What could be more stimulating than continuously dealing with the consequences of bad or unlucky decisions? It made a guy's existence fairly spark with a sense of challenge, calling on quick wits and a subtle manipulation of other people through clever excuses and confusing explanations. At any rate, he always paid off his debts, even if a bit belatedly, thus he didn't have a reputation as a deadbeat.

Dwayne was at the rooming house where he rented small living quarters that sported a narrow bed, dresser and wardrobe. A miniature bookshelf was along the wall, holding some three dozen paperback books as worn out from being carried around as from being read. He had picked them up during his wartime service in Europe when inexpensive novels were made available to the troops. These books had exposed him to recent bestsellers, adventure stories, mysteries and even poetry.

A single sink with a mirror had been installed in one corner of the room, but for other toilet and bathing needs, he had to use the bathroom at the end of the hall that he shared with other renters. However, he preferred showering at the OK Barber Shop downtown near his office rather than use the house bathtub. At the moment, he was busy applying Wildroot Hair Cream for a quick combing of his thick locks before departing for downtown. The first order of the day was to either scare up some work or float a loan. The latter alternative was unlikely as he already owed money to his usual sources of financial aid.

At that moment, the last thing he wanted to do was alert his landlady Mrs. Busch that he was up and awake. She was a humorless large woman in her middle-years and would be wanting the coming month's rent of fifteen dollars. Unfortunately, all the money Dwayne possessed at that time was a single fifty-cent piece; and fifteen cents of that would be going toward the purchase of a pack of Lucky Strike cigarettes. He had already put a dollar's worth of gas in his car the night before, and he would need those five and a half gallons added to the one that was already in the tank.

He tiptoed across his room to the closet and opened the door to get his clothes for the day. He chose one of his two worn suits; the gray was a bit fresher than the blue and would have to do. After getting his brown oxford shoes, Dwayne went to the dresser to retrieve a pair of black socks and a white shirt fresh from the laundry. After quickly dressing, he picked up a battered satchel in which he kept extra underwear, socks, toilet articles and other assorted items of his lifestyle. Then he set his fedora on his head, and checked in the mirror over the sink to make sure it was at a rakish angle.

Now ready to leave the house, he pressed an ear against the door of his room listening for sounds of Mrs. Busch out in the hall. After a few long moments of silence, he eased out of the room to tiptoe down to the backdoor. He deftly slipped outside, and hurried to the street, turning in the direction where he had parked his car the evening before.

It took a couple of minutes to get the old coupe's engine to turn over, but after coughs of protest, it eventually began to chug heavily thought somewhat unevenly. Duane slipped the floor gearshift into first, and eased away from the curb, heading south on Estelle Avenue. When he reached East Douglas, he made a right turn and drove straight downtown.

DWAYNE WHEELER WAS TWENTY-SEVEN-YEARS-OLD, six feet tall with a slim muscularity, and had close-cropped light brown hair. His blue eyes betrayed his Anglo-Saxon ancestry, and the young man was considered attractive by women. However, he eventually turned them off by his lackadaisical attitude toward life, and lack of prosperity as well as his habits of gambling and drinking too much at times. Dwayne also had a slightly felonious side to his make-up that sometimes got him into unpleasant predicaments that most conventional females found unacceptable. And the fact he drove a battered 1935 Pontiac coupe was further evidence of his precarious economic condition. His profession was not particularly attractive either. Dwayne was a private detective.

Dwayne's boyhood while growing up in Wichita,

Kansas was fairly normal during his early years. His father was a barber at a large shop downtown and made a fair living cutting hair of well-to-do businessmen who had survived the ravages of the Great Depression. Mr. Wheeler, his wife and son lived in a nice house on Green Street just south of Kellogg Street. Unfortunately, this pleasant lifestyle came to an abrupt end when the elder Wheeler met his end under the wheels of a taxi cab. He had been more than a little inebriated on a Saturday night, and he stepped off a curb while attempting to cross a downtown street against a red light. This tragedy left Dwayne and his mother destitute and desperate. They went "on the county"—the depression era terminology for welfare—and life was tough. The boy dropped out of classes at Wichita High School East when he was sixteen and worked odd jobs to bring money into the household.

In 1940, at the age of twenty, Dwayne became a full-fledged orphan when his mother died from a particularly vicious form of stomach cancer that killed her in the three months between diagnosis and death. Left completely on his own, Dwayne enlisted in the small professional army of pre-World War II days, and the young man ended up as a military policeman at Fort Benning, Georgia. When hostilities broke out with Nazi Germany and the Japanese Empire in 1941, he was shipped to the European Theater of Operations. He was never in combat because of his MP battalion being assigned to such chores as traffic control in the rear areas, guarding installations, and transporting German prisoners of war to holding camps.

After VE day, in post-war Germany, Dwayne, who had carried his old habits of not making wise choices into the military from civilian life, became involved in various black market dealings in the chaotic atmosphere of the defeated German nation. He was drawn into the activity by his company executive officer Lieutenant Peter Van Dyke. Van Dyke was from a once wealthy New York banking family who had lost it all in the Depression. He had been forced to leave Yale University and go to work at whatever jobs he could find. When the war broke out, he was drafted into the army and was commissioned a second lieutenant in one of the short turn-around officer candidate programs. Van Dyke did not become an officer out of a desire to be a leader. Rather he looked upon the higher rank as offering more opportunities to score in schemes to advance himself financially enough to return to civilian life in grand style after the war.

Van Dyke chose Dwayne for the black market activity because of his assignment in the investigative unit of their battalion. It was an assignment where the Wichitan could develop leads to larcenous opportunities. The temptation to make a lot of extra money seduced this young man who had known such abject poverty in his boyhood. Bribery, outright burglary, and the transportation of stolen goods pulled him deeply into serious illegalities. Dwayne ended up getting caught in a deal involving the sale of U.S. Government property.

He could have ratted out Van Dyke, but ironically the officer had been appointed his legal counsel, so Dwayne wisely let him handle his defense since the lieutenant had as much to lose as he did if his part in the black market came to light. The charges against Dwayne were eventually dropped, but not because of any clever legal maneuverings by Van Dyke. He merely pointed out off the record that Dwayne could name names and cause a lot of embarrassment to certain factions in the civil and military governments. Consequently, worried authorities offered Dwayne a "general discharge for the convenience of the government" from the Army instead of a prison sentence. He wisely accepted the offer.

When Dwayne returned home to Wichita in early 1946, he decided to take advantage of the investigative experience he had in the military police and attempted to join the Wichita Police Department. However, he was turned down because of the less than honorable discharge from the United States Army. Since he couldn't be a cop, Dwayne decided to settle for second best, and applied for a private investigator's license. The Kansas state government, like many bureaucracies in those hectic days after the war, was harried to the point of acute ineptness, and he was approved as a PI without their discovering the truth behind his military service. He simply claimed an honorable discharge on his application form.

Thus Dwayne Wheeler became a licensed investigator with a seedy office in a rundown building in downtown Wichita. He moonlighted by manhunting for local bail bondsmen, running liquor for bootleggers, and acting as a bag man for bookies. But as of that moment, the door to his office was padlocked and his telephone turned off; all for nonpayment of rent and bills.

———

NOW, HAVING GOTTEN SAFELY AWAY FROM THE rooming house and his landlady's attention, he continued on his way to begin the day. He crossed Broadway where East Douglas became West Douglas and continued until he spotted the Jayhawker Restaurant on the north side of the street. In truth, the establishment was not a restaurant *per se;* it was actually a diner with a counter that ran the length of the narrow building.

After parking, he walked toward the eating place,

pausing at the door to look in. He could see Donna Sue Connors and the other waitress Maisie Burnett working behind the counter. He entered casually and gave Donna Sue a nod as he sat down.

Dwayne and Donna Sue had begun dating a couple of months before. The waitress was in her early thirties, making her five years older than Dwayne. She was country girl pretty with blond hair, green eyes, and light freckles. Although a bit plumpish, her figure gave her the look and sexiness of the quintessential 1940s "sweater girl." Donna Sue, although married twice, had no children and was an independent, somewhat audacious woman. She didn't expect much out of her relationship with Dwayne, and her main attractions to him were his good looks, sexual prowess, and the fact he took her out for good times on Saturday nights; all in that order.

She walked up to him. "Hey, hon, how're you doing?"

"Oh, pretty good," Dwayne replied.

"Mmm," she mused. "You combed your hair kind of careless like, didn't you?"

"I was in a hurry," he said.

"Mmm," she mused again with a nod. "And you need a shave."

"I'm going to shave and shower over at the barbershop."

"Okay," she said. "Are you ready for your usual breakfast this morning?"

"All I need is a cup of coffee."

She rolled her eyes. "Are you broke—again?"

"Nope," Dwayne said. "It's just that I ain't hungry. I ate yesterday."

Maisie, a short, plump blonde with a liking for men, walked by to turn in an order at the kitchen window. She giggled. "Sounds like things are back to normal."

Donna Sue's face assumed a look of exasperation. "Dwayne! What am I going to do with you? I'll spot you to a breakfast."

"I really couldn't eat nothing," Dwayne said dolefully.

"Oh, God, Dwayne!" Donna Sue exclaimed under her breath. "Do we have to go through this every time you're down on your luck?"

"This is only the second or third time since we met," he protested.

"Actually, it's the fourth," Donna Sue said. "Which makes me think this is going to be a regular habit with you."

Dwayne looked at Donna Sue with his blue eyes casting a humble glow. "Now, baby, you don't have to buy me nothing to eat." He tried to affect a heartrending expression on his face, but only managed to make himself appear as if he had a gassy stomach. "I ain't worth the sixty-five cents."

Donna Sue turned toward the kitchen window. "Number seven," she called out. "Eggs over easy, link sausages and rye toast." Then she added, "With French fries."

Arnie Dawkins the cook looked out the window into the restaurant. "Hey, that means Dwayne's here."

"Howdy, Arnie," Dwayne said with a grin.

"Howdy, Dwayne. I'll fix that right quick for you."

Donna Sue leaned toward Dwayne and whispered irritably, "It's a good thing you're cute, Dwayne Wheeler. That's all I got to say."

He showed a crooked grin. "You're pretty cute yourself."

Donna Sue smiled and winked, then turned to take care of another customer who had just wandered in.

When he was served, Dwayne ate slowly to savor the

meal. There was a good chance that he would not eat again until he returned to the Jayhawker the next morning. As usual he saved the French fries until last. That was his favorite food, and he preferred them even to hashbrowns for breakfast. After leisurely finishing the catsup-soaked spuds, he stood up. "I'll see you later, Donna Sue. I'm going over to the barber shop."

Maisie spoke up. "You already told her that."

"Mind your own business," Dwayne snapped at her. He didn't like Maisie because she went out on dates with customers even though she had a husband in the air force serving in Japan. He turned back to Donna Sue. "I'll prob'ly be there all day."

"Is your office locked up again?" she asked.

"Yeah," he said. He couldn't lie since he used the OK Barbershop, located directly across the street from the restaurant, as a substitute headquarters. That was where his father had once cut hair, and the owner Ernie Bascombe let him use the phone.

He went through the door to return to his car. After ample use of the choke, the old vehicle kicked into life, and Dwayne quickly whipped a U-turn over to the south side of the street where the barbershop was located. He pulled up a couple of doors down from the tonsorial establishment to park. After retrieving his satchel, he hurried toward his destination.

The OK Barbershop had plate glass windows on both sides of the front door displaying the name of the establishment in gaudy letters of red and blue. It was twenty-plus feet wide with six barber chairs on the right as one entered the place. Waiting customers shared a long wooden bench with a large coffee table holding magazines to their direct front.

Toward the rear, on the other side of the haircutting

area, was a working center for bookmakers earning their money through a trio of phones along the back wall. Beyond that were two doors; one leading to the restroom and the other to a showering area where soap and towels were available.

The gambling activity at the barbershop was an open secret in Wichita. The customers, mostly successful downtown businessmen who had prospered well during the wartime economy, went to the place for haircuts because of its risqué reputation. They got secret thrills from being in the company of "bad guys," and put down a few bets themselves now and then. The results from the various tracks around the country came over a short-wave radio, and each announcement of the wins, places and shows caused a muted silence to settle over the place as the bettors settled into a collective hopeful mood. Most of the time it was the bookmakers who were able to grin happily at the results. The Wichita police left the shop alone as long as the gambling did not become too apparent.

Ernie Bascombe, the bald chubby owner, was at his first chair as usual when Dwayne walked into the place. He looked up from his haircutting, waving his scissors in greeting. "Hey, Dwayne. How're you doing?"

Dwayne responded, "I need a shower. On the cuff, okay?"

"Sure," Ernie said. "You know where the soap and towels are."

"I brought my own," Dwayne said.

"Hey," Ernie said as an afterthought. "Did you hear about Stubb Durham? He got killed last night."

"No shit?" Dwayne said. "What happened?"

"Somebody shot him," Ernie said. "Longshot's back at the phones. He said he wanted to talk to you if you came in this morning. I think it's got something to do with Stubb."

Dwayne walked toward the rear of the shop where a couple of bookies by the names of Longshot Jackson and Ollie Krask lounged in chairs next to the phones. Longshot Jackson, so called for his propensity of pushing horses with long odds on his customers, was a slim, short, crafty looking man who dressed in a dapper manner, favoring zoot suit styles with broad-brimmed hats, jackets with pads in the shoulders, and pegged trousers. A carefully shaven, pencil-thin moustache amplified his rather wily appearance, and there were noticeable bags under his constantly shifting eyes. He turned his uneven gaze on Dwayne as he walked up

"Did ya hear about Stubb?"

"Yeah. Ernie just told me."

Ollie Krask, an extremely corpulent man, had his own reinforced chair that no one else was allowed to use. He spoke in a bubbly baritone. "Godamn shame," he said after swallowing a hunk of Tootsie Roll he was chewing.

"The shame," Longshot said, "is that them flatfeet have already stopped looking into it."

Ollie snuffled. "They don't give a shit about a poor dead bookie. Good riddance is what they think."

"Stubb was a good guy," Longshot said. "We want to find out who shot him. So listen, Dwayne, about a half dozen of us kicked in to hire you to do an investigation. What's your going rate?"

Dwayne, who didn't actually have a going rate, was generally happy to take whatever was offered for his services. He shrugged and replied. "Twenty-five bucks a day and expenses."

"Fuck a whole bunch of expenses," Longshot said. "We'll pay you a straight twenty-five bucks a day."

Dwayne's only real expense would be eighteen-cent a gallon gasoline. He agreed to the terms. "Okay. Twenty-five dollars a day. I want a hunnerd in advance."

Longshot reached into his shirt pocket and pulled out some bills. After counting out a hundred dollars, he handed them over. "When do you start?"

"At noon today," Dwayne answered, taking the money. "I got to get my office and phone back."

"All right then," Longshot said. "But we want reg'lar reports, see? At least ever' two or three days."

"And don't drag your feet," Ollie warned him. "There's a limit to our patience as well as our money."

"I understand," Dwayne said. "Well, I'm going into the back to shit, shower and shave, then I'll visit good ol' Bell Telephone to settle up then trot over to my landlord at the Snodgrass Building."

―――

By a quarter to noon, Dwayne had paid off his telephone bill, settled his meal tab with Donna Sue, and looked up the three guys he owed money to pay off the loans. After that he turned to having his office reopened. His landlord Twig Clanton, who owned three of the most rundown buildings in downtown Wichita, led the newly funded private detective up to the second floor. They stopped at a door with a hand painted plywood sign nailed to it. Dwayne had done it himself using a stencil sheet of letters.

DWAYNE WHEELER
PRIVATE INVESTIGATOR
CONFIDENTIAL SERVICES

The fact that outside hasps were on the doors of all the offices in the run-down edifice gave stark evidence of the monetary unreliability of Clanton's tenants. He undid the padlock and pulled it off. "The phone guy was downstairs at the switchboard and turned you back on."

"Thanks, Twig," Dwayne said. "Maybe I can go six months before you lock me out again."

"Try to do six weeks and I'll be happy," Clanton said. The man was reputed to be extremely rich and had donated a lot of money to various Wichita charities over the years, but he ran his business with a miserly tightness. He pocketed the padlock and walked back toward the stairs to descend to his own office on the first floor.

Dwayne stepped into his agency and took a deep breath of the musty air before opening a window. The only furniture he had was a battered secondhand desk with mismatched chairs; one behind for him, and another in the front for the rare client who might walk in needing his services. Dwayne went to the phone and picked it up, pleased to hear the buzzing sound of a live instrument. After sitting down, he stuck his finger in the dial and turned out a number he knew by heart.

"Homicide," came a voice on the other end.

"Is that you, Gallagher?" Dwayne asked.

"*Sergeant* Gallagher to you, shamus," scolded the other man who recognized the caller's voice.

"Get me Ben Forester, *Sergeant* Gallagher."

A few moments later another voice came on the line. "Hey, Dwayne. What's up?"

"I got no information for you today," Dwayne said, who kept Forester up to date on happenings on the street. "But I'd like some from you for a change. What's the story on Stubb Durham's murder?"

"The guy got himself shot," Detective Sergeant Ben Forester replied. "That's the story."

"Some of his ol' buddies are under the impression that you cops don't particularly care about what happened," Dwayne said. "They hired me to look into the case."

Forester's voice lowered to almost a whisper. "Take some advice, Dwayne. Keep your nose out of that business. It looks like somebody very important wants it swept under the rug."

"I'm getting paid for this, Ben," Dwayne said. "I need the money."

"I can't help you."

Dwayne sighed, knowing better than to press the issue. "Okay. Thanks just the same."

He hung up the phone and leaned back in his chair. He had at least hoped to get a copy of the police report on the killing. After a moment he remembered another source and got to his feet and left the office. He drove to the corner of Market and William where the Wichita Eagle Building was located. The *Wichita Eagle* and the *Wichita Beacon* newspapers served the city with both morning and evening editions. Dwayne was good friends with Bud Terwilliger the police reporter on the *Eagle*.

Dwayne went up to the second floor where the editorial offices were located and was glad to see Bud hunched over his typewriter at his desk. Bud, like Dwayne, was a war veteran, but he had been in combat as a marine infantryman and was seriously wounded in the Pacific Campaign. He walked with a limp, drank a lot, and was a crack crime journalist. He gave Dwayne a grin.

"What's going on, ol' buddy?"

Dwayne grabbed an empty chair and pulled it up. After plopping down, he said, "Stubb Durham."

Bud wordlessly opened a desk drawer and pulled out a

photograph. He handed it to Dwayne. It was a flash picture taken at night and showed Stubb sprawled awkwardly in death across a sidewalk with his jacket and shirt soaked in blood.

"Not much to tell," Bud said. "He was shot by person or persons unknown while walking from his car to his house at about two in the morning. *This* morning."

"I got it from good sources that the cops aren't real interested in this," Dwayne remarked.

"Prob'ly not. He was more'n likely done in by somebody that owed him money or that he owed money. All that bookie stuff is really undercover, and it's hard to find out things. That crowd doesn't talk much."

"It was bookies who hired me to investigate this," Dwayne said. "And that tells me there's a hell of a lot more to this than just what's floating on the surface."

"Well, you know all I know right now," Bud said. "But if I hear anything interesting, I'll clue you in."

"Thanks," Dwayne said, getting to his feet. "I think I'll make a personal call on the grieving widow."

"The killing just happened," Bud reminded him. "It might be a bit early to go over there."

"You're right," Dwayne agreed. "I'll wait until tomorrow morning."

Bud grinned slightly. "Yeah. That'll be a lot better."

"I'm hoping she knows something she'll share with me when she learns I've been hired by his friends," Dwayne said.

Bud pulled his wallet from his pocket and fished out a ten dollar bill. "Give this to her, will you? I owe this to Stubb from the third race at Hialeah last Sunday."

Chapter 2

The residence of the late bookmaker Stubb Durham was located in the northeast part of the city, close to the Wichita University campus. It was a middle-class neighborhood of homes that were almost fifty years old. They were roomy two-story frame dwellings built solidly by craftsmen at a time when ornate turreted Victorian gingerbread houses had begun to go out of style. The yards were slightly elevated above the sidewalks with cement steps leading up to the lawns and walkways to the front porches.

After parking his semi-trusty old Pontiac, Dwayne Wheeler made his way up toward the Durham house from the sidewalk. He stopped when he saw the rust-colored spot on the cement where Stubb Durham had fallen and bled heavily after receiving four lethal bullets in his body. The closeness of the neighboring houses meant the assailant had used a silencer on his weapon; otherwise, someone would have been awakened by the shots. Although Dwayne hadn't been able to obtain an actual police crime report on the incident, he guessed the caliber was probably a .22, and the ammunition had been hollow point to give a maximum of soft tissue injury. From the position of Stubb's body in the photograph Bud Terwilliger showed him, Dwayne figured the shooter had been to the left side of the house, which put him on Stubb's right as he walked toward the front door from the street. Dwayne strode over to where the killer must have stood in the bushes, but there was nothing unusual to note. The Wichita Police had been over the area thoroughly in their investigation of the incident.

Dwayne went up on the porch and pressed the doorbell. A few moments later a middle-aged lady answered the summons. She was a small and frail woman with gray hair, wearing a simple housedress and an apron. Her face was drawn and pale, and she said nothing to the caller, waiting for him to identify himself.

Dwayne could see the suppressed grief in her eyes, and he gave the woman a smile of greeting. "Missus Durham? I'm Dwayne Wheeler, and I don't mean to trouble you, but I'm looking into your husband getting shot."

"He was more than just shot," Mrs. Durham said in a low voice. "They killed him." She looked beyond Dwayne at the stained sidewalk, then spoke in a soft voice with a faraway look in her eyes. "I must get that cleaned up."

"Yes, ma'am."

The lady gave him a puzzled gaze. "Are you a policeman?"

"No, ma'am. I'm a private investigator," he said, pulling a flat leather pouch from his inside jacket pocket. His official Kansas private investigator I.D. card and a badge were on the inside. The badge was not state issue; instead, he had purchased it in a pawn shop to make his identification look more authoritative. "Longshot Jackson and Ollie Krask hired me to find out who did it."

Mrs. Durham showed no inclination to let him come into the house. "Why'd they do that? The police were here swarming all over the place. They can find the fellow."

"Well, ma'am, I hate to say this, but they're not showing much interest in the case anymore," Dwayne explained. "That's why Longshot and Ollie hired me. A couple of other bookies chipped in, too."

"Why aren't the police following up on this terrible thing?"

Dwayne shrugged. "I don't know. But I called a pal of mine who's a police sergeant, and he said that there wasn't an on-going investigation anymore."

Mrs. Durham opened the door wider and stepped back. "Come in, Mr. Wheeler."

He entered the house and she led him down a short entryway into the parlor. It was typical of the neighborhood with an old sofa and easy chairs circa 1920s. The curtains over the windows were heavy and fringed, and various bric-a-bracs and portraits were on shelves and end tables. Dwayne guessed the most recent photograph had probably been taken fifteen or twenty years before.

"Sit down, Mr. Wheeler," Mrs. Durham said, settling in an easy chair that faced into the center of the room.

Dwayne chose the sofa and took off his hat as he sat down. He pulled a notebook and mechanical pencil from his shirt pocket. "Can you tell me what happened that night?"

"Well, I was sitting in this same chair and listening to the radio," she said. "Late at night I can pick up Del Rio, Texas if the weather's clear. Or I can always find some late night music on KFH."

Dwayne hadn't started taking notes yet.

Mrs. Durham continued, "I always waited up for Stubb. It was a habit we had for years, I guess, and when he got home, we always went into the kitchen for cocoa and a little talk." She paused and took a breath. "So I was listening…" The lady lost her composure, but not in a sudden sort of way. She eased into quiet weeping, pulling a handkerchief from her apron pocket, and dabbing at her eyes.

"I'm real sorry, Missus Durham. I sure wished this hadn't happened. I knew Stubb and liked him a lot."

"You'll have to excuse me, Mr. Wheeler," Mrs. Durham said after a moment. She cleared her throat, taking a deep breath. "I was raised in this house and stayed until I married Stubb. The idea of such an awful thing happening where I grew up is hard to accept."

"Did you and Stubb always live here?"

"No," Mrs. Durham replied. "When we were first married, we purchased a house down on the south side of the city on Oliver."

"When did you folks move in here?" Dwayne inquired.

"It was right after the Crash of Twenty-Nine," the lady replied. "Daddy had a hardware store on Central and he lost it along with all the stock he had invested in over the years. It hurt his pride to ask Stubb and me to move in here. But if we hadn't, he and Mama would have lost the place."

"I take it your dad didn't approve of Stubb's being a bookmaker."

Mrs. Durham smiled sadly. "No. Stubb and me had to run away to get married down in Oklahoma. Daddy was furious…" She stopped speaking and turned to gaze out the window a moment before continuing. "We were married in nineteen-twenty-five. I was thirty…an old maid, I guess."

Dwayne could tell that the woman had wed beneath

herself from her manner of speech. It was obvious she had at least finished high school, and Dwayne knew for certain that Stubb Durham never got past the sixth grade.

She grew quiet again, and Dwayne experienced a feeling of discomfort creeping into his consciousness. He was beginning to sense her pain in a very personal way.

Mrs. Durham turned back to her visitor. "Daddy died in thirty-three and Mama passed away a couple of years later. Stubb and I have been here ever since." Then she added in a low voice. "We never had children."

"Can you get back to the night of the shooting?" Dwayne asked as gently as possible. "You said you was listening to the radio. Then what?"

"I heard some sort of pops or sharp clicks over from the side of the house. I was curious and went to the front door and turned on the light. I saw Stubb lying there on the sidewalk. Well, I ran out as quickly as I could." She paused for another sharp inhalation. "He was bleeding heavily, and his face didn't have any expression. His eyes were just...just staring up. I went back in and called the ambulance." She pointed to the nearby phone on a table in the hallway. "The Bell Company gives out free lists of emergency numbers for the police and fire and ambulance."

"Did you call the police?"

"No," Mrs. Durham replied. "But the ambulance people did, I guess. They came up here from Wesley Hospital. It's just down Hillside a ways, but I guess you know that. Anyway, ten minutes after they got here, a police car drove up. As soon as the policemen figured Stubb had been shot, they got on their radios. It wasn't long before two more carloads came. There were a couple of fellows from the *Eagle*. One had a camera and started taking pictures until the lawmen shooed him off. Then one policeman in a suit gave them an interview or something, and they left."

"What did the cops do after that?"

"They asked me some rather brief questions, then the ambulance fellows put Stubb on a stretcher and drove away with him," Mrs. Durham said. "When I asked where they were taking him, they said to the morgue and that I should have our funeral home call down there and find out when they could pick him up." She glanced out the window for a few more moments, before turning back to Dwayne. "We haven't had much to do with anybody dying after my parents passed away, so we didn't have a funeral home exactly. But Mrs. Stevenson next door told me what to do earlier this morning. She buried Mr. Stevenson about six months ago. I called the undertakers or morticians or whatever they were, and they said they'd take care of everything. So here I sit."

"Did Stubb have anybody that was mad at him?"

"Stubb always got along with everybody. But he did say he'd had a run-in with another bookie a couple of weeks ago."

Now Dwayne began scribbling in his notebook. "Did he say what the trouble was about?"

"Only that the other fellow wanted Stubb to throw in with some other bookies in some sort of a set-up, and Stubb didn't want to."

"Did Stubb tell you who the other guy was?"

Mrs. Durham nodded. "Arlo Merriwell. I've seen him a couple of times. I never cared for him much."

Dwayne knew Merriwell. He was a big tough unpopular guy who personally collected from deadbeat bettors rather than hiring enforcers like most bookies did. He liked to hurt people. "Who were the other guys in with Merriwell?"

Mrs. Durham shrugged. "I don't have any idea."

Dwayne replaced the notebook in his pocket and stood up. "Well, I'm obliged, Missus Durham. You've helped me a lot." He produced the ten dollars that Bud Terwilliger had given him. "This is for you. The guy that owed it to Stubb wanted to pay off."

"That was nice of him," Mrs. Durham said. "I can use all the help I can get."

"Some of the other bookies will prob'ly come over to buy Stubb's action," Dwayne said. "Do you know where he kept his lists of bets and customers?"

"I know where they're hid," she said a bit suspiciously.

"Well, they'll offer you some money for 'em," Dwayne said. "You should get around fifteen hunnerd bucks. Maybe as much as two thousand."

"That's nice to know," she said as she walked him to the front door. "And I hope you find whoever killed Stubb."

"I'll do my best, ma'am," Dwayne promised. He put on his hat, then headed for the street. When he reached his car, he got in but didn't drive off right away. Instead he lit up a cigarette and gazed out the windshield. The feeling he had experienced during the long moments Mrs. Durham stared out the window, returned suddenly. It brought back memories of his mother with painful clarity.

They had been living in a cheap hotel on East Douglas by courtesy of Sedgwick County, and his mother was employed in a large laundry a few blocks down the street. He could remember her walking to work in the winter, the thin coat she had gotten from the Salvation Army pulled tight around her. That was the most miserable time of his entire life, and even that culminated in more despair when she died so quickly after becoming ill.

Mrs. Durham must have felt the same awful shock

when Stubb was murdered. She was left alone with no children and Dwayne was left alone with no brothers or sisters. He recalled leaving the hospital that last time, going back to the small hotel room. He was too dulled by reality to weep, and he sat wide awake all night by her empty bed. When the morning came, he went to the post office at Third and Broadway where the army recruiter was located. Dwayne didn't break down and cry until a month later after he had been shipped to Fort Benning, Georgia. He was alone in a barracks furnace room taking his turn as fire orderly. Dwayne had just shoveled more coal into the water heater and had sat down to rest. It was then that the weeping came on him unexpectedly and the tears flowed as he sat there in that lonely place on a cold Georgia night, motherless and far from his Wichita hometown. The sobbing had gone on for a full ten minutes before subsiding.

Now Dwayne wiped at his eyes, then stepped on the starter while working the choke to get the Pontiac's engine going. He had work to do.

DWAYNE KNEW THAT ARLO MERRIWELL'S hangout was the Uptown Billiard Parlor on East Douglas. It was a block past the large Hillcrest Apartment Building that rose from the surrounding cityscape with the majesty of an Egyptian pyramid. The neighborhood was a combination of small businesses and modest homes and the large edifice always seemed out of place to him.

Merriwell had once worked out of the OK Barbershop like Longshot Jackson and Ollie Krask, but after a couple of altercations between Merriwell, the other bookies, and some customers, Ernie Bascombe gave him the heave-ho. Merriwell was now the resident bookie in the billiard room where he sat beside a pay telephone and took his bets.

When Dwayne approached the Uptown Billiard Hall, he did so cautiously. He paused just to the side of the big plate glass window in the front and took a quick peek inside. Sure enough, Arlo Merriwell was at his post beside the payphone, while the owner Delmar Watson manned the counter next to him. All seemed normal although there were no pool players at the moment.

Dwayne entered the place and Merriwell looked up at him with a scowl. He had no use for anyone who was associated with the OK Barbershop. Delmar Watson, who was reading the *Racing Form*, looked up and shifted the toothpick situated in one corner of his mouth to the other. "Hi, Dwayne."

"How're you doing, Delmar?" Dwayne replied. He nodded to Merriwell. "Hi, Arlo."

"What brings you uptown, Wheeler?" Merriwell asked.

"I haven't been over here for awhile," Dwayne said. "I thought I might run into somebody I knew."

Delmar laughed. "Well, you found two of us."

"Yeah," Merriwell said.

He was a large man, two inches over six feet tall, with a solid body that went two hundred and fifteen pounds. His hair was coal black as were the thick eyebrows over his cold eyes. His nose had been broken several times during a short career as an unsuccessful heavyweight boxer, fighting in tank towns in the Midwest. The few fights he won were by being able to take so much punishment that his opponents wore themselves out trying to knock him down. Most of the time the referees stopped the matches after Merriwell had been beaten so bloody and stupid it appeared he was close to death. His last bout was in Omaha where he actually punched the referee in a rage for stopping the carnage. He lost his pugilist license and was declared unfit to continue his boxing career because of both mental and physical causes.

The most unusual thing about Merriwell was his phenomenal memory. In spite of beatings in the ring, he could remember bettors, their bets and odds on the wagers without writing down the details. On the few times he was arrested, the police never found as much as a single scrap of paper on him indicating any type of bookmaking activity.

Dwayne walked over to the pop cooler and pulled out a bottle of Orange Crush. He came back to the counter and dropped a nickel on the glass top. "Who's been in here lately that I might know?"

"Nobody special," Delmar said. "Want some peanuts to go with that?"

"Sure," Dwayne said, laying down another five cents. Delmar handed him a thin cellophane bag, and Dwayne opened it, pouring the contents into the bottle of pop. He took a quick swallow, chewing the peanuts. "Quiet today, huh?"

"It'll pick up later this afternoon," Delmar said.

Dwayne glanced at Merriwell. "Want to shoot a game of eight-ball?"

"Sure," Merriwell answered. "Dollar a game?"

"You're on."

Merriwell got his own private cue from behind the counter and began assembling it while Dwayne walked back to the tables and selected one from the wall racks. When he was ready, Merriwell joined him.

The bookie won the lag for the break and positioned himself to start the game. He blasted the cue ball into the triangle of striped and solid balls. They split violently, bouncing off the rails, and careening around the table. The two and fifteen went into pockets.

"I take the stripes," Merriwell said, having a choice between them and the solids.

The game began with the quiet concentration of both players. Merriwell had a distinct advantage since he had his own cue that was built specifically for his style of shooting. Dwayne used a house cue but managed to play well. Merriwell won the game, sinking the eight ball after calling the pocket, while Dwayne had the three and six balls left. He dutifully pulled a dollar out of his wallet, laying it down for Merriwell to pick up.

They split the next two games, leaving Dwayne a buck in the hole. But he won the next one to catch up, while Merriwell took the fourth. Dwayne finished off his pop and peanuts. "You want something to drink?" he asked Merriwell. "I'm buying."

"Get me a Coke. I don't like that orange shit."

Dwayne went to the pop cooler and came back. "It's your break, ain't it?"

"Yeah," Merriwell said, taking the Coke.

From that point on they sipped pop between shots and carried on brief periods of quiet conversation. Then Dwayne asked, "Did you hear about Stubb Durham?"

"What about him?" Merriwell asked, lining up a shot on the nine ball in a corner pocket. He missed.

"He's dead," Dwayne remarked. He walked around the table to take his turn.

Merriwell didn't say anything for a moment, then mumbled, "Uh...who done it?"

"Who said anybody done it?" Dwayne remarked dryly.

"All right then, what happened to him, smart ass?"

"He got shot," Dwayne said.

"Then, godamn it," Merriwell blurted, "I'll ask again! Who done it?"

"The only guy who can answer that question is the shooter himself."

They each made a couple of more shots. "Yep," Dwayne remarked. "Ol' Stubb is dead." Merriwell missed on his next turn, and stood back.

Dwayne got ready to shoot, but hesitated. "I heard tell that you and Stubb wasn't getting along too good."

Merriwell's face wrinkled into a furious frown. He took a step toward his opponent and grabbed him by his shirt collar. "What the fuck do you mean by that?"

"Hey!" Dwayne said. "What's the big idea? Let go of me."

"Are you here as a gumshoe?"

Dwayne tried to wrestle free while saying, "I just heard you and him had an argument or disagreement."

"Are you trying to say something?" Merriwell growled. "D'you think it was me that shot Stubb?" He shoved Dwayne hard against the wall.

Dwayne recognized the danger he faced and responded by swinging his pool cue and hitting the other man on the side of his jaw so hard that the cue broke. Merriwell barely blinked. Dwayne was fascinated he could strike the man with all his strength with absolutely no physical consequences.

Merriwell immediately tossed his own expensive custom cue down on the table. He quickly grabbed another from a nearby rack and whipped it around at Dwayne's head. But the nimble private eye managed to duck, and Merriwell's assault resulted in the improvised weapon breaking against the wall. Dwayne charged forward and slammed the heel of his right hand as hard as he could into Merriwell's jaw. That was a punch he had learned as a military policeman, and it usually was enough to render the victim unconscious. Once more Merriwell only blinked. Then he attacked.

Now Dwayne was seriously worried. He realized he could spend the whole day pounding Merriwell on the head with pool cues, and the guy wasn't going to be fazed a bit. The private eye back-pedaled around the table, holding the broken cue in his right fist. He feinted and dodged, trying to keep Merriwell on the defensive. But the big bookmaker pressed on, taking some hard whacks on the head. Dwayne knew his only tactical choice was to wait for an opportunity to rush toward the door.

"Hold it, you son of a bitches!" Delmar Watson yelled, running up to them. He held a Smith and Wesson .38 revolver in his hand, covering the two combatants. "I'll shoot you, by God! You ain't tearing up my place! I mean it, godamn your eyes! You just try me!"

Dwayne and Merriwell stepped apart, each warily eyeing the infuriated man. "Take it easy, Delmar," Merriwell said with a hint of urgency in his voice.

A year before, Delmar had shot and killed a lowlife who had wandered into the pool hall and tried to stick him up. Delmar pulled out all the money in his cash box and handed it over. The guy grabbed the bills and rushed for the door. Delmar retrieved his revolver from under the counter, and followed him out to the street, running after him. He pulled the trigger twice, both rounds hitting the man's back. The guy sprawled to the sidewalk to never move again.

No charges were ever filed against Delmar Watson although he was chastised by the police for shooting a firearm in a public place. Fortunately the slugs, after going complete through the guy's torso, fell harmlessly to the sidewalk twenty feet ahead. That was the end of the incident, since Wichita did not impose limits on citizens when they protected their lives or property with firearms.

Now Delmar pulled back the hammer on the pistol. "And I want ten bucks from each of you for them busted cues."

In spite of Delmar's reputation for being a bit on the trigger-happy side, Merriwell was defiant. "You didn't pay ten bucks for any of your godamn cues. I know for a fact that you bought 'em second-hand in a big batch when Eastside Recreation went out of business last year."

"Then each of you cough up three bucks and lay it on the table," Delmar ordered.

The pair complied while keeping their eyes on the man who had thrown down on them.

Delmar continued, "Dwayne, get your ass out of here. And before you come back again, you look inside before you walk through the door. If you see Arlo, don't bother to come in. I don't cotton to have my pool hall turned into a battleground by a couple of shitheads." He would have run them both out to the street, but Merriwell paid him a fee for using his place to conduct bookmaking.

Dwayne tossed the remnants of the cue stick to the table and backed away. He watched both men until he was near the door, then turned and rushed outside.

Chapter 3

It was slow in the OK Barbershop when Dwayne Wheeler walked in after his busy morning of visiting the Widow Durham, tussling with Arlo Merriwell, and having a pistol aimed at him by Delmar Watson. Only two of the six barbers had customers to serve, and the others sat in their chairs waiting for walk-ins to appear. Ernie Bascombe, reading at his usual position nearest the door, looked up from a two-month-old copy of *Argosy Magazine*, and nodded to Dwayne. "How's it going?"

"Oh, I guess I'm managing to stay busy," he replied. "It's gonna take awhile."

"Well, I guess that's to be expected," Ernie allowed, turning back to his reading.

Dwayne continued toward the back of the shop to the bookies' bailiwick. He always avoided looking at the fourth barber chair. That had been his father's, and seeing where the old man had once worked, it gave him an uneasy feeling; something between nostalgia, regret and anger at his dad for getting drunk enough to stagger out in front of a speeding taxi.

Back by the three phones, Ollie Krask the fat bookie was eating a *Baby Ruth* candy bar, and he chewed it with undisguised pleasure as Dwayne approached him. Ollie quickly shoved the remainder of the bar into his mouth. "Making any progress, Dwayne?" he asked in a voice muffled by the hunks of chocolate.

"I'm learning a little bit," Dwayne said. He looked around. "Where's Longshot?"

"He's taking a piss."

Almost as if on cue, Longshot Jackson stepped out of the restroom. When he saw Dwayne, he hurried over to join him and Ollie. "Find out anything?"

"A little bit of information that might mean something or not," Dwayne replied. "Missus Durham told me that Stubb hadn't been getting on with Arlo Merriwell. Fact of the matter, she says Stubb was real upset about the way Merriwell had been acting lately. Merriwell was trying to get him to join some set-up for bookmaking."

"I've heard talk of that," Longshot said.

"That's news to me," Ollie remarked.

"It don't make any difference," Longshot said. "We don't need no organization no how. We're all doing fine on our own as individuals."

Ollie reached in his shirt pocket and pulled out an *O Henry* candy bar. "Merriwell's wasting his time. He ain't got a lot of friends among us bookies. That's why Ernie kicked him out of here. Nobody in their right mind is gonna join up with him in anything. I don't know why he'd even bother to try."

Longshot settled into his chair. "Maybe he's working for somebody else."

"They'd have to be somebody looking for a mean guy as an enforcer," Ollie commented.

"Yeah," Dwayne agreed. "Anyhow, I went over to the

Uptown Billiards to talk with him. We was playing eight-ball when I sort of asked him about Stubb real casual like. I said that I'd heard him and Stubb had been arguing about something."

"Whoa!" Ollie exclaimed. "That was kind of a direct way to talk to that mean son of a bitch."

"I guess it was," Dwayne said with a grin. "He tried to lay a cue stick up the side of my head. It made me kind of suspicious."

"Jesus, Dwayne!" Longshot exclaimed. "Were you crazy enough to get into a fight with Arlo Merriwell?"

"It just sort of happened."

"You may have hit a real tender nerve with Arlo by what you said, Dwayne," opined Longshot.

"Delmar Watson pulled a gun on us and said if we didn't stop fighting, he'd shoot us," Dwayne said.

Ollie laughed. "I remember about him shooting that hold-up man. He just might have pumped some bullets into you two."

"He invited me to take a hike," Dwayne said. "I think he took Arlo's side."

"That ain't no surprise," Longshot said. "Him and Arlo have a business agreement."

"I don't know why Delmar lets a mean bastard like him use his place," Ollie commented. "I suppose it's because the Upton Billiard Parlor being on East Douglas is kind of removed from the main action."

"Yeah," Dwayne said. "Maybe it was Delmar who shot Stubb. And Merriwell could be mixed up in it." He paused thoughtfully for a moment. "Well, I'm gonna see what I can dig up on Merriwell until somebody more interesting turns up."

"Both those son of a bitches is mean," Longshot allowed. "But it'd still have to be something pretty serious before they'd turn to outright murder. Such as a business arrangement that didn't turn out good."

"Maybe the two of 'em did have a reason," Dwayne suggested. "If I can discover a motive for killing Stubb, I'll be that much closer to finding the perpetrator whether it's Arlo or not."

"What the hell is a perpetrator?" Ollie asked, now fishing a *Butterfinger* out of his other shirt pocket since the *O Henry* had been consumed.

"I learned that in the military police," Dwayne said. "A perpetrator is the guy that done it."

"Well, Dwayne, we're counting on you catching that *per-per-trator*," Longshot remarked.

"I ain't gonna be working this weekend," Dwayne said. "So you don't have to pay me for Saturday and Sunday."

Longshot grinned. "You want to spend some time with Donna Sue, right?"

"I plead guilty," Dwayne said, looking at his watch. "I guess I'll wander across the street to the Jayhawker Restaurant and get me some lunch."

Ollie spoke up quickly. "Have 'em send me over four hamburgers."

"Do you want cheese on 'em?" Dwayne asked.

Ollie shook his head. "I don't want to make a pig of myself."

"I'll take a chicken salad sandwich," Longshot said.

Dwayne left the shop and jaywalked across Douglas to the restaurant. He went to the counter and sat down. A couple of minutes later Donna Sue came up to him after waiting on another customer. "I already put in your lunch order," she said, knowing that Dwayne would want his usual of a grilled cheese sandwich, French-fries and an Orange Crush.

"Send four hamburgers over to the barbershop for Ollie," Dwayne said. "And a chicken salad sandwich for Longshot."

"Right," Donna Sue said. "Does Ollie want them to be cheeseburgers?"

"Nope," Dwayne replied with a grin. "He says he doesn't want to make a pig of himself."

Maisie Burnett, who had been listening, interjected, "How could he do that? The guy already eats like a horse."

Dwayne frowned at her. "Don't butt into other peoples' conversations."

Maisie made a face at him, then went down the counter to wait on a customer.

Donna Sue looked at Dwayne. "Will you be able to take me to the club tomorrow night?"

"Yeah," he answered. "I decided not to work the caper this weekend." The couple regularly went to a place called Western Danceland on Saturday nights.

Some more diners walked in, and Donna Sue left him to put in the two bookmakers' orders, then turned her attention to the usual busy lunch crowd of downtown businessmen and workers that would be streaming in for the next half hour.

―――

It was early Saturday evening as Dwayne sat in the living room of Donna Sue's small apartment, leafing through a *Collier's* magazine. They had just had a quickie in her bedroom; what Dwayne referred to as a "Wham! Bam! Thank you, ma'am!" Now she was dressing after the brief lovemaking. This coupling was because Dwayne staying late after the dance was out of the question. Donna Sue had a strict landlord who did not allow late male callers in his female renters' rooms.

Now she was in the bathroom, primping for an evening of dancing to country western music, and the ashtray at Dwayne's elbow had several cigarette butts showing how long she had been taking.

He was attired in his sports jacket with rodeo pockets and shoulder patches. It went well with his brown slacks that were appropriate for a visit to Western Danceland. All he lacked was a Stetson hat and a pair of cowboy boots.

He looked up from the magazine occasionally, a little impatient with Donna Sue's habit of getting ready slowly for an evening out. He had to admit she could really make herself attractive once she had shucked her waitress uniform. She was constantly getting requests for dates as well as out-and-out propositions from the male customers who patronized the restaurant. Now and then he wondered what he would do if she decided to go out with another guy. Donna Sue and Dwayne hadn't exactly declared themselves as official steadies yet, but he knew he'd be crazy jealous if she did accept a date. He had to admit that Donna Sue Connors was somebody very, very special to him though he wasn't quite sure what it all meant at that point in their relationship.

Dwayne looked toward the bathroom door. "Are you going to be much longer?"

"A minute or two more," she replied.

DONNA SUE, LIKE DWAYNE, HAD A ROUGH LIFE AS a child after her father had deserted her mother and the four kids. Since Donna Sue was the oldest, she had to quit school to help her mother at her job of cleaning offices in downtown Wichita during those lean depression years. Saturdays were spent doing long hours of laundry and ironing. It was hard work filling their old washing machine with water, putting in the Rinso soap flakes and the clothes then turning the appliance on. When that part was finished, then came draining for the next load while soaking the clean duds twice in rinse tubs before running them through the ringer. Then they all had to be taken out and hung on the line outside for drying. After that everything had to be ironed.

The pay was skimpy, but between that and the cleaning job that paid fifteen dollars a week, Mrs. Connors managed to keep her brood fed and a roof over their heads.

Donna Sue had begun working at the Jayhawker Restaurant before the war when she was eighteen following her first divorce. She had married a truck driver ten years older than she at the age of sixteen. He had a bad habit of coming home drunk and raping her, smothering any notions that she had been carried away to some castle-in-the-sky by a prince charming. The lout wandered away and was never heard of again, and the divorce was a mere matter of paperwork.

She hated waitressing, but relief from the drudgery came after the December 7, 1941 sneak attack on the American naval base at Pearl Harbor, Hawaii by the Japanese Navy. She was able to quit slinging hash when the Boeing Aircraft Company published a want ad for workers in their Wichita factory, and, with the war time draft on, the manufacturer was hiring women as well as men. She wasted no time in applying for a position, joining the ranks of those working females who became collectively known as "Rosie the Riveter."

Donna Sue was a fast learner and impressed her supervisor enough for him to choose her for the company training program as a welder. When the short but effective apprenticeship ended, she was assigned to work on B-17 bombers. She was rated a Class A welder and was making a hefty ninety cents an hour with plenty of overtime. She had an advantage in that she could squeeze into small spaces to do her work. Eventually she became an inspector doing quality control of other welders. This was quite an accomplishment for a woman, and it was written up in the company newsletter. She saved a copy of the publication but rarely looked at it because of the anger and frustration it stimulated.

Donna Sue met her second husband at Boeing, who had been deferred from the draft because of his skills as a tool-and-die maker. They worked different shifts, seeing each other mostly on Sundays. The arrangement worked out well for their relationship, but one day she came home early because of a production delay, and found her hubby in bed with a neighbor woman. He and his paramour fled her wrath, and a divorce followed within a year.

When the war ended, Donna Sue was let go like all the other women at the plant. With jobs cut, only the men were kept on. All her hard work and accomplishments were wiped out in an instant. She went back to waiting the counter at the Jayhawker and was not happy about the unfairness of the situation. With very little education and no hopes for better employment, she developed a rather jaded outlook on the world. In truth, Donna Sue had no desire for a permanent relationship with a man; but that feeling dissipated a great deal after she met Dwayne Wheeler. He actually never tried to pick her up when he came into the restaurant, but she thought he was cute with his boyish handsomeness and charm, and always hoped he would ask her out. They ran into each other one Saturday night at Western Danceland when she was with her girlfriend Wanda Riley. A guy picked up Wanda, and Dwayne ended up giving Donna Sue a ride home. They made a date for the coming week, and going out together became a habit.

After a few weeks her feelings of affection for him were growing, but sometimes she felt it was similar to the fondness for a younger, somewhat irresponsible and immature brother.

———

WHEN DONNA SUE WAS MADE UP AND DRESSED up, she came out of the bedroom. Dwayne laid down the magazine, and looked at her appreciatively. She wore a dress she had purchased for eight dollars that morning at Buck's Department Store. It was a cadet blue whirl-skirt frock of rayon crepe romaine that showed off her figure from the way it draped from shoulders to be caught at the waist. Donna Sue knew that the skirt, although reaching to mid-calf was free enough to swing out while dancing to show off her shapely legs. Unfortunately, because of the shortage of nylon that lingered after the war, she had no hose to wear. Instead Donna Sue turned to her jar of stocking lotion, a creation rushed to the market as an answer to the dearth of silk and nylon. She rubbed the light suntan shade on her legs to give the look of "silk stocking glamour" as the advertisements promised.

"You're looking hot, babe," Dwayne said, getting to his feet. "I've never seen that dress."

"I got it this morning," she said giving him a bit of a smile.

Dwayne grabbed the sack holding the pint of bootleg

whiskey off the side table, and stuck into his inside jacket pocket. Thus, prepared, the couple left the apartment for the drive south down Broadway to Western Danceland located just across the city limits.

Their destination was a rough establishment typical of where the less sophisticated elements of Wichita society went to carouse. It was a large and wild redneck joint where music and dancing broke out occasionally during fights. It had been established soon after the start of the war by a rustic entrepreneur by the name of Jessie Pickens. He saw the need for a place where the less skilled war plant employees from Arkansas, Oklahoma and Texas could blow off steam with their peers. There was a killing every couple of months in the place when a couple of the dull-witted celebrants would take a drunken argument to the ultimate limits.

The parking lot was already crowded when Dwayne and Donna Sue arrived. He found a spot on the far outskirts of the unpaved, rutted area that could turn into a sea of mud when it rained. Donna Sue had to walk carefully across the rough terrain in her high heels as they approached the club entrance. The roar of celebration could easily be heard even at that distance.

There were no greeters when they arrived at the door, and the patrons were expected to find their own tables. However, they saw Benny Gordon one of the bouncers, and he walked up to say hello. Benny was an ex-paratrooper sergeant who had punched out a couple of MPs during a memorable three-day pass in Paris right after the war. Rather than being sent to the stockade, he had been given a "convenience" discharge similar to Dwayne's. In his case it was because he had been awarded the Silver Star for bravery in combat. The army didn't want the bad publicity of giving a genuine hero a dishonorable discharge.

"Hey, Dwayne," Benny said, issuing a friendly greeting and giving a wink to Donna Sue. Dwayne got him extra jobs now and then when somebody needed muscle for a specific project. Generally it was debt collecting for bookies.

"How do things look?" Dwayne asked.

"Pretty quiet now," Benny answered. "But things should liven up once the band starts playing."

"Who's the band tonight?" Donna Sue asked.

"It's the Kansas Kowboys," Benny answered.

"Oh!" Donna Sue exclaimed. "They are really good!"

After splitting off from Benny, the couple went around to the rear of the club to look for a place to sit. The usual loud, raucous crowd, made up mostly of tough-looking men and women, were well into that Saturday night's gala. Their manner of dress ranged from the type Dwayne and Donna Sue wore, to stags dressed in Stetson hats, flowery western-style shirts, jeans and cowboy boots. But most of the celebrants sported attire of tacky gaudiness as well as work clothing. This latter garb bore the names of the employers on the backs, showing that the wearers had jobs. These were the guys who attracted a lot of women. There was nothing these females enjoyed more than going out with free spending men with regular employment, and they showed their gratitude with sex to their generous escorts at the end of the evening.

After a couple of minutes of looking, Dwayne and Donna Sue found a place off to one side. When one of the rustic waitresses arrived at their table, they ordered set-ups of soda water. This was the method for imbibing alcohol in a dry state. The customers ordered mixes called set-ups in which to pour the bootleg liquor they had brought in with them. The various soda, tonics and others cost a dollar a glass, which went a long way in financing the payoff of the local law to stay away from the place. The only trouble with Western Danceland was that when a customer ended up knifed or shot in the parking lot, the publicity of the incident forced the sheriff's department to take extra measures. It usually meant being closed down for a couple of weeks.

"Hey, you two!"

Both Dwayne and Donna Sue looked up to see Jessie Pickens standing by the table. Dwayne had done several jobs for Jessie, mostly having to do with keeping tabs on his wife and seventeen-year-old daughter. Both females were more than a little on the promiscuous side, and the daughter loved nothing more than to go off with truck drivers. Mrs. Pickens was the sort to drink until she blacked out, then find herself abandoned in a cheap hotel or motor, wondering how she had gotten there.

Dwayne nodded to the owner of Western Danceland. "How're you doing, Jessie?"

"Business is good," Jessie replied. "Too bad about Stubb Durham. I hear you're working on the case."

"Yeah," Dwayne said. "The cops don't seem to care much about it one way or the other."

"You'll get 'em, Dwayne," Jessie said with a wink. "Well, have a good time." He wandered off to look for more regulars to chat with.

The band for the evening had not yet arrived, and the jukebox blared out an old Bob Wills tune that no one was paying much attention to. The interior was dominated on one side by a long, scarred bar where the patrons sat on scuffed wooden stools. A line of battered booths stood along the opposite wall on the far side of the tables, and there was a large dance area in the middle.

Dwayne and Donna Sue had just been served their set-ups when one of the patrons had decided to answer the challenge ritual of another at the bar. The encounter was short-lived as the challenger went down to ignominious defeat with the crowing of the victor in his ears. Benny Gordon, who hadn't arrived on the scene quick enough to break up the altercation, picked up the loser and pushed him toward the door for ejection. A couple of females at a nearby table cackled. After being regularly roughed up since girlhood by the men in the lives, they loved to see a male get a good hiding. It was almost as satisfying as doing it themselves.

A half hour passed before the Kansas Kowboys arrived with their instruments in tow. They immediately went to the stage and began setting up for the evening's show. There was no sound system at Western Danceland, not even a microphone for announcements. Benny Gordon went up and pulled the large, heavy-gauge steel screen across the stage, and latched it shut. This was the barrier needed when things were thrown at the band if unruly rednecks didn't like a particular song or objected to the artists' interpretation of some piece of music they had a special affinity for.

When the band was ready, they launched into their rendition of *Down Mexico Way*. Dwayne and Donna Sue got to their feet and walked out to the dance floor as others crowded the space to begin the evenings' program. For the next four hours—when there weren't any fights—the crowd waltzed, two-stepped and improvised through *Moon Over Montana, Red River Valley, You Are My Sunshine,* and everybody's favorite *San Antonio Rose* among others.

It was two a.m. when Dwayne and Donna Sue finally decided they'd had enough. Her feet, fatigued from waiting the counter at the restaurant all week, ached along the arches with sharp pains from all the dancing she and Dwayne had done. Because of her discomfort they walked slowly along the rows of cars back to Dwayne's coupe.

It was when they arrived at the auto that the incident occurred.

A man stepped out of the shadows and grabbed Donna Sue, clamping his hand over her mouth to keep her from yelling. Just as Dwayne moved to her rescue he was seized by two other men; one on each side. A fourth appeared immediately and hit him hard in the solar plexus. He would have fallen to his knees if the other two hadn't held him up. The guy continued to hit him fast and hard in the stomach and ribs. Dwayne, through his pain and disorientation, was aware he was being given a skillful beating; just enough to hurt without doing serious damage.

When the assailant finally quit, he stepped back and growled, "Lay off, shamus, understand? Or the next time you'll end up like Stubb Durham."

The headlights of a car driving down the next row lit up the area for a split second. It was long enough for Dwayne to catch a glimpse of the man who had been punching him; and he recognized the attacker as a guy named Billy Joe Clayton from Kansas City.

When the guys holding him let him go, Duane fell to his knees. The thugs disappeared into the darkness, and Donna Sue ran over to him. "Are you hurt, Dwayne, honey?"

He struggled to his feet, unable to speak.

Dwayne sat shirtless on the chair in Donna Sue's tiny kitchen as she held an ice bag to the part of his ribs that were the sorest. There had been no damage to his face, but his body bore several large bruises from the fists of Billy Joe Clayton.

"Maybe you should go to the hospital, Dwayne," she said.

He shook his head.

"You might have some busted ribs."

"Naw," he groaned, getting to his feet. "They didn't work me over that hard. This was just a warning."

"Are you sure you're okay?" she asked. He had been so badly shaken up that she had to drive them back to her apartment house with Duane sitting hunched over on the passenger side of the seat.

"I ain't gonna die," he said. "Let's go into the living room."

She held his arm as he walked slowly down the short hallway to her parlor. He carefully lowered himself onto the sofa as Donna Sue went into the kitchen and came back with an Orange Crush. She handed him the bottle. "What the hell was that all about?"

"Well," he said after a sip of his favorite pop. "It's got to be about Stubb's shooting. They mentioned his name."

"I heard them," she said, sitting down beside him. "It sounded like they want you to stop working on the caper." She had picked up the terminology from Dwayne who had picked it up from the *Sam Spade* radio show.

"Yeah. I would say they're upset about me getting involved."

"God, Dwayne! Can't you get in another line of

work? You're really a smart guy even if you do a lot of dumb things."

"Thanks," he said. "That gives me lots of confidence."

"Well," she said. "You're gonna quit this Stubb Durham thing, right?"

"Hell, no, I ain't gonna quit," he said.

"Then you should ask Longshot and the others for more money if you're gonna get the shit beat out of you."

Dwayne shook his head. "A deal is a deal." He took a deep breath and winced at the pain it caused. "By the way, I recognized the guy who had been pounding on me. His name is Billy Joe Clayton, and he's from Kansas City. He comes down to Wichita a couple of times a year."

"What for?"

"He works for an outfit up there in K.C.," Dwayne explained. "They're into various types of businesses. Like bootlegging and bookmaking. And hookers."

Donna Sue frowned in puzzlement. "I don't get it."

"I'm beginning to," he said. "Stubb's widow told me that he had been having trouble with Arlo Merriwell over that bastard wanting him to join some organization or other. Now that Stubb has been shot and I got my ass kicked by Clayton, I got it figured out. The Kansas City mob wants to move in on Wichita." He paused. "I got to talk to Ben Forester about this. It could end up being something big."

Dwayne sank into a contemplative mood, and Donna Sue remained silent as he pondered the situation. Finally he sighed loudly and looked at her. He smiled and leaned over to kiss her, letting his free hand slip into her dress top.

"Dwayne! Do you want to have sex after getting beat up like this?"

"Sure," he said. "What's that got to do with anything?"

"And you're not supposed to be here this late," she reminded him.

"Since I am here anyway, why waste the opportunity?"

Donna Sue thought for a moment, then relented. "Okay. But I have to wash my stockings off. I don't want that lotion all over the sheets." She stood up. "And you can't stay 'til morning. You know that Mr. Greeley will get upset and both him and his wife have already warned me once about you."

"Landlords or not, they should mind their own business," Dwayne complained.

"They have to obey the law," Donna Sue remarked.

As she walked toward the bathroom, he took a sip of his Orange Crush.

Chapter 4

Dwayne was still stiff and sore on the Monday following the beating he'd been given in the parking lot. When he left the rooming house to start the new week's work, he walked stiffly down the street toward his car, experiencing a good deal of discomfort; particularly in his rib and abdominal areas. His plans for the day were to make a couple of visits to the right people and places to obtain more detailed information about the activities of the K.C. mob in Wichita. It was conceivable that he would be able to link that troubling situation to Stubb Durham's murder. There was also the possibility that if Arlo Merriwell was the killer he might have done in Stubb for some reason not connected to Clayton or Kansas City. But at this point Dwayne thought it best to operate on the premise that the murder was involved in the potential takeover.

Because of the physical discomfort he felt, the private eye wasn't looking forward to climbing in and out of the small coupe during the course of the day. His first planned call was at the Harry Street Medical Arts Center just east of Hillside, but it wasn't for treatment of his injuries. All wasn't as it seemed to be in the complex, and his visit concerned the murder case as well as the Kansas City mob.

It only took ten minutes to drive to the intersection of Harry and Hillside, and he turned east on Harry, going down two blocks to his destination. The one-story buildings on the property were less than a year old, and still had a new-built look about them. Dwayne pulled into the parking lot, going to a space at the far side of the site. He took a deep breath, and opened the door, easing out of the small automobile. Dwayne gritted his teeth and slowly walked down to the last office in the building. The venetian blinds in the large picture window were drawn shut, but he knew there would be somebody inside. This was the clandestine communications system of an enterprise that operated twenty-four hours every day of the week.

He pressed the buzzer by the door twice, then gave a longer three-count push, followed by another quick two. He hoped the signal pattern was still in effect for entrance. Then he stepped back so that he could be easily seen through the peep lens in the door. In a half minute, he was admitted into the interior.

"Hi, Dwayne," Rachel Brooks said. She was a small, slim brunette in her middle-years, dressed and made up in a semi-flashy style wearing a red sleeveless blouse, yellow slacks, and high heels. She walked back to her chair behind the desk. "What brings you around?"

"Business," Dwayne replied. He eased himself down into a chair opposite her. "My business. Not yours."

Rachel was the telephone receptionist for Wichita's

number one call girl ring known as Venus Services. "That's too bad. We have some new talent you should try. Exotic war brides brought back from Europe and Asia. I suppose their husbands are having a tough time getting their lives restarted in civilian life, so the couples need the extra cash. Does that sound like something you're looking for?"

"I have a steady nowadays," Dwayne said. "Well, we're close to going steady, I guess."

"Good for you," Rachel said. She had been a call girl herself for several years, earning big bucks because of her good looks. But a serious car crash had left her legs badly scarred. Whores were required to be as unblemished as angels for their customers, even if some of the guys were overweight, sweating slobs. Rachel looked at Dwayne closely, noting he wasn't entirely comfortable. "Are you all right?"

He managed to both grimace and grin at the same time. "A guy told me to *shut* up, and I thought he said to *stand* up."

"Oh, Dwayne!" she said. "You've got to be more careful."

"I agree."

"Well," Rachel said. "Are you investigating something or other?"

"Yeah," he replied. "A bookie got shot dead about a week ago. I've been hired to look into the case."

"And you think we can help you?"

"I'd like to find out if anyone from Kansas City has contacted Missus Davies."

"I haven't heard anything," Rachel said. "Wait a minute." She dialed a number and waited for an answer. When it came, she said, "This is Rachel. I need to speak with Mrs. Davies." She picked up a pencil and idly tapped it on the desktop for a couple of moments. "Hi, Mrs. Davies. Dwayne Wheeler is here and he's investigating some case or other. He wants to know if you've been contacted by anybody from Kansas City...yeah...he just walked in...okay." She looked up at Dwayne. "She says she wants to talk to you. But not on the phone. She'll send Karl to pick you up."

Mrs. Davies' reaction surprised Dwayne. Evidently something unusual must have occurred. He had done some work for her in the past, but she never contacted him personally. In fact, she was pretty much a recluse. "Sure. That's fine."

Rachel turned back to the phone. "He's says okay... right." She hung up. "Karl will be by in twenty minutes or a half hour."

Dwayne settled back to wait. He had done a job six months ago for Mrs. Belle Davies that involved a would-be blackmailer who had arrived from out of her past. He was an elderly man demanding an inordinate sum of money to remain quiet about an incident he did not fully explain. Dwayne had used Detective Sergeant Ben Forester for help in getting a positive identification on the old guy. He turned out to be a former Hollywood press agent who had drunk himself out of clients and a good reputation. Dwayne acted as the go-between for Mrs. Davies, and it didn't take him long to figure out the geezer really didn't have much on her. Dwayne would have followed the usual protocol for such cases by beating the would-be blackmailer up, then run him out of town, but the poor old guy wouldn't have survived it. So he merely threatened him enough to scare him witless, and that was that. Mrs. Davies had given the efficient private eye a hundred dollar bonus.

While Dwayne waited in the office, Rachel got two phone calls from clients. She answered each with a cheerful "Hello! Venus Services. How may we serve you?" Both contacts had been from a bellboy who needed a couple of the girls at the Riverview Hotel before noon. Dwayne knew that meant out-of-town businessmen were wanting a little early action before heading out for the day's sales calls.

It was close to forty minutes before the coded buzzing at the door sounded. Dwayne saved Rachel the trouble of getting up by going to the peephole for her. "It's Karl," he said, opening the door.

A tall gaunt man with a mournful expression on his face stepped into the small office, wearing an old fashioned chauffeur's outfit complete with billed cap but without the leather gaiters. Even though Karl Lund was Swedish, his hair was raven black, and his brown eyes under the bushy dark eyebrows had a decidedly humorless appearance. When he spoke, his voice was deep and low. "Mrs. Davies is in a hurry to see you."

"Are you taking me to her house?" he asked incredulously.

"That is correct," Karl replied.

"Then let's went," Dwayne suggested.

Karl held the door open, and Dwayne limped through it over to the 1934 Duisenberg limo. It was as pristine as it had been on the showroom floor in Saint Louis when it was purchased brand new. Dwayne slipped into the back seat, knowing that the chauffeur didn't like anybody in the front with him. The big car's twelve cylinder engine kicked over, and Karl headed for the exit from the lot.

Mrs. Belle Davies lived on a secluded semi-country estate in an open area just past Thirty-Seventh Street in the northwest part of the city. The large two-story house was almost invisible from the road because of a high wall and tall trees. A narrow private road led from the street to a heavy iron gate that was always manned by a guard.

Dwayne leaned forward for a better view as Karl drove up to the gated entrance. The iron portal was instantly opened, and the limo eased through. Karl head down a gravel driveway leading up to the small front porch that was covered by an overhang supported by two massive granite columns. A butler was waiting at the steps and walked down to the automobile when Karl braked it to a halt. The man opened the passenger door, and Dwayne gingerly got out, trying not to show his physical discomfort.

The greeter was heavy set and had an expression on his round face as if he smelled something unpleasant. "This way, Mr. Wheeler. I am Carson."

"Lead on, Carson," Dwayne said, noting the man had an English accent. He was surprised the guy was wearing a business suit and bow tie rather than the normal butler's attire.

They entered the house, crossed a foyer and went down a short hallway to a door. Carson indicated Dwayne was to go through it, and he stepped into a waiting room. The butler said, "Make yourself comfortable, Mr. Wheeler. I shall collect you presently."

Dwayne was in a small but well-furnished parlor with a deep carpet. A rather large portrait of a young woman dressed as a flapper of a bygone era dominated one wall. She looked out from the painting with a semi-serious expression on her face as if she found her existence a lackluster, boring experience. Dwayne admired the lady's beauty for a moment, then sat down on a sofa to wait to be called into the presence of his hostess. He had never seen her before, but he knew quite a bit about her; or at least a little more than other people.

Belle Davies ran Wichita's most select call girl service. Her circle of friends, acquaintances and associates was small as much for security as for her penchant for privacy. None of the people who knew her was sure of her age, but she had been in silent movies before, during and after World War I, appearing in minor roles with such notables as Vilma Banky, Mabel Normand, Douglas Fairbanks and even Rudolph Valentino. No one was sure how she ended up in Wichita, but it was said that she had been paid off in a small fortune to get out of Hollywood because of some inside knowledge of the true cause of a famous personage's death. Others said that a wealthy man had died of a heart attack in her swank bordello in Los Angeles, and his infuriated widow had used her influence to get the madam run out of the state.

The butler appeared in the door. "Mrs. Davies will see you now, sir."

Dwayne followed him out into the hall, and farther into the interior of the house. Once more Carson stopped and indicated that Dwayne was to enter a room. This one was much larger and more elegantly furnished. A woman looked at him from where she stood beside a table on which set an antique classical bust of a beautiful Roman or Greek woman, the shoulders white and smooth.

Mrs. Davies offered a slight smile. "How do you do, Mr. Wheeler." Her voice was gracious and feminine but there existed a commanding tone in it.

"Hello, Missus Davies," Dwayne said, quickly recognizing her as the young woman in the painting hanging in the sitting room.

The beauty of her youth was still evident and because of her dignified appearance, she could demand respect with only the slightest of gazes. Her gray hair was not colored or enhanced in any manner and she wore it in the outdated mode of a flapper of the roaring twenties. Dwayne couldn't figure out why she chose that fashion other than it must have reminded her of an exciting glamorous youth. The dress she wore also reflected the 1920s although it was obviously newly-made. The garment had a plunging rolled collar over a net bodice, and the tight skirt went down to her knees. Dwayne noticed her legs were shapely and slender.

"Please sit down, Mr. Wheeler."

Dwayne waited while she settled on a settee, then he eased himself down into a plush easy chair. He felt as if he had stepped back in time. "What can I do for you, Missus Davies?"

"When Rachel called, she said you were interested if I had lately been in contact with anyone from Kansas City," Mrs. Davies said. "May I inquire as to the reason for your interest?"

"Of course," Dwayne said. He gave her a quick rundown on Stubb Durham's murder and the beating and warning he had received from Billy Joe Clayton. He summed it up by saying, "It looks to me like the K.C. mob is aiming to muscle in on the Wichita scene. I have a strong hunch the Stubb's killing may be tied to it."

"And what are your intentions if it is?" she asked.

"I'll figure out a way to find the killer, then stop them," he said, then added, "I have a certain contact within the Wichita Police Department. He don't want them guys moving into town either. Right now I'm pretty sure they killed Stubb and that they have some inside help from somebody in Wichita."

"Then you think it possible to thwart their plans?"

Now Dwayne knew she had received a threat involving her call girl operation from a person or persons in Kansas City. He nodded. "I ain't saying it'll be easy. But if I can dig up enough on 'em I'm pretty sure they can be stopped. Especially if I can hang Stubb's murder on one of those guys." He paused. "Right now a couple of bookies have hired me to look into this. But they could run out of patience if I don't produce any evidence. That means they'll stop paying me."

"How much are they paying you, Mr. Wheeler?"

"Twenty-five bucks a day," he replied in his guileless way. It would never have occurred to him to try to squeeze some extra money out of the lady if she wanted to hire him by exaggerating the deal he had made with the bookies.

"I will match them dollar for dollar, Mr. Wheeler," Mrs. Davies said. "And if they cease reimbursing your efforts, I shall then take up where they left off. Is that satisfactory?"

"Yes, ma'am." He cleared his throat. "I take it you want me to see that the K.C. guys get out of Wichita."

"That is exactly what I desire," Mrs. Davies said. "I will advance you five hundred dollars."

Dwayne was stunned, and it took him a moment to respond. "That certainly sounds fine to me," he replied. "It will be a lot of help. I take it that you'll want progress reports."

"You may make them through Rachel," she instructed. "However, due to the seriousness of this situation, I may require you to visit me here occasionally. Again, all arrangements will be made through Rachel."

"I understand, ma'am," Dwayne said.

She stood up and went over to a table, pulling out a drawer. She fetched some bills and stuck them in an envelope. "That will be all for today," Mrs. Davies said. "Karl will drive you to wherever you wish to go."

At that point Carson appeared to lead him back to the front door.

After retrieving his car at the medical center, Dwayne immediately headed for the downtown area. His destination was on Mosley Avenue north of Douglas where Elmer Pettibone ran his bootlegging business. He was the premier bootlegger in Wichita, and leased a small warehouse. The building was an operations and administration center. Bootleggers kept their liquor in various places; such as garages, basements, barns or other buildings in various locations. Wichita's warehouse district was perfect for incoming deliveries and brief storage before distribution to customers. Elmer also had a half dozen automobiles parked in the back.

When Dwayne reached the neighborhood, he went to a gas station to use an outside payphone. His physical discomfort hadn't gotten any better, and he once again had to ease his way out of the coupe, then hobble over to make a call. After dialing Elmer's number, he informed him of his intended visit. Bootleggers did not appreciate or receive unannounced visitors, even when it was a friend.

"Hey, Dwayne, is this important?" Elmer asked. "I'm kind of busy right now."

"Yeah, it's important," Dwayne replied. "But it won't take much time."

"Okay."

Dwayne hung up the phone, then limped back to his vehicle. He was beginning to think Donna Sue had been right when she wanted him to go to the hospital.

Steel shutters covered the windows of the bootlegger's headquarters, preventing anyone from getting a look inside. Dwayne knocked, and Elmer quickly opened the door. Dwayne walked in and went directly to the nearest chair and gently sank down.

Elmer gave him a studious gaze. "What the hell's the matter with you? You walk like you've got a corn cob shoved up your ass."

"I think I'd prefer that. Truth is, I got my clock cleaned Sunday morning over at Western Danceland."

"You shouldn't ought to tangle with them rednecks," Elmer said, going behind his desk and settling into a chair.

"It wasn't a redneck that done it," Dwayne said. "Billy Joe Clayton worked me over with a little help."

"The guy from Kansas City?"

"The same," Dwayne replied. "I guess you heard Stubb Durham got killed, right? Well, I've been hired by Longshot Jackson and Ollie Krask and some other guys to look into it."

Elmer, his thinning gray hair brushed straight back over his head, mentally processed what Dwayne had just said. The bootlegger was a tough-looking individual who was known for his pleasant personality, and was popular in certain crowds around Wichita. He got his illegal liquor from a syndicate in Dallas, Texas, and also dealt now and then with Oklahoma moonshiners. He pulled a Chesterfield cigarette from the pack in his pocket and lit it. "How come you're looking into it?"

"The cops have lost interest."

"Is that why you've come to see me?"

"In a way," Dwayne replied. "Has there been anything unusual happening where you're concerned?"

"Yeah," Elmer said. "I ain't got my usual delivery from Dallas yet. It's three days late. I called down there and can't get anybody."

"I may know why," Dwayne said. "It appears to me that the Kansas City mob is muscling in on Wichita. I have reason to think that Stubb Durham was approached to join up with them, and he refused."

"Okay," Elmer said, obviously deciding to reveal something. "Here's what's happened. Clayton got ahold of me earlier this morning by phone. He asked if I'd be interested in buying my liquor from his outfit." He tapped the ashes off his cigarette into an ashtray at his elbow. "And the price is higher. And I ain't stupid. The K.C. bunch have either bought off my Dallas source or leaned hard on 'em."

"This is all bad news for Wichita bootlegging, huh?"

"Hey, no shit," Elmer remarked.

"I've been hired to do another little task, too," Dwayne said. "There's interested parties that want me to bust up K.C.'s efforts. It's gonna be tricky setting them up for a fall. But it can be done. I have a good source of help and information on the Wichita P.D. to give me a hand. And I could use some help from you and your guys if you keep me informed of what's going on where you're concerned."

"No problem," Elmer said. "If you can't pull this off, Wichita is gonna have to cave in to Kansas City." He paused. "So. What's your next step?"

"I'm gonna find Billy Joe Clayton and follow him

around for a couple or so days," Dwayne said. "I need to get a handle on where he's hanging out and with who."

Elmer chuckled. "Damn! I hope he don't pick another fight with you."

"Did I mention he wasn't alone Sunday morning?"

"You better be careful anyhow," Elmer cautioned him. "He's one mean son of a bitch."

"There is one more thing," Dwayne said. "I'm pretty sure Clayton knows my car. I'd like to leave it here and use one of yours."

"I don't see a problem with that since I can't make any pick-ups or deliveries," Elmer said. "I've got a forty Ford two-door sedan you can use. Go get your car and drive it around to the back of the building. I'll open the door for you."

Dwayne pushed himself to his feet. "I'll be only a minute or two."

He left the office and limped a half block to the Pontiac coupe. Then he drove around the corner and pulled up just as Elmer pushed the garage door open. Dwayne drove into the building and pulled into an open space, then got out of his car.

Elmer handed him a pair of keys, pointing to a black Ford. "There she is. I keep all my cars gassed up at all times. Bring it back like that."

"Will do," Dwayne promised. "I'll keep in touch. You got my office phone number, right?"

"I've tried reaching you there before," Elmer said. "How's come you don't have a secretary like them private dicks in the movies?"

"Yeah, that's a problem," Dwayne admitted. He was thoughtful for a moment. "I tell you what. If you need to talk to me, call the OK Barbershop and ask for Longshot Jackson or Ollie Krask." He pulled out his notebook and wrote their names and the phone number on a slip of paper. "Here you go."

"Okay," Elmer said. "And you better be careful around Clayton. Just remember what I said. The guy is no dummy and he's tough as hell."

"Nothing in this life is easy, Elmer."

Chapter 5

It was a few minutes past one o'clock when Dwayne limped into the Jayhawker Restaurant just after the lunch rush. Maisie Burnett gave him a close scrutiny. "You're walking kind of goofy, ain't you?"

"I'd rather walk goofy than look goofy like you," he said.

The waitress, who knew he disliked her for some reason, sneered back, then turned to Donna Sue. "I'm gonna take a break," she said, walking back to the kitchen.

Dwayne sat down at the counter. "I'm ready for lunch."

Donna Sue shouted out the usual order for an Orange Crush, grilled cheese sandwich and French fries. From the kitchen, Arnie Dawkins the cook, yelled, "Hey, Dwayne!"

"Hey, Arnie!" he answered, looking at the Plexiglas box by the cash register holding slabs of pie. He pointed at it. "I'll take the apple."

Donna Sue wordlessly tended to the request, and then she crossed her arms and looked at him. "I can tell from the way you're sitting that you're really hurting."

"It ain't so bad," Dwayne said. Then he added with a wink, "It only hurts when I laugh."

"You could have some busted ribs, Dwayne. A doctor ought to take a look at you."

"I got better things to do with five bucks," Dwayne said.

She glanced out the window. "Where'd you park your car?"

"I got another for the caper," he said. "A nineteen-forty Ford sedan. From Elmer Pettibone."

"What's that all about?" she asked.

"I got some surveillance to do and there's some folks that know my Pontiac," he explained. "I left the old coupe with Elmer and he loaned me the Ford." He pulled a pair of sunglasses from his inside coat pocket. "I picked these up in my room on the way over here, so I won't be recognized." He looked around, then pulled the jacket open revealing his .45 Colt semi-automatic pistol in a shoulder holster. "This, too."

Donna Sue frowned. "Don't you get into any trouble!"

They were interrupted when Arnie announced the food was ready. Donna Sue fetched it off the kitchen window and set it down on the counter. Dwayne took a bite of the sandwich. "I'll tell you something," he said, chewing. "If I'd had this piece with me over at Western Danceland there'd have been four dead son of a bitches laying in that parking lot."

"I got a bad feeling about this whole thing or caper or whatever you call it," Donna Sue said under her breath. "I think you'd be better off just forgetting about it."

He picked up a French fry and pointed it at her. "Listen here. This is a big caper, and I got some money backing me up on this. Big bucks. Know what I mean?" He finished off the hunk of potato.

"So what are you going to do next?"

"I'm gonna find Billy Joe Clayton," Dwayne said. "He was the one that pounded on me."

"And how're you gonna find him?"

"I already thought about that," Dwayne said. "If I'm right about the K.C. mob's intentions here in Wichita, and if I'm also right about some of the locals helping 'em, I'll bet Arlo Merriwell is up to his ears in this shit. And since Arlo hangs out at the Uptown Billiard Parlor that's where I'll find Clayton sooner or later."

Donna Sue sighed. "And what're you gonna do once you find him?"

"Put him under surveillance," Dwayne said. "I want to find out where he goes. Who he sees. Things like that so I can work out some leads."

A couple of construction workers came into the restaurant, and Donna Sue went to wait on them. Dwayne turned to finishing his lunch then stood up and dropped seventy-five cents on the counter just as she walked up. "I'm taking off," he said. "Watch out the window. I'll drive by in the Ford. It's really a neat machine."

———

AFTER DWAYNE PARKED THE CAR A FEW YARDS east from the pool hall on the opposite side of Douglas Avenue, he settled down to watch the place. At first he thought about going up and peering through the plate glass window, but if Clayton was there and spotted him it would ruin not only that day's surveillance, but make any future work extremely difficult if not outright impossible.

He tipped his hat forward to keep his face in a shadow, and lit up a Lucky Strike. He smoked slowly with his eyes peering through the sunglasses at the entrance to the Uptown Billiard Parlor.

The majority of detective work is tedious, boring and time-consuming. This particular stake-out was no different and there was a good possibility that the rest of the day would be a complete waste. For all he knew Billy Joe Clayton might have gone back to Kansas City.

A trio of teen-age boys wearing Wichita High School East sweatshirts appeared from around the corner and went into the pool hall. Dwayne grinned at the sight. When he was attending the school, he used to cut classes with his buddies and go to that same place to shoot a few games. They did it at least once or twice a week.

A few more minutes eased by, and an old guy that he recognized as a friend of Delmar Watson's came out and walked slowly down to Hillside Avenue then turned and disappeared from sight.

Twenty minutes later Dwayne lit another cigarette. An elderly couple that he guessed were residents of the Hillcrest Apartments walked toward him, then passed by lost in conversation with each other.

After another quarter of an hour, the truant school boys came rushing out of the pool hall, heading for a car probably parked around the corner. Dwayne figured they must have played eight ball longer than they intended and were going to be late to their next class. The detention room at East High, a place he knew well, would have three additional internees after school that day. Another five minutes crawled by with nothing remarkable happening.

Then Billy Joe Clayton stepped out onto the street.

This was almost too good to be true, and the sight of the dark, squat hoodlum made him forget his physical discomfort for a happy moment. Dwayne watched him walking east down the opposite side of the street. He switched his gaze to the rearview mirror, tracking the subject of his stake-out. Clayton jaywalked over to Dwayne's side of Douglas, and he rightly figured the thug was going to a car. A half minute later, a Chevrolet pulled out from the curb and came down the street with Clayton at the wheel. Now Dwayne started up the Ford, and eased into the street to follow the Kansas City gangster.

Clayton went north a block on Hillside, then whipped east on First Street before turning south on Rutan Street. This took him back to Douglas, and now he headed east at a steady clip. As Dwayne tailed him, they continued on Douglas for several minutes until crossing Woodlawn Boulevard into a section of the city known as Eastborough. The private eye was surprised since this was where the wealthiest and most prominent of the local citizenry lived. He wondered what would bring a low-life into such a prestigious neighborhood. However, Clayton drove through the area, then turned north on Rock Road. They went a mile or so farther, before Clayton turned into a private drive that led to a gate.

Now Dwayne was really surprised. This was the Prairie Wind Golf and Tennis Club where Sedgwick County's *crème de la crème* came for recreation, exercise, dining and posh social events. He pulled over and watched as Clayton drove up to the gate. The mobster stopped and exchanged some words with the guard, then was permitted to continue on. Obviously some very well-to-do club member had invited Clayton as his guest. After a few moments of thought, Dwayne came up with an idea, and put the Ford into gear, driving slowly toward the entrance, coming to a stop.

"Good afternoon, sir," the guard said. "What can I do for you?"

"I have an appointment with a Mister…ah, a Mister…" He went through the motions of looking through his pockets. "I can't find the letter. It was an interview for employment."

"Oh, sure," the guard said. He pointed at a large building with a parking area around it. "That's the club house there. You'll find a door at the rear marked 'employee entrance.' You go through there and you'll find an office on your right. They'll take care of you."

"Thanks, buddy," Dwayne said.

He followed the directions exactly and within three minutes, was walking through the door as indicated. A sign on a portal to the right showed it was the bailiwick of the staff supervisor. He knocked and opened it.

A young woman sat at a desk, and she showed a friendly smile. "What can I do for you?"

"I'd like an application for employment," he said. "I'm a waiter."

"Who recommended you?"

"It was a gentleman by the name of Johnson," Dwayne lied, figuring there had to be at least one Johnson somewhere among the membership.

"Oh, yes!" She reached in a metal box on her desk and pulled out a form. After attaching it to a clipboard, she said, "Fill this out and write the name of your sponsor on the bottom. If you leave it here with me I can pass it on to the supervisor. He'll get in touch with you."

"Thanks a lot," he said. He took the application and went over to a chair. He sat down and began answering the questions. After a moment, he looked up. "Excuse me. Is there a restroom nearby?"

"Down the hall, past the kitchen on the left."

Dwayne, with the clipboard in hand, went out into the hall. But instead of going to the rest room, he stepped into the kitchen. A cook wearing a chef's cap gave him a quizzical gaze. "Yeah?"

Dwayne showed the clipboard. "I'm applying for a job, and I'd like to take a look around first."

"Sure. Just be quick and keep out of the way."

Dwayne walked along the stainless steel stoves and cabinets, acting as if he was checking out how things were done amid the bustle of cooks and waiters coming and going. Over in a far corner, a lone dishwasher worked at a sink, scraping dirty plates, rinsing them then putting them in racks to go through the steamer. Dwayne empathized with him; he'd done his share of the unpleasant job in local restaurants as a boy, sometimes grabbing leftovers off plates to eat before washing them.

When he reached the door leading to the dining room, he stopped and gazed out into the eating area. If he was astonished at seeing Billy Joe Clayton being admitted into the Prairie Wind Golf and Tennis Club, he was positively amazed at seeing him at a table having a mid-afternoon snack with no less a personage than Harry Denton. Denton, although having moved to Wichita in 1944, had quickly established himself as a local real estate executive, and was well-known among Wichita's upper crust. He and his wife Miranda were featured regularly in the *Eagle* and *Beacon* society pages and were members of several organizations dealing in charities and civic improvement.

Dwayne watched the pair for a couple of minutes, noting they were carrying on as equals in an informal, friendly manner. Now he had a third suspect to add to Arlo Merriwell and Billy Joe Clayton. In truth, this one made him more nervous than the hood or the bookie. To Dwayne's way of thinking, there are both tough and powerful men in the world, and Harry Denton was definitely the latter, making him a hundred times more dangerous that some brawler like Clayton.

He turned from the door and went back through the kitchen. He stopped at the girl's desk, thanked her and returned the clipboard after removing the application. "I changed my mind," he explained.

———

It was evening and Dwayne picked up Donna Sue at the restaurant as he usually did to take her to her apartment house. "Wow!" she said as they rolled along in the Ford. "This is a lot nicer than the old Pontiac. Why don't you buy one?"

"I probably can when this caper is finished," Dwayne said. "But I think I should wait until forty-eight. Detroit had to make military vehicles during the war, so they'll have to spend this year retooling to go back to making civilian cars again. That'll be the first chance to get a brand new set of wheels since forty-two." He was thoughtful for a moment. "O'course I read in the paper that the forty-eight models won't be much different, but the forty-nines are going to be sleek and modern with new styling."

"Dwayne, the minute you get your hands on enough money to buy any kind of car you better make the deal just as quick as you can. You and dollar bills don't stick together long."

He chuckled. "I can't argue with you on that."

When they reached the apartment house, he pulled up in front but didn't kill the motor. "I got some work to do this evening."

"Okay," she said, opening the door. "Will you be by later?"

"I'm not sure. I might be able to."

"If it's after ten o'clock, forget it," she said. "Mr. Greeley's been giving me those looks again."

"I won't be able to make it then," he said. "I'll pick you up in the morning and take you to work. I'll stay by the curb and honk so the old bastard can see I've just driven up."

"I'll be watching for you." She got out of the car and headed for the building.

Dwayne drove away, going around the block to head back downtown. He knew that the offices of Denton Commercial Real Estate Enterprises were situated on the top floor of the exclusive Hotel Riverview. The hostel was located where West Douglas crossed the Big Arkansas River, and was one of the three most exclusive lodging establishments in the Wichita area. Dwayne had an excellent contact there in Jimmy Thompson a bellboy. Jimmy earned big tips from businessmen guests by obtaining bootleg liquor and call girls for them. As the longest employed member of the bell staff, he used his seniority to work the preferred night shift where the most money could be earned.

DWAYNE WHEELER STRODE IN THE LOBBY OF THE hotel just in time to see Jimmy Thompson exit an elevator. Jimmy was eighteen years old with red hair and blue eyes. He was short and stocky, built like a middleweight boxer. When he spotted Dwayne waving at him, he came over with a big grin. "Hey, Dwayne!"

"Hey, Jimmy," Dwayne responded. "Listen I got a

favor to ask of you. It's worth a couple of bucks."

"Who do you want killed?" the bellboy asked, winking.

"All I need to do is get on the top floor where the business offices are," Dwayne said.

Jimmy pointed to the elevator. "Well, hell! Just get in and tell the operator to take you there."

"It's ain't that easy," Dwayne said. "I'll need a lookout."

"How long is it gonna take?"

"Fifteen or twenty minutes."

"Okay."

They went over to an elevator and Jimmy pressed the button. It appeared within a minute or two. Jimmy nodded to the operator. "Take a break."

The operator, glad for chance to get a smoke, happily surrendered the conveyance. Dwayne and Jimmy entered, and the bellboy turned the elevator lever to **UP**, and they began the climb to the eighth floor. When they arrived, the bellboy locked the doors open. "Where are you headed?"

Dwayne pointed down the hall. "That way. Be sure and wait for me." He walked past a couple of offices to a frosted glass door with a sign identifying the business behind it as the Denton Commercial Real Estate Enterprises. Dwayne reached into his inside coat pocket and pulled out the small leather pouch that held his lock pick set. He slid the pick into the lock, followed by the tension wrench. As he worked the pick farther into the device, he pressed down on the wrench. The hotel lock was so old it was almost an antique, and it took less than five minutes for him to lower the pins down from the shear line. With that done, he turned the doorknob and pushed.

The last thing Dwayne wanted to do was ransack the

place, so he moved slowly and carefully as he began his search to avoid leaving any sign of his visit. He wasn't sure what he was looking for as he pulled out his pen light, but hoped to find some correspondence or something that would link Denton with Kansas City. He was surprised when he noted only one filing cabinet. There was hardly anything in it but some rental receipts for office furniture and hotel bills that included room service. Not one thing was in the container that had anything to do with real estate. Dwayne considered this extremely strange for what was supposed to be a big operation. He actually had more paperwork than this in his own small enterprise. In his crummy little office, he kept copies of reports he'd had typed up for clients at a steno service along with his own notes, receipts and other bits of documents. But there was no administrative paper of any sort here.

Next he went through the desk drawers, finding most empty. Desperate for something, he examined the trash baskets. Nothing. The last thing he hadn't scrutinized were the in-and-out boxes on top of the three desks. All were empty. Then he spotted a piece of paper crammed under a corner of a desk blotter. He pulled it out and saw it was a written message that read, "Schomp called and wants you to call him back. Hobart 3325."

Dwayne took in a deep satisfying breath and smiled widely. R.K. Schomp was head of the main crime syndicate in Kansas City. He put the memo into his inside jacket pocket, his fingers trembling with excitement. This could end up giving him a great deal of help.

After a careful examination to make sure he'd left no evidence of his rummaging around, he went to the door. Then, turning the lever that would lock after he pulled it shut, he left the office and went back down to the elevator where Jimmy waited for him.

Chapter 6

Dwayne Wheeler woke up extremely early on Tuesday morning. He had slept fitfully the night before because of his eagerness to try the phone number he had picked up in the Denton real estate offices. If the memo was correct, it would connect him directly with R.K. Schomp's headquarters or maybe the guy's home in Kansas City. By representing himself as Denton, Dwayne could possibly glean some useful tidbits of information if not a hunk of valuable intelligence on the K.C. mob and their intentions.

Dwayne congratulated himself on having the presence of mind to take the memo with him. That way Harry Denton would be unaware that he was to return a call to the crime boss. The K.C. people would eventually realize that an unknown person had contacted them, but that would take some time.

By six a.m. Dwayne knew that he was so eager to get the ball rolling on this latest development, he would not be able to sleep any more. He got out of bed and quickly did his morning grooming routine and dressed before hurrying from the rooming house to the borrowed Ford parked at the curb.

He forced himself to drive slowly as he headed downtown to avoid a long wait on the street for the Jayhawker's opening at seven. Even then he would have two hours with nothing to do since the most feasible time to place the call to Kansas City would be around nine a.m. By that time it would be a sure thing somebody would be around to answer it. He didn't want to chance getting on the telephone too early, then having to place another call. Denton might make contact with the K.C. boss on other matters, so the timing had to be just right.

DWAYNE CHAIN-SMOKED IN THE CAR IN FRONT OF the restaurant, feeling a bit foolish, but he figured he might as well be there as tossing and turning in bed. He had gone through four cigarettes before he spotted Arnie Dawkins showing up to open the place at a quarter till seven. Arnie had just unlocked the door when Dwayne walked up. The cook was surprised to see him. "Hey, Dwayne, what's going on?"

"I'm getting an early start this morning," Dwayne explained, following him into the eatery. "I could use a cup of coffee."

"It'll take a few minutes," Arnie said. "I've got to get the kitchen ready and the grill fired up before I do anything else."

"That's okay," Dwayne said. "I know how to make coffee." He walked over to the large metal urn and began the routine of filling it with water and putting coffee into the metal basket that set on top of the hollow percolating stem. With that taken care of, the only thing left to do was turn on the burner and wait.

There was a rapping on the front door glass, and Dwayne turned to see Donna Sue peering inside. He let her in, and she gave him an inquiring look. "What are you doing here so early?"

"I've got things to do today," he said, going to a nearby stool at the counter. "And I'm anxious to get started."

"How come you didn't drop by to give me a ride? I had to walk pretty fast to keep from being late."

"Oh, God, I forgot," Dwayne replied. "I'm sorry, honey, but I got my mind focused on some things I got to do."

"You're moving around a little better now, I see," she remarked, taking off her coat.

"The stiffness is all but gone, but I'm still a little sore."

She disappeared into the backroom and re-emerged with her apron on. "Hey, who made the coffee?"

"I did," Dwayne said. "Does that mean I get a couple of free cups?"

"You get free coffee every time you come in here," Donna Sue said. She walked over to the kitchen window and peered in. "Hi, Arnie. I guess you know Dwayne's out here."

"Yeah," came back his voice. "I'll have the number seven ready for him in about ten minutes. With French fries o'course."

"O'course," Donna Sue said. She turned back to Dwayne. "So how's the caper going?"

"Better than expected," he said. "I've come across a couple of big leads. That's why I'm starting early." He lowered his voice and motioned her to come closer. "It looks like at least one member of the local upper crust is in on this. I can't quite figure the connection yet, or if Stubbs' murder is part of it. But it must be since Clayton mentioned it while he was whaling on me in Danceland's parking lot. And, listen to this. The big shot I'm talking about doesn't seem to be in the business everybody thinks he is."

Donna Sue knew when to be discreet, and she whispered. "Who're you talking about?"

"Harry Denton."

"C'mon!" she exclaimed in a sotto voce. "Him and his wife are always in the Sunday society pages. I read where they're talking about him running for mayor."

"That'd make the crooked elements of the local high society real happy. That's better than having a judge in your back pocket."

"I don't like this at all, Dwayne. It's one thing when you're following a cheating wife for some guy, but this is something that can get out of hand if you bump heads with powerful people. They don't have to do anything to you themselves; those swells can hire somebody do it for them."

"This is something that can make me a big-time detective," he countered. "I could be another Pinkerton."

"Who's he?" she asked.

"Only the guy that started up the biggest P.I. agency this country's ever seen."

The conversation was interrupted when Arnie called out, "Number seven with French fries."

The door opened and Maisie walked in. She looked down at Dwayne's plate. "Oh, goodie! The local French fry gourmet is here."

"And so is the town punchboard," he rejoined.

"What's that mean?" she asked angrily.

"If the shoe fits, wear it."

"One of these days that big mouth of yours is gonna get you in trouble," Maisie said. "I'll have my husband beat the hell out of you when he gets back from Japan."

Dwayne snorted. "You'll be the one he pounds on after I clue him in on a few things."

Maisie angrily hurried to the back room to take off her coat.

Donna Sue glared at Dwayne. "That was a hateful thing to say."

Dwayne looked back at her with a shrug. "She's fucking other guys while her husband is overseas. I didn't have that problem when I was in the army 'cause I didn't have a girl back home. But I seen some guys that got 'Dear John' letters and it was real tough on 'em. The worst was when the wife of a good buddy of mine wrote and told him she was pregnant. She said he'd be coming home to a readymade family."

"Dwayne," Donna Sue said softly. "Maisie isn't a very pretty girl. She's flattered when some guy asks her out."

"Ha! Why don't she put a mattress on her back and run around the streets offering curb service?"

Donna Sue gave him a glare of pure fury. "I never want to hear you say anything that horrid again!"

Dwayne wiped his plate clean with the last piece of rye toast, then stood up. "I'm off. See you later."

———

IT WAS NINE O'CLOCK IN HIS OFFICE BEFORE Dwayne finally picked up the handset off the phone. He took a deep, steadying breath, then dialed zero and waited.

"Operator," a feminine voice announced.

"Long distance, please," Dwayne said. When he was connected, he continued. "I'd like to place a station-to-station call to Kansas City. The number is Hobart three-three-two-five."

"Is that Kansas City, Kansas or Missouri, sir?"

"Let's try Missouri."

A few moments passed, then long distance announced, "Your number is ringing, sir."

After three rings, a man answered. "Yeah?"

"Yeah, hi," Dwayne said. "This is Harry Denton in Wichita. I found a message on my desk to call Schomp. I guess he wants to speak to me."

"He ain't come in yet," the man said. "Wait a minute." He left the phone, and Dwayne could hear him in the distance speaking with what seemed like two other men. Then the guy came back. "Schomp wants to know what happened to that private dick."

"Clayton whipped on him a little bit in a nightclub parking lot," Dwayne said. "The guy has decided to butt out of the hit on the bookie."

"All right," the man said. "That's good news."

"Yeah," Dwayne agreed. "Listen, I'm a little mixed up. I can't get ahold of Clayton, and I'm not sure what's going on."

"Well, just let Clayton make his rounds and see what he can set up," the man advised. "When it's time to send some more guys down there, you'll be told. Schomp will be there, too."

"Gotcha," Dwayne said.

"We ain't exactly got a time table here, but the boss can't stall them Eye-talians forever. They'll only wait so long for us to clear out."

Dwayne's eyes opened wide in surprise. He cleared his throat. "Are they...well, getting...impatient...maybe?"

"Not yet," the man said. "But if they do, we'll know

about it when one or more of us get bullets in the back of the head."

"Yeah," Dwayne said. "This is serious all right. Well, I've got things to tend to. Thanks for the info."

He hung up and leaned back in his chair. So that was it! Some Italian gangsters from Chicago or some other place back east wanted to set up in Kansas City, and they had no intention of sharing business with Schomp's syndicate. It was obvious that Schomp was able to negotiate a graceful exit since the Mafia wouldn't want anything like a gang war to break out to call public attention to their ambitions. The K.C. mob was definitely coming to Wichita because they had no choice in the matter. It was either that or fold up their operation. And that made them doubly dangerous. There could even be more killings to hurry things along before the Italians really started putting on the pressure.

Dwayne grabbed the phone again and dialed.

"Homicide, Sergeant Forester."

"Hi, Ben," Dwayne said. "Listen up. I got some big news. Kansas City is moving down here. They got to, because the Mafia is running them out of K.C. And, get this, his nibs Mr. Harry Denton is up to his ears in this caper. We got to have a meet."

"*You* listen up, godamn it!" Forester hissed back. "My boss Lieutenant Cordell is aware you're nosing around. And he knows you're one of my street informants. He *told me* to *tell you* that you'd better back off or you'll be arrested for interference in police business."

"He can piss up a rope," Dwayne said. "As a licensed private detective, I got a perfect right to investigate Stubb's murder. Jesus Christ! I'm willing to share whatever I find with the cops. Ain't I talking to you?"

A loud sigh sounded from Sergeant Ben Forester.

"Dwayne, this is too big a deal for you to handle. Things could suddenly turn real unpleasant where you're concerned. I'm telling you to get out while the getting's good. You're gonna be a real sorry son of a bitch if you don't."

"Would the Wichita Police be in on this thing?"

Forester hesitated, then replied, "You don't know when to shut up do you? You're gonna be found dead in some back alley. Do you realize that?"

"Well, Ben, thanks for the warning," Dwayne said. "I got some things to tend to today." He hung up with a feeling more of inquisitiveness than fear.

A HALF HOUR LATER, DWAYNE PULLED THE FORD up in front of the flower shop across the street from Wesley Hospital. He chose the place because it was always prepared to handle small orders for people visiting patients. He walked into the shop and was nearly overwhelmed by the sweet fragrances.

A slim young woman, with her back to him was working on a floral arrangement. She turned around, holding a pair of small shears in one hand. "What can I do for you, sir?"

"I need some flowers," Dwayne said. "Nothing real big or fancy. I want to take 'em with me. And I'm in kind of a hurry."

"Well, we have some pink lilies available," she replied, taking off a pair of garden gloves. "I can fix you up a bouquet in a small glazed bowl."

"How much would that cost?"

"Three dollars plus sales tax," she said.

He paused a moment, then shrugged. "Sure. That will be fine."

"It won't take long."

Dwayne turned around and gazed out the window, watching the traffic on Hillside. Then his eyes turned to the hospital, and he looked at the windows in the building. He wondered how much suffering and dying was going on behind those panes at that exact moment. It made him think of when his mother had been in Saint Francis when she died. They had doped her up pretty good because of her pain. Dwayne had wished he could talk to her, but she was completely out of it. When he left her that final time, he leaned over and kissed her tenderly. Her flesh was taut and pale, and the boy knew the touch of death was on her.

"Here you are, sir."

Dwayne twisted around, noting the bouquet of four pink lilies, their broad petals overlapping in the little vase. "That's pretty."

"I'm glad you like it, sir," the small woman said. "That will be three dollars and six cents."

He was able to produce the exact change, then picked up the floral display and walked out the shop toward his car. After carefully placing the flowers on the front seat next to him, he started the engine. When a lull came in the passing traffic, he eased onto the street and headed north on Hillside.

———

Dwayne pressed the doorbell and stepped back. A couple of moments later, Mrs. Stubb Durham opened the door. "Oh, hello, Mr. Wheeler," she said, eyeing the bouquet. "Please come in."

"Thank you," he said. He held out the vase. "I brought these for you."

Her quick smile showed she was genuinely pleased. "Why, how nice! How very nice!" She led the way into the parlor, setting the gift down on a table by an easy chair. "Please, sit down, Mr. Wheeler."

He took off his hat and settled on the sofa as he had done on his first visit. "You can call me Dwayne, if you want to, Missus Durham."

"All right, Dwayne," she said, giving the flowers a quick glance. "Thank you."

"You're welcome," he said.

"Well, what can I do for you?"

"I just came by to see how things were going for you," Dwayne said. "I thought if you needed anything, I could take care of it."

"That's really sweet of you," Mrs. Durham said. "My neighbors have been giving me some very kind and helpful attention. They took me shopping over at the Dillon Supermarket, and the lady next door has brought me some hot dishes a couple of times." She smiled at him. "It's sort of sad to be preparing meals for one."

"I bet it is."

"How has your investigating been going?"

"I'm making progress," he answered. "Detective work is slow and plodding." Then he added, "Not like in the movies or on the radio."

"I suppose not," Mrs. Durham said. "I spend so much time alone, and that was while Stubb was alive, too. He was gone a lot, and the radio was my only company."

"I like the *Sam Spade* and *Richard Diamond* programs," Dwayne said. "They're private detectives like me."

"My favorite program is *Fibber McGee and Molly*," Mrs. Durham said.

"I like them, too."

"They're always having people come to their door," she said. "Since I never had visitors, I suppose I felt like they were calling on me, too."

"Yeah," Dwayne said. "And the programs are pretty funny."

"Did you know that Molly also plays the part of Teeny the little girl that pesters Fibber?"

Dwayne shook his head. "I didn't know that." There was a pause in the conversation, and he said, "My mother always liked the soap operas."

"Which ones does she like best?"

"I don't remember," Dwayne said. "She died when I was twenty. My dad's dead, too. He got run over."

"I'm sorry to hear that," Mrs. Durham said. "Are you married, Dwayne?"

"No, ma'am, but I have a girlfriend."

"That's nice."

He looked at his watch. "Well, I got to get moving here. There's several things I'm going to be tending to." He stood up and pulled out his wallet. "I'm going to give you my business card. My office number is on that. I'll write down a couple of other places on the back where you can reach me. If you need anything, please call, okay?"

"All right, Dwayne."

He handed her the card and stuck his hat back on his head. "Well, I'll see you later, Missus Durham."

"Thank you for the flowers."

"You're welcome."

She led him to the door and opened it. Dwayne gave her a smile, then headed out, going down the steps toward his car.

Chapter 7

When Dwayne left Mrs. Durham's house, he drove straight over to his surveillance spot across from the Uptown Billiard Parlor. He knew he should have gotten there a bit earlier, but he had wanted to give her the flowers as soon as he could. At any rate, thugs like Billy Joe Clayton and bookies like Arlo Merriwell were not exactly early risers, so he doubted if he had missed much.

This day's parking place was in front of the Kings-X Burger House, putting him some twenty feet closer to the pool hall than the day before. Dwayne settled back after some gentle twisting of his torso to check out the left-over pain from his beating. He was pleased to note it had subsided substantially, and he pulled out his pack of Luckies and Zippo lighter to begin a period of surveillance that might or might not produce results.

As Dwayne kept his eyes on the door of the target building, his mind drifted back to Mrs. Durham. Buying her flowers had not been quite as impetuous as it seemed. The new widow had remained in the background of his thoughts since that visit he paid her a week before. There had been no word of a funeral or memorial service for Stubb, so she must have made simple arrangements with no guests. More than likely there was no one she wanted to invite.

Dwayne sincerely felt a sympathetic twinge for what she was currently enduring, as he compared her bereavement with what he had felt when he'd lost his mother seven years earlier. The main dissimilarity between what Mrs. Durham suffered and his own grief had to do with their difference in age. He had been only twenty with his life ahead of him when he lost his mother, and his sorrow was dulled somewhat by the underlying knowledge that the passage of time would ease the pain as he progressed through the long remainder of his existence on earth. There was none of that for Mrs. Durham.

He remembered she'd said she married Stubb in 1925 when she was thirty-years-old. Dwayne did some figuring in his head coming up with the facts that she'd been born in 1895, making her fifty-two now. Suddenly, after a violent murder, her twenty-two year marriage had come to an abrupt end. And she was alone in the world with no children or relatives. All she had now was a big empty house that contained not only memories of her late husband but of her dead parents, too.

It also occurred to him that his visit on the Tuesday so soon after the Sunday night killing had been more than a little thoughtless on his part. But it had been imperative that he get his investigation rolling as quickly as possible. A delay of a week or more could have cooled off any hot leads.

Now, sitting in the car, Dwayne was glad he had purchased that little bouquet for her.

———

Only a few people had come and gone from the Uptown Billiard Parlor, and as far as Dwayne could figure, Arlo Merriwell or Billy Joe Clayton might not be inside or even planning on visiting the place. He pulled out the last cigarette, and lit it. There was a fresh pack in the glove compartment to assure the continuance of his chain smoking. One advantage to cigarettes was that they dulled hunger somewhat. If he did begin to get a growling in his stomach, he could go to the Kings-X for a hamburger. They served them in small individual cardboard boxes for takeout.

He suddenly sat up straight when both Arlo Merriwell and Billy Joe Clayton came out of the pool hall together. This was better than he expected. The two walked slowly down the street chatting in a friendly manner. Evidently they were in a good mood. The pair got into a Pontiac sedan that Dwayne recognized as belonging to Merriwell. Wherever they were headed had to be important, since the bookie was ignoring his betting business at a time of the day when most wagers came in. It occurred to Dwayne that perhaps the K.C. mob was handling his business for him.

Within a few moments, Merriwell made a quick U-turn from the curb, and headed west on Douglas. Dwayne fired up the Ford, and pulled out into the street to follow. Traffic was light, so he kept at least a two-block distance as he trailed them toward downtown.

When they turned north on Mosley Avenue, he thought they might be headed for Elmer Pettibone's place, but they went a couple of blocks farther. They pulled up in front of another warehouse building, and went into an office that Dwayne knew was where a bootlegger named Mack Crofton ran his operation. He parked a block away, and killed the engine. Since they were paying a visit to Mack, Dwayne figured this could mean more menacing activities in the takeover.

Dwayne knew Mack Crofton fairly well. He was a quiet little guy, who had the demeanor of a church deacon. He was a bald, pudgy bachelor and seemed a bit on the mild-mannered side, and conducted his liquor business without any ballyhoo. Although not as big an operator as Elmer Pettibone, Mack ran a significant operation that included some of the larger towns north of Wichita such as Salina, Emporia and Hutchinson.

Dwayne lit another cigarette, wishing he'd gotten a hamburger. As he waited in the car, the usual number of large and small delivery trucks came and went among the businesses in the area, and a couple of semis wound through the streets on the way to the loading docks in back of the buildings. Dillon, Kroger, Safeway and other grocery chains operated their warehouses in the vicinity as did some manufacturing and food processing plants. Dwayne's view of Mack Crofton's front door was cut off several times when heavy vehicles rolled slowly through the district to pick up or drop off large loads.

Merriwell and Clayton were in Mack's building for a bit more than three-quarters of an hour before they emerged. Dwayne watched them get into Merriwell's car and drive away. He waited until they turned off Mosley onto Central before he got out of the Ford and walked down to Mack Crofton's door. He knocked and waited for the bootlegger to respond. Mack looked at him in surprise. "Hey, Dwayne."

"Hey, Mack. I need to talk to you."

Mack let him in, and closed the door. "What's up?"

Dwayne walked over to a chair in front of the desk and sat down. "I guess you heard about Stubb Durham, huh?"

"I was told he got shot."

"He got shot all right," Dwayne said. "The cops lost interest in the killing, so Longshot Jackson and some other bookies chipped in and hired me to look into the situation."

Mack went over to the filing cabinet and pulled a fifth of bourbon from the top drawer. He poured some of the liquor into a couple of paper cups, and brought them over to the desk, setting one down in front of Dwayne. He took a sip from the other. "Have you found out anything yet?"

"I've found out plenty," Dwayne said.

Mack sat down in the chair behind the desk. "Sounds interesting."

"I noticed Arlo Merriwell and Billy Joe Clayton were here," Dwayne remarked, lifting the cup to his lips and taking a swallow. "I followed them from Delmar Watson's pool hall, and waited until they came back out."

"Yeah?"

"Yeah," Dwayne said. "And I know why they came to see you. You got an offer to throw in with the Kansas City mob, didn't you?"

Mack remained silent.

"They've already approached Elmer Pettibone, and it seems he told 'em to go fly a kite." Dwayne leaned forward, continuing, "But Elmer admitted to me that he's gonna have to cave in sooner or later. The Dallas source has suddenly gone quiet."

"Mmm," was all Mack said. He drained the cup and tossed it into the wastebasket at the side of the desk.

"Stubb Durham was killed because he wouldn't cooperate with 'em," Dwayne said. "At least that's what I think right now."

Mack was thoughtful for a moment. "Then maybe Elmer is gonna get killed by them guys."

"Maybe," Dwayne allowed. "At any rate, I'm gonna need some help in my investigation."

"It sounds like it."

"Merriwell and Clayton did offer you a deal while they were here, right?"

Mack didn't answer right away. He stared down at the desktop for close to thirty seconds before raising his head. "Yeah. They offered me an arrangement where I'd be the only bootlegger in Wichita. They're gonna edge Elmer and all the other Wichita guys out of business. Clayton told me that his pals up in Kansas City are moving in down here."

"Did he tell you why?"

Mack shook his head.

"The Mafia is taking over K.C. and they told R.K. Schomp to get his ass out of there if he didn't want to end up dead," Dwayne explained. "Evidently Schomp was able to buy some time because them Eye-talians didn't want any messy gang war or killings to draw attention to what they was up to."

"Clayton didn't say nothing about that."

"I ain't surprised," Dwayne said with a chuckle. "The Mafia is a big, rich organization with lots of clout. They're all over the place. The K.C. mob don't want anybody to know they cut and run." He finished off his cup of bourbon. "What did you tell 'em, Mack?"

"I told 'em to give me a few days to think things over."

"Were you stalling them or didn't you want to be in their organization?" Dwayne asked.

"A little of both," Mack admitted. "I didn't know what was going on."

"You're a Wichita guy, Mack," Dwayne said. "You

don't want them pricks from K.C. taking over our town, do you?"

"Hell, no!"

"All right then," Dwayne said, standing up. "They can be stopped and I'm the guy that can do it. I got a couple of contacts in the Wichita Police. But I could use some help from you, too. Are you willing to give me a hand?"

"Aw, shit," Mack said softly. He looked up into Dwayne's face, hesitating for a moment. "Oh, I guess so."

"Good," Dwayne said. "So here's what you got to do. Tell 'em you're in on the deal. Go along with whatever they tell you to do, but keep me informed about everything. *Everything*! Get it? I need to know every single solitary detail so's I can pass it on to the law. I'll give you calls now and then to check in with you."

"All right."

"Good!" Dwayne said. "Thanks a lot, Mack. I prob'ly won't see you in person again for awhile."

Mack nodded mournfully. He really didn't like what was going on.

When Dwayne left the office he was practically skipping down the street. Now he had an ally who could keep him informed of all the bad guys' actions and intentions. He went to the Ford to drive to the O.K. Barbershop, then have lunch at the Jayhawker. At that moment he was really hungry.

———

THE BARBERSHOP WAS HUMMING WITH ITS USUAL Tuesday business. Since the place was closed on Sunday and Monday except for the bookies, a lot of customers showed up on the following day to have their ears lowered. Dwayne nodded to the busy barbers as he went back to the bookie area. Both Longshot Jackson and Ollie Krask were there with another colleague Rory Talbert who ran a small wagering operation. As soon as the trio sighted the private detective, they sat up straighter in their chairs.

"What's going on, Dwayne?" asked Longshot.

"Plenty," Dwayne said. "I don't want to get into details right now, but this caper is widening up like a fat gal climbing out of her girdle."

Ollie spoke up, handing him a piece of paper. "You got a phone message. It's from a broad name of Rachel."

Dwayne read the scribbled note that asked him to call her the first chance he got. Since the phones in the back were for bookie use only, Dwayne had to go up to the one at the front. He fed it a nickel and dialed, listening to the ringing on the other end of the line.

"Hello," said Rachel Brooks. "Venus Services. How may we serve you?"

"Hi. This is Dwayne. I got a note to call you."

"Hi, Dwayne. Mrs. Davies wants to see you as soon as it's convenient for you. Karl will drive over here to pick you up."

"Okay. I'll be there in about an hour." He hung up, then walked back to the bookies.

Ollie gave him a straightforward look. "How much longer is this gonna take?"

"I got to be honest with you," Dwayne said. "I can't give you an exact time, but there's gonna be some big happenings in good ol' Wichita before this month is up. And I need another hunnerd bucks."

Ollie and Rory glanced over at Longshot, who slipped a hand into his jacket pocket. He pulled out some bills and held them out. "Do you know who killed Stubb? That's what we're really concerned about."

"Not yet," Dwayne replied candidly. "But I'm close to it, you guys. And I ain't lying, okay?"

The bookies exchanged glances among themselves, then shrugged. Dwayne put the money in his wallet. He didn't really need it at that time, but felt the case was progressing fast enough to allow for some extra funds to use in unexpected circumstances.

With that taken care of, he hurried out of the barbershop and trotted across to the Jayhawker Restaurant. When he walked in, Maisie took time to give him a dirty look before walking down to the far end of the counter. With the regular lunch hour over, he was able to get immediate attention from Donna Sue. She put an Orange Crush in front of him and turned in the order for a grilled cheese sandwich and French fries.

"It's been a long time since you left this morning," she said. "Things must be going good. You're grinning."

"Yeah," he said. He motioned her to lean closer. "I got a spy working for me."

"A spy?"

"Yeah. A snitch. An inside guy. An informer."

"Sounds like he's gonna be busy," she remarked.

"Didn't I tell you this was a big caper?" he asked. "And you remember what I said about this gonna make me a big shot around town, don't you?"

She started to reply when Arnie Dawkins voice sounded, "Grilled cheese and French fries!"

Donna Sue picked up the order and sat it down in front of Dwayne. "Are you done for the day?"

"Ha! Are you kidding? I'm just starting."

———

The parking lot of the Harry Street Medical Arts Center was crowded when Dwayne drove into it. He had to pull into a spot a few doors away from Rachel's office. She let him in and went back to her desk. "I'll call for Karl to come pick you up."

"I'm glad Missus Davies wants to see me."

"I think she just wants a progress report or something," Rachel said. "You guys must have something big going on, huh?"

"You bet," Dwayne said. He took a seat across the office as she made the call. When she finished and hung up, she said, "He'll be here directly."

"Fine."

"I notice you're moving better now."

"I'm a fast healer," he said.

It took Karl the chauffeur only fifteen minutes to make the drive down to Harry Street. He hurried Dwayne out of the office and into the backseat of the Duesenberg. He sped out of the parking lot, barely slowing down at the intersection with Hillside, then turned north. Dwayne sat in the back, holding on to one of the hand straps mounted by the window. They cut a trio of yellow lights, and actually ran a red as Karl worked his way over to Thirty-Seventh Street.

When they reached the gate leading to Mrs. Davies' house, the chauffeur honked to indicate his rush to get inside. When they went up the drive to the front porch, the butler Carson went down the steps and opened the door for Dwayne. "Follow me, please."

This time Dwayne wasn't put into a waiting room; he was taken directly to the parlor where Mrs. Davies was standing by the table as she had been on his first visit. She was garbed in another out-of-fashion dress that looked as fresh and new as the one she wore before. Now Dwayne knew for sure that the dated garments were all newly made. That wasn't too surprising since a lady with Mrs. Davies' taste would never buy second hand.

The expression on her face was one of deep concern. "Please sit down, Mr. Wheeler."

He settled on the sofa and she joined him. "I have received some important news from a friend of mine in Kansas City who is in the same business as I am here."

Dwayne nodded. "Would it involve the Mafia moving into K.C.?"

"Ah!" she said. "It is obvious that you have been extremely busy." She tinkled a bell that was on a table by her elbow. "Perhaps you can fill me in on your latest activities."

Before he could speak, Carson appeared in answer to the ringing. "Yes, madam?"

"Fetch drinks for Mr. Wheeler and me," she said. "What's your pleasure, Mr. Wheeler?"

"Scotch and soda," he said.

They waited while the butler went to the bar at the side of the room. After he had tended to the chore, he served them, and quietly departed. Mrs. Davies took a sip of her vodka martini. "Please continue, Mr. Wheeler."

"I've been watching one of the Kansas City bunch by the name of Clayton," he said. "He's closely allied with two Wichita locals. One is a bookmaker by the name of Arlo Merriwell." He paused and took a swallow of his drink. "The other is Harry Denton."

Her eyes opened wide in surprise. "*The* Harry Denton?"

"No one else but," Dwayne replied. "Do you know him?"

"Not only by reputation," Mrs. Davis replied, "but as a client."

"Well, ma'am, I broke into, uh...that is to say, I visited his office late one evening. I discovered that he has absolutely no files or papers regarding real estate."

"I see," she said. "So Harry isn't what he seems to be then. It makes one wonder where he gets all his money."

"I'm not sure, but it's obvious he has something to do with R.K. Schomp up north."

"I am not acquainted with that gentleman," Mrs. Davies said.

"He's the big shot in Kansas City that's being run out of town by the Eye-talians," Dwayne explained.

"I am curious as to how you discovered this situation."

"I called Schomp's office and struck up a conversation," Dwayne explained. "One of his boys let that interesting bit of information slip out."

"How did you come to do that?"

"I found a message on Denton's desk while I was searching his office," Dwayne said. "It said for him to call Schomp. I took the memo with me, and called long distance the next morning saying I was Denton. Schomp wasn't there, but some of his guys were. And they were nervous about getting out of town by the deadline the Mafia had laid out."

"That was very clever of you, Mr. Wheeler. I am pleased with the results of your efforts."

"Thank you, ma'am," he said. "There's one more thing. I got a spy working for me inside the K.C. bunch. He's a Wichita bootlegger, and he don't want them moving in on him either. So he's gonna keep me informed of all their plans."

Mrs. Davies stood up. "When you were here before, you mentioned a contact or contacts within the Wichita Police Department. Do you trust them?"

"I've known a certain sergeant since I was a boy," Dwayne replied. "We've helped each other out quite a bit since I became a private detective. I give him stuff I pick up on the street, and he gives me tips on certain cases that aren't common knowledge."

She shook her head. "Never trust a cop. Not a single, solitary godamn one of 'em."

He was a bit taken aback by this side of her personality.

The woman began pacing slowly back and forth in front of the sofa as she spoke. "And now there is the Mafia to deal with. I put up with them in Los Angeles, and they had the cops and just about every judge and politico on their payroll. If they're not stopped, they'll be moving into Wichita soon."

"In my opinion, if we bust up the K.C. mob here, the Mafia won't want to get involved with Wichitans."

"That could be," she said. "The people here aren't like the miserable little weasels in big eastern cities." She smiled. "This is still a frontier town, and a lot of the locals have guns, don't they?"

"I guess so, ma'am."

"Well, those Italians or Sicilians or whatever they are, aren't used to dealing with an armed population," she said.

"Y'know," Dwayne said. "That's kind of a curious situation. When I was in the army I knew a lot of guys with Eye-talian last names. They seemed like they was from normal decent families."

"I wouldn't know about that," Mrs. Davies said. "All I know is that a certain group of gangsters are Italians. And so was Mussolini."

"I guess so," Dwayne allowed. "But if they do come down here they'll find that Wichita folks are willing to use their guns." He remembered the angry Delmar Watson throwing down on him and Arlo Merriwell in the pool hall.

"I don't know why people don't allow gambling, liquor and brothels," Mrs. Davies said. "At least that way there's no corruption. My girls would be better off in a bordello, but they have to go out to meet johns in hotels and other places. That can be dangerous, and I use the Speed-ee Taxi Service to safely get them where they must go."

"I can see your point," Dwayne said.

Mrs. Davies continued, "If it wasn't for prohibition all those Mafiosos would still be petty thugs back east. They came out of that fiasco with millions."

"Yes, ma'am."

She walked over and sat down beside him again. Dwayne watched as she sipped the martini, then ate the olive off the stick in the drink. "Mr. Wheeler, you do appreciate the danger you face, do you not?"

"I don't quite know what you mean by 'appreciate'," he said.

"I mean to say that you are 'well aware' of the danger you face."

"Sure," Dwayne said. "And if I forget, my girlfriend reminds me of it."

"I'm sure she does," Mrs. Davies said. "I'm going to give you another five hundred dollars. I'm quite happy to realize that my confidence in you as an efficient and effective agent is well placed." She got up and went over to the table to fetch the money.

Dwayne tipped back the scotch and soda and drained it. That was a thousand dollars he had gotten from her. He was in the big time now; just like Sam Spade on the radio.

Chapter 8

Sunday evening was a time that Dwayne Wheeler and Donna Sue Connor particularly enjoyed when he visited her apartment. Her landlord and landlady, Mr. and Mrs. Eb and Mae Greeley, were religious people who went to church regularly in the morning and evening of that first day of the week. On other evenings when the couple's single female tenants had male visitors, they made sure the callers did not stay too long, hoping the young people wouldn't have time to engage in any sexual activity. This was Mrs. Greeley's main concern, and she spent summer evenings on the porch swing of the apartment house, timing when young men came and went. During the cold months of winter, she positioned herself on an easy chair at the front window to conduct these vigils of morality. If more than an hour slipped by, she dispatched her husband to the offenders' premises to knock on the door. As an added incentive for the girls to conduct themselves appropriately, a lithograph of Jesus Christ praying in the wilderness was mounted on the wall of each apartment bedroom.

But Sundays from seven to nine-thirty p.m. the Greeleys were at their church's evening services, and several of the apartments fairly rocked with lovemaking. And it was on one of these happy occasions that Dwayne and Donna Sue were locked in a sexual embrace, lost in their mutual passion.

Donna Sue's breathing quickened, then she suddenly commanded, "Stop!" A moment later, her voice was calm; almost a whisper. "Wait. Don't move."

This was the way it always happened, and he obediently ceased his love plunges until she settled down. After a moment or two, she recovered and spoke softly. "Okay. Finish up."

And he did exactly that.

They separated and rolled to opposite sides of the small bed. "What time is it?" Donna Sue asked.

"Eight fifteen," he replied after looking at his watch.

"Time to spare."

"Yeah," Dwayne agreed. "*Sam Spade* will be on in fifteen minutes."

She gave him a playful slap. "I was more concerned about the Greeleys coming back from church."

They eased themselves out of bed and began dressing. When they were decent, they went into the living room and Dwayne turned on the radio. Donna Sue hurried to the kitchen to retrieve a Royal Crown Cola for herself and an Orange Crush for Dwayne. Then Dwayne turned on the radio as the eight-thirty hour arrived, and the crime drama began:

(Sound of a phone ringing, followed by the handset being picked up.)

"Sam Spade Detective Agency," answers Effie Perrine the secretary.

WICHITA PAYBACK 101

"It's me, sweetheart," Sam Spade says over the phone. "And I've wrapped up another caper."

"Oh, Sam," says Effie with admiration. "I hope we made some money on this one."

"We sure did!" Sam assures her.

"Nobody shot or stabbed you, did they, Sam?"

"You'll find that out presently, sweetheart," Sam says. "I'll be right down to the office to dictate my report on the Dead Clown Caper."

This was followed by a Wildroot Hair Cream commercial, then the story began as Sam started dictating the report on his latest caper to Effie who would then type it up and mail it to their client. At this point the detective's voice faded away, and the dramatized story of the adventure commenced, and Detective Sam Spade's latest case was launched for the radio audience.

Donna Sue knew to keep quiet as Dwayne sat mesmerized by the unseen story that was broadcast with only narration, dialogue and sound effects flowing over the airwaves into the listeners' consciousness. This was what was known as the "theater of the mind" in which the audience formed the appearances of the characters, costumed them, and designed the sets; all mentally while sitting by their radios.

The program ended just before nine, and Dwayne switched the radio off. "Man! That was a great caper tonight. I really like that show."

"No kidding," Donna Sue said. "When you're listening to that damn program you don't even know I'm around."

"Sam Spade is the kind of detective I want to be," Dwayne said, ignoring her sullen declaration. "Y'know what I mean? With a real office and a secretary. That's what this latest caper could do for me."

"I'll be your secretary," Donna Sue said. "You don't need a floozy like Effie."

"Effie's a nice girl," Dwayne protested. "And she's loyal to him."

"I tell you what," Donna Sue said. "If this caper you're on pays off, I'll go to work for you."

"Okay."

"Sam Spade always names his capers," Donna Sue said. "What are you gonna call this one you're on right now?"

He thought a moment. "The Payback Caper because we're gonna pay back them K.C. pricks for trying to muscle in on Wichita."

"Call it what you want," Donna Sue said. "I'll just be glad when the whole mess is over and done with. Then we can start going to Western Danceland again."

"We could have gone Saturday night," Dwayne said. "It was your idea not to."

"Damn right I didn't want to go," Donna Sue snapped. They had gone to see the movie *Gentleman's Agreement* at the Orpheum Theater downtown instead of to the nightclub. "You would've got the shit beat out of you again." She looked at the clock over the stove. "The Greeleys will be back soon. Maybe you better go."

"To hell with the Greeleys."

"I like this apartment," Donna Sue said. "It's close to work and the rent's reasonable. Well, fairly reasonable. Anyhow there's no landlord that's gonna let women entertain men friends 'til late at night."

"Maybe you should rent half of a duplex."

"What would I do with all that room?" she asked.

"And I don't want to have to ride the bus to work. I can even walk to downtown in cold weather from here."

"I guess you're right," Dwayne relented. Then a thought occurred to him. "Wait a minute! They don't know that Ford is mine. If they don't see the Pontiac, they won't know I'm here."

"Don't be silly," she said. "You can bet that Missus Greeley took note of what you were driving the first night you had the Ford."

"Okay." He stood up and walked over to the coat rack and got his hat and jacket. After slipping them on, he joined her where she waited at the door. "I'll see you tomorrow at the Jayhawker."

They exchanged a lingering kiss, and Dwayne slid his hand around to her buttocks and squeezed. "Go!" she said. "You'll get all worked up again."

Dwayne winked and left the apartment. He went down the stairs to the landing at the front door and let himself out. The car was close by, and he slipped inside and put the key in the ignition. Just as he pulled out into the street he spotted the Greeleys' Nash approaching the apartment house. A quick glance as they drove under a streetlight revealed Mrs. Greeley looking pointedly his way. Donna Sue was right. The landlady had already made the Ford.

When he reached Douglas and turned west, he lit a cigarette, thinking of the sex he had just enjoyed with Donna Sue. He was pretty sure she had never come before doing it with him. He remembered how surprised she had been the first time, breathing hard after it happened, asking, "Where the hell did *that* come from?"

The red light of the police car behind him illuminated the interior of the Ford in a deep rosy glow. He pulled over, puzzled at being stopped. He could see the cop getting out and approaching him. It was someone he didn't know, and Dwayne asked, "What's the problem, buddy?"

"I ain't your buddy," the guy growled. "Gimme your license."

Dwayne fetched the white-on-black Photostat from his wallet, and handed it over.

"Gimme the registration."

Dwayne looked down at the steering wheel column where the small document was in a leather holder that was attached by a couple of spring wires. He pulled it off and surrendered it.

"How's come the name on the registration isn't the same as on the license?"

"Why do you think?" Dwayne said. "Any fucking idiot would know that meant this ain't my car."

"Get out of the vehicle, you wise-ass son of a bitch," the cop said, jerking the door open.

Dwayne obeyed and was pushed up against the car. At that point a plainclothes man joined them who he recognized. "Well, well! And a good evening to you, *Sergeant* Gallagher."

The cop turned to the sergeant, saying, "The name on the license is differ'nt than the one on the registration."

"Oh, yeah?" Gallagher said. He wasn't a tall man, but he was extremely muscular with a bull neck and heavy shoulders. He looked at Dwayne. "Where'd you steal this car, Wheeler?"

"You know godamn well I didn't steal the fucking car, Gallagher," Dwayne said angrily. "And don't tell me you ain't noticed the name Elmer Pettibone on the registration either. You know him as well as I do. I borried it from him. That means he knows I'm driving it around."

"Why would Pettibone loan you a car?"

"Because I *asked* him to loan it to me," Dwayne said. "My Pontiac ain't running at the moment."

"Why would it be running when you swiped a better car to drive around in?" Gallagher shot back. He looked at the cop. "Call in for a tow truck."

"Hey!" Dwayne exclaimed. "What's the big idea?"

"I'll tell you the big idea, shamus," Gallagher said. "You're under arrest for grand theft auto. Turn around and put your hands behind you."

Dwayne started to resist, then thought better of it.

When Gallagher frog-marched Dwayne through the back door of the police station, he bypassed booking, going straight to an interrogation room. The sergeant switched on a large lamp with a 250-watt bulb that sat on a table. That, and two chairs, was the only furniture in the place.

"Okay, Shamus. Empty your pockets."

Dwayne complied, laying out his wallet, private investigator I.D., keys, cigarettes and lighter. Since he hadn't been fingerprinted or photographed, he knew he wouldn't be charged with anything. This wasn't an arrest at all. But the thought wasn't very comforting; he knew this situation was going to be special and unpleasant for him.

Gallagher grabbed Dwayne and propelled him across the room, slamming him face first into the wall. Dwayne started to spin around and fight back, but the policeman gave him a sharp punch to the kidneys.

"Oof!" Dwayne exclaimed with the acute consciousness that all the hurts from the Danceland beating hadn't completely gone away. "Godamn you, you chickenshit son of a bitch!"

"Keep your opinions to yourself," Gallagher said. He chuckled. "I'll bet that hurt, huh? Still sore from the ass-kicking over at Western Danceland?"

"I ain't surprised you know about it," Dwayne snapped back. "I bet you was over in the shadows skulking behind a car and watching the whole thing."

Gallagher gave him a rough patting down, then walked over to the table and picked up the items that Dwayne had surrendered. "Sit down, shamus."

"How about leaving me my cigarettes?"

"How about kissing my ass?" the cop shot back. He walked out the door slamming it hard.

Dwayne went to the chair and slumped down in it. He turned the lamp and aimed its illumination directly at the room's entrance. Whoever walked in first would get an eyeful of brilliant light. It wasn't much revenge for the contrived arrest, but it was better than nothing.

―――

"Hey!"

Dwayne had dozed off, and woke up with a start at the sound of the exclamation. He blinked when the light was turned around in his direction.

"You're a real wise-ass, Wheeler," Gallagher said. "I was gonna give you back your cigarettes, but I ain't gonna do it now."

"Oh, woe is me, asshole!"

Gallagher sat down opposite him, turning the lamp in a neutral direction. "We're gonna have us a little talk, shamus. It has to do with you looking into Stubb Durham's murder."

"I'm a licensed private investigator," Dwayne said. "I

been hired to find out who did it. And I told that to Ben Forester, too."

"Who hired you?"

"Now, Gallagher, even a dipshit like you knows that's confidential information."

"All right, suit yourself," Gallagher said. "But here's the word for you. You are interfering in police business. Even a private eye can't do that no matter what he's been hired for. Now you can do something smart for the first time in your life, and drop the case. Things will be a lot easier as far as you're concerned, and people won't be coming around to pound the piss out of you."

"Or harassing me on the street with a false traffic stop."

"Right!" Gallagher said. "Now you're getting the big picture."

"Okay. I'm going to quit looking into Stubb's murder. I promise. As sure as there's a God above, I'll put it completely out of my mind. I'll even move away to another state. I'll get me a new identification and start my life over somewhere far, far away. Maybe I'll enlist in the French Foreign Legion and go to a war in some distant exotic country and die for France. How's that?"

Gallagher's voice was taut with anger. "You're really asking for it, Wheeler. Y'know it's a matter of public record that when you applied for a position on the Wichita Police Department, you was turned down on account of your punk-ass discharge from the United States Army."

"So?"

"So how come you claimed it was an honorable separation from the service when you applied for you P.I. license?"

"I don't recall doing that."

"We got us a copy of the application from the State of Kansas," Gallagher said, grinning. "All we got to do is march over to the courthouse and have some judge declare your license revoked." He leaned back in the chair. "That should take, say, all of fifteen minutes."

"Y'know, Gallagher, it's guys like you that give rotten bastards a bad name."

"I'm done talking with you, shamus," Gallagher said. "You're on your way down. One of your friends wants to talk to you before you're released."

He went to the door and opened it, and Sergeant Ben Forester walked into the room. Ben nodded to Gallagher as he left, then he approached the table and looked down at Dwayne.

"You've been given the word, Dwayne."

"Yeah."

Ben sat down. "I've already told you twice that there's some big happenings going on in Wichita, and you're getting in the way. In fact, you been stomping on the shoes of some pretty important and powerful folks hereabouts."

"It's all like I already told *you*," Dwayne said in an angry undertone. "The Kansas City mob is moving in on Wichita, Ben. The Mafia is taking over K.C., and they've given Schomp some time to get out of town. The Eyetalians don't want a big hullabaloo when they move in. You can be sure they've greased some wheels, but if things don't go their way they'll be dead bodies found all over."

"You've really been digging, haven't you?"

"I lack a few bits of information, but I can get 'em," Dwayne said. "If—that is—*when* I find out who killed Stubbs, I'll be able to start putting enough together to go to the D.A."

Ben stood up. "Fuck it. I ain't gonna worry about

you, Dwayne. You're on your own." He took a paper sack out of his side jacket pocket and dumped Dwayne's belongings on the table.

The first thing Dwayne did was get a cigarette and light it. He exhaled smoke, looking at Ben as he picked up the rest of the things. "I guess I can't depend on much help from you, huh, Ben?"

"Get the hell out of here."

Dwayne stepped out into the hall, then headed for the exit. When he walked out into the alley, he was surprised to see the Ford parked next to the police station. A quick look inside showed the key was in the ignition. Dwayne got into the car, and started the engine. A glance at his watch indicated it was seven thirty a.m.

A good time for breakfast at the Jayhawker Restaurant.

Chapter 9

The moment Dwayne stepped through the door of the Jayhawker, Donna Sue turned toward the kitchen window and hollered the order for his favorite breakfast.

Arnie Dawkins' voice sounded from the kitchen, "Hey, Dwayne!"

"Hey, Arnie," Dwayne said, sitting down. He noticed Maisie was ignoring his presence in a very obvious fashion. He had begun to regret the impulsive way he'd insulted her and decided it would be best if he simply paid no attention to the waitress in the future.

"Jimmy Thompson called about fifteen minutes ago," Donna Sue informed him. "He wants to talk to you. It's urgent."

Dwayne said got to his feet. "It must be important if he called at this hour. Normally he'd be sleeping after work." He walked over to the pay phone and dropped a nickel in the slot, then dialed the bellboy's home number.

"Izzat you, Dwayne," came a sleepy voice.

"Nobody but."

Jimmy cleared his throat. "Some bad shit's going on at the hotel, man. A couple of guys came in last night and told me that I was to use a differ'nt phone number for call girls. I asked 'em what's up, and they said they was a new operation and that we had to call their girls instead of Venus Services."

"Okay."

"I tried to ignore 'em but when one of the regular hookers showed up at the back entrance to the hotel, they was in the alley, and went up to her and told her to leave," Jimmy said. "She and the taxi driver that brung her was scared shitless. After they took off, them guys got another broad and brought her to me. They said if I pulled that shit again I'd end up back by the trash cans with my head kicked in. I didn't have no choice. The rest of the night I called their number if a guest wanted a woman. At least they ain't said nothing about bootleggers yet."

"I understand," Dwayne said. "You said there was two of 'em?"

"Yeah."

"Now listen, Jimmy," Dwayne said. "I'm gonna take care of this. The only thing you got to do is play along with 'em. I'll be at the hotel about ten o'clock tonight in the alley to take care of those bastards."

"I'll be looking for you."

Dwayne hung up and was thoughtful for a moment. The K.C. guys were beginning the takeover of the Riverside as a prelude to moving in on other hotels. He fed the phone a nickel for another call. When a sleepy voice exhibiting obvious irritation answered, he said, "Hey, Benny. This is Dwayne. D'you want to make fifty bucks tonight?"

Benny Gordon, the ex-paratrooper and Western Danceland bouncer, forgot his annoyance at being awakened, and gave a cheerful reply. "Damn right! What's going on?"

"There's a couple of guys forcing their whores on the bellboys at the Riverview," Dwayne explained. "They need to be taken out."

"Count on me," Benny said. "I got to get somebody to cover for me at Danceland tonight, but that's no problem."

"I'll be by to pick you up at your place at nine thirty," Dwayne said.

"I'll be waiting with bells on, along with my brass knucks."

Dwayne hung up and went back to the counter where his breakfast waited. Donna Sue poured him a cup of coffee. "What's going on?"

"It looks like I'll be busy tonight," Dwayne replied, stabbing a slice of a French fry. "I got to get home after I eat and get some sleep."

She eyed him suspiciously. "What the hell have you been up to?"

"I didn't get any beddy-bye last night," Dwayne explained. "I spent the night at the police station."

"What the hell did you do?" Donna Sue demanded to know.

"I didn't do nothing," Dwayne protested. "I was stopped by a patrol car and ended up stuck in an interrogation room while Ben and his pal Gallagher harassed me all night. They suggested I forget my investigation."

"Oh, God!" she said. "And o'course you're not going to, are you?"

"What do you think?"

"Dwayne!" she hissed angrily. "There are times when I don't think you got any more brains in your head than there are in a horse's ass."

He chuckled. "Well, you're prob'ly right, sweet thing." He turned his full attention to the food.

Dwayne went to the rooming house, going straight to bed. He slept until noon, then forced himself to get up. After throwing on a bathrobe, he padded in bare feet out to the hallway payphone. His total contribution to Ma Bell for that day went up to fifteen cents for yet one more phone call.

"Venus Services," answered Rachel Brooks. "How can we—"

He interrupted her. "This is Dwayne. How's business?"

"Things went to hell last night," she reported. "No calls came in."

"Phone your boss lady and tell her I'm on it," Dwayne said. "And say I'm gonna need fifty bucks in extra expenses."

"Mrs. Davies is very, very upset about these unexpected developments," Rachel said. "If you clear this up, you'll get a bonus."

"I may need it for a hospital bill," Dwayne said, then hung up. He went back to his room and bed for some more shut-eye. The coming evening promised to be one filled with violent exercise.

It was ten minutes before ten p.m. when Dwayne and Benny Gordon pulled up on the side of the hotel next to the alley entrance. "Hey, Dwayne, I brought some brass knucks for you, too," Benny said. He reached in his pocket and pulled out the weapon.

"Jesus!" Dwayne said. "They're big."

"Yeah," Benny said, producing his own that were identical. "These babies were attached to a couple of trench knives I brought back from the war. See the holes on the end? There was a brass nut that held the blade in place. You unscrew it and the blade comes out. So you got nothing left but the knucks." Then he added, "I could've brought 'em with the blades attached, but I didn't figger we wanted to kill anybody."

Dwayne slipped his fingers through the openings, noticing the four pointed protrusions sticking out. "Yeah! These'll do the job."

"Then let's go," Benny suggested.

They walked from the car, and around the corner to the front entrance of the hotel and went into the lobby. An anxious looking Jimmy Thompson headed over to them. "Them guys have already brung two whores over, and should be showing up again within a few minutes or so."

"That'll be at the back entrance leading to the alley, right?" Dwayne asked.

"Yeah," Jimmy replied nervously. "We can't walk 'em through the lobby, y'know. He looked at Benny. "Hi ya."

Dwayne didn't introduce Benny since that would have been an unforgiving *faux pas* in this type of activity where serious injury or even death was possible. Instead he said, "Okay take us to the door and we'll be waiting just inside. As soon as them guys and the whore show up, you get out of the way."

Jimmy snorted a chuckle. "You damn right I will!" He led them through the lobby past the elevators to an exit.

Dwayne and Benny slipped on the metal knuckles, took a couple of shadowboxing type swings, then settled down to wait. Jimmy stuck his head out the door and kept watch on the alley, being careful not to expose himself too much. After a few minutes passed, he stepped back inside the entrance. "Here they come. Them guys don't use taxis. They drive the whores themselves."

A few seconds later the door opened and a somewhat attractive young woman stepped through it. She was immediately followed by a couple of husky thugs, who nodded a greeting to Jimmy.

Then Dwayne stepped forward and plowed his armed fist into the face of the guy, while Benny did the same to the one nearest him. The metal knuckles crunched into the victims' jaws, cutting through flesh and shattering bone. Dwayne was shocked and a little frightened at the physical damage caused by the heavy knucks. He hadn't expected to feel the crush of splintering cheeks and jaws.

"Grab the cunt!" Dwayne yelled at Jimmy, who immediately grasped one of the whore's arms and held tight.

Benny's victim was on the floor, but Dwayne's had managed to keep to his feet. He was the unlucky one. Another punch by the private eye crashed into his nose, smashing it flat in a spray of blood and snot. His legs gave way and he collapsed flat on his back to the floor. The other man had struggled up to his knees, and Benny hit him again; this time in the kidneys. He went down to join his buddy.

Dwayne walked over to where the thoroughly frightened prostitute stared down in horror at her battered escorts. "Listen, sweetheart," he said. "You came here with a driver, right?"

The woman was scared witless.

"*Answer me!*"

"Uh...oh...y-yes," she stammered, gulping as one of the men threw up. "He's waiting for...those guys there."

"Okay," Dwayne said. "You run over to your driver, and tell him to get down here and fetch these hunks of hamburger, and to tell his boss not to send any more K.C. pricks or whores. If they do, there'll be some dead shit-heads for the cops to find. That'll cause a big ruckus here in town." He glared at her. "And it'd be a good idea if you told all your girlfriends to get their cute little asses back to Kansas City. The next time any of you show up at a hotel in Wichita, you'll get what your bodyguards got. D'you understand?"

The woman was a red head with freckles and a nice figure. "Please don't do nothing to me!"

"We're gonna drag these two dumb bastards out in the alley," Dwayne said. "Go get the driver quick!"

Jimmy let the prostitute go, and she rushed through the door. Dwayne turned to the bellboy. "Okay. You can call Venus Services for a replacement."

Jimmy hesitated. "Man! I think maybe you guys just started a war."

"Don't worry about it," Benny said with a wink. "We're both veterans."

They stood back in the shadows behind the door watching as the driver walked into view. He stopped short at the sight of his battered buddies. After looking around, he grabbed one and helped him to his feet. The second victim got up unsteadily, and followed after them.

Dwayne had worn his pistol in a shoulder holster for the evening's activities. Now he knew he had better continue the habit, along with carrying a couple of extra magazines of ammo.

The next morning Dwayne went to the Jayhawker for breakfast, then hurried over to his office to put in a call to Mack Crofton. He knew enough time had passed for Mack to have picked up the Kansas City group's reaction to the beatings the night before. He settled down at his desk and dialed Mack's number. When the bootlegger answered the phone, his voice trembled with excitement as soon as Dwayne identified himself.

"Jesus, Dwayne!" he said. "Did you have anything to do with those two guys who got fucked up last night?"

"Tell me about it."

"Somebody must've beat 'em half to death with sledge hammers! They borried one of my cars to drive them poor bastards back up to K.C. to see a doctor on their payroll. He don't make police reports."

Dwayne decided that it was time to give Mack an injection of confidence with some encouraging exaggeration. "I was in on the action, Mack. There was some other guys there with me. Them K.C. pricks don't seem to realize that there's a strong organization in Wichita that don't want 'em moving into town."

"Well, I can tell you for sure that those guys are really pissed off," Mack said. "They swear they're gonna get even."

"Have they said anything else they might have in mind regarding this little situation?" Dwayne asked. He pulled his pistol from the holster and casually aimed it at the doorknob.

"Naw," Mack said. "I think a strong message has been delivered to 'em. They've decided they ain't gonna send any more whores out anywhere in Wichita. At least not for awhile."

"If those son of a bitches know what's good for 'em, they'll forget taking over our town," Dwayne said.

"They're kind of confused about something else," Mack said. "The boss R.K. Schomp has been in a town for the last couple of days or so. I met him, and there was a phone call to him up in K.C. from somebody who claimed to be Harry Denton. But Denton said he didn't call. Schomp checked with Bell Telephone and found out the call had originated in Wichita, but couldn't find out the number."

"That shook 'em up, huh?" Dwayne asked with a grin, reholstering the pistol.

"It sure as hell did," Mack said. "They figure somebody knows their intentions."

"Well, Mack, *somebody* does," Dwayne assured him. Then he realized that Mack had revealed something. "How did you know about Denton? Has he been at the meetings, too?"

"He sure as hell has," Mack said. "And it's obvious as hell that he knows Schomp really good. I would say them two were old buddies from way, way back. And our pal Arlo Merriwell is around all the time. I don't think he's minding the store when it comes to his bookie business anymore. He's a big part of this thing. It looks like he's gonna be one of the bosses."

"Have you met any Wichita cops at these meetings?"

"Nope," Mack replied. "And nobody's mentioned any."

"Okay," Dwayne said. "But keep your eyes open. I think that Sergeant Gallagher may be on their payroll." He didn't want to mention Ben Forester's name even though the cop was obviously in on the takeover. Mack knew Dwayne was a friend of the detective, and the truth would have shaken his resolve to continue as a snitch.

"I'll let you know as soon as I find out anything," Mack promised.

"How're they treating you?"

"Pretty good," Mack replied. "In fact, they're promising me big things as soon as they nail Wichita down."

"You got to stick in there, Mack," Dwayne said. "When the time is right for you to cut and run, I'll let you know."

"Yeah," Mack said. "I don't want them to get wise to me. I'll get what Stubb Durham got."

"Has anyone mentioned him?"

"No," Mack replied. "I haven't said anything about him either."

"Keep it that way," Dwayne said.

Mack didn't speak for a moment, then he said, "I'm scared shitless, Dwayne."

"Listen up. There's some big shots behind me here, Mack. And this is gonna take a little time. You just hang in there and keep me informed on ever'thing that's going on. That's all you gotta do. It's real simple. Okay?"

"You can count on me, Dwayne."

"Okay, Mack. I'll be in touch later. Remember to phone me if you get any important news. I think it would be best if you called Ernie Bascombe at the OK Barbershop to get ahold of me. He knows how to keep a lid on things. There's too many bookies around there, and they got a tendency to yak it up."

"I understand," Mack said. "G'bye, Dwayne."

"Bye."

Dwayne hung up and leaned back in his chair, swiveling around so he could look out the window. Mack Crofton was now the key to his case since he was the only one who would know exactly what the K.C. pricks were up to. The only thing Dwayne could do at this point was wait to see what developed before deciding his next step in the caper.

Chapter 10

An hour after ending the phone call with Mack Crofton, Dwayne was still thinking over the latest happenings of the caper in his office. He had just decided to let things slide quietly by for a couple of days and turned his attention to the *Racing Form*. Less than ten minutes passed, and his perusal of the latest horseracing news was interrupted when his telephone jangled.

"Dwayne Wheeler, private investigator," he intoned.

"Dwayne, this is Rachel." She had three phone numbers on her list where to reach him; his office, the O.K. Barbershop, and the Jayhawker Restaurant. She had called his office first; surprised not only to get him, but that the telephone rang. Most of the time it didn't. She wasted no time, and cut to the chase. "The boss lady wants to see you, Dwayne. Right away."

"Okay," he replied, glad for the opportunity to get reimbursed the fifty bucks he'd spent on Benny Gordon. "I'll be over for Karl to pick me up."

"Not this time," Rachel said. "It looks like you've gotten on her sweet list, my boy. She wants you to drive yourself. Tell the guards at the front gate who you are. They'll be expecting you and will let you in."

"Guards?" he said. "There was only one, as I recall."

"There are two now," Rachel said. "Mrs. Davies has become nervous since the unpleasant incidents at the Riverview Hotel."

"I am on my way," Dwayne said, pleased at this turn of events. It looked like he was now in like Flynn with Wichita's premiere madam. He fairly skipped out of his office and down the stairs as he made his way to the street.

DWAYNE DROVE UP TO THE GATE LEADING TO Mrs. Davies' house after turning off Thirty-Seventh Street. When he came to a stop, two men approached the barrier. One stepped through a small door, and walked over to the car. His companion stood off to one side, keeping a close eye on the visitor. The first guy peered into the car window. "Yeah?"

"The name is Wheeler," Dwayne said. "Missus Davies wants to see me. I was told you guys would be expecting me."

"Oh, yeah," the guy said. "You've come here before with Karl, right?"

"Twice."

The guard signaled his buddy to open the gate, then motioned Dwayne to drive into the interior of the compound. The private detective continued on his way down the gravel driveway to the house.

When he reached the front porch, Karl the chauffeur motioned him to pull up and park. Dwayne did as he was instructed, then got out of the car, waiting to see whatever protocols for his visit had been dictated by Mrs. Davies.

Karl took him into the house and deposited him in the same waiting room where he had cooled his heels during his first visit. "Make yourself to home."

"Thanks," Dwayne said. He settled down on the sofa and turned his eyes to gaze at the portrait of Mrs. Davies as a young flapper. He wondered what her personality had been like in those days. Although the expression on her face in the painting displayed a sort of world-weariness, there was also an aura of confidence in her beauty, her intelligence and her future. She probably would have already made a load of money at that time, if she could afford to have an artist paint her likeness. Dwayne wondered if she had ever been a working whore. He was no expert on luxury bordellos, but he had heard that some of the more intelligent of the beautiful courtesans were brainy enough to realize the advantages of having other women service johns for them. This saved their bodies from the encroaching ravages of countless sexual contacts along with emotional stress that many times led to drug addiction. And, of course, there were also the lingering risks of venereal diseases.

"Mr. Wheeler."

The deep feminine tone startled Dwayne, and he turned abruptly toward the door to see a rather severe yet not unattractive woman gazing at him. She was tall and slim with her raven black hair pulled back in a bun. She appeared to be about Donna Sue's age.

He stood up. "That's me."

"I am Miss Caruthers," she said. "Mrs. Davies' secretary. Please come with me."

Dwayne was led down a long hall to some stairs past the room where he met Mrs. Davies his previous two visits. He ascended to the next floor behind Miss Caruthers, and they emerged into another, wider hall.

The prim secretary kept up a steady pace to a door at the end of the corridor. She opened it and stepped inside, stopping to allow him to go past her. When he entered the chamber, he saw it was an office with a large, ornate mahogany desk, file cabinets, and several chairs.

"Wait here," Miss Caruthers said.

Within a minute she returned with Mrs. Davies. The older lady gave him a surprisingly friendly smile. "So nice to see you again, Mr. Wheeler."

"Hi, Missus Davies."

"Take a seat," Mrs. Davies said as she sat down in a nearby chair.

Miss Caruthers went behind the desk and made herself comfortable as she settled into a silent, listening posture.

"You have done me a great service, Mr. Wheeler," Mrs. Davies said. "Without you, my arrangements in this city might easily have been completely compromised. And I understand that you have requested a fifty dollar bonus."

"Not a bonus, ma'am," Dwayne said. "It was an expense. I had to hire somebody to help me sort of put a stop to the interference that had started."

"Am I to assume there was violence?"

"Oh, yes, ma'am," Dwayne assured her. "Things could have turned against us in a really bad way."

"But you succeeded," Mrs. Davies said. "Rachel has informed me that my business activities are completely back to normal. I am speaking of those at the Riverview Hotel, of course. Thanks to you, this unpleasantness did not spread to my other points of interest."

"I'm glad to hear that, ma'am."

"I am most grateful," Mrs. Davies continued. She turned to her secretary. "Miss Caruthers, if you please."

The secretary reached into a desk drawer and withdrew an envelope. She held it out, and Dwayne got up and walked over to take it.

"You will find five hundred dollars there," Mrs. Davies said.

"Oh, that ain't necessary at all, Missus Davies," Dwayne protested. "In fact it's okay to forget that fifty bucks for the guy that helped me."

"Nonsense," Mrs. Davies said. "I want you to know that my gratitude for your good services goes further than cash. I hope you will consider me a friend, Mr. Wheeler. And I mean that most sincerely."

"I'm truly grateful, ma'am," Dwayne said, thinking of using the unexpected funds to place some bets on a couple of good horses he saw in the *Racing Form* that morning.

"If you are ever in a situation where I might render you some aid, do not hesitate to call upon me."

"Thank you kindly, ma'am."

She walked back through the door she had used to enter the office as Miss Caruthers stood up. "I shall take you back downstairs, Mr. Wheeler."

Dwayne, more than a bit flabbergasted, numbly followed after his refined escort.

Dwayne went straight to the O.K. Barbershop, hurrying past the working barbers to Longshot Jackson. "I got three bets on tomorrow's races I want to put down."

Longshot, with plenty of past money made on Dwayne's wagers, took out his notebook. "What pleasures you today?"

"One hunnerd dollars on the nose on each one," Dwayne asked. He turned to the *Racing Form* in which he had circled his choices. "Belmont Park, third race, number four horse."

"Gotcha!" Longshot said.

"Pimlico," Dwayne said. "Second race, number ten horse."

"Gotcha!"

"And finally Churchill Downs, fourth race, number six horse."

"Gotcha!"

Ollie Krask, sitting nearby munching a Hershey Bar, grinned. "Hey, Longshot, d'you want to lay any of that off?"

Longshot scribbled in his notebook, working out the odds. "Well, the total possible winnings is nine hunnerd dollars. So normally I might, but this is Dwayne so I don't think it'll be necessary."

Ollie burst out in heavy laughter that was so loud, the barbers and their customers turned to see what was so funny.

Dwayne smirked at the fat bookie. "You'll be laughing out the other side of your mouth tomorrow." He looked at Longshot. "I ain't giving you a marker. This is cash!"

"Now I know I ain't laying any of this off!" Longshot exclaimed.

———

Early the next evening after driving Donna Sue home from work, Dwayne returned to his rooming house three hundred dollars lighter. He wisely did not mention the big loss of cash to her. The horses he had bet on ran out of the money; sixth, eighth and dead last to be exact. He had just slipped the key into his door when the payphone in the hall rang. He walked over and lifted the receiver. "Hello."

"Godamn, Dwayne! Thank God I found you!"

"Hey, Mack, what's up?"

"Them guys is moving on you, man!" Mack Crofton exclaimed. "They're gonna snatch Donna Sue. I heard 'em talking, and they know where she lives. God only knows what they'll do to her."

"Oh, shit!"

Dwayne slammed the receiver back down, racing from the house and out to the car. He tried to control his emotions as he raced up to Central, wheeled a quick left through a yellow traffic light, and headed for Donna Sue's street. He was damn glad he had the Colt pistol and extra magazines with him.

When he pulled up in front of the apartment house, he paid no attention to Mrs. Greeley sitting in the swing on the porch in the waning daylight. He raced from the car and up the steps, charging through the door to climb the stairs to the second floor. He reached Donna Sue's apartment and knocked hard and rapidly.

"Donna Sue! Donna Sue!"

She answered the frantic pounding, and stared at him with a puzzled expression. "What in the hell?"

He pushed her back as he rushed through the door. "Pack a bag quick! I got to get you the hell out of here."

"Jesus! What's going on? Are you crazy?"

Dwayne stopped and took a couple of breaths. "Some guys are coming after you to get at me. Understand? They're gonna snatch you!"

"That don't make sense, Dwayne!"

"Listen, godamn it!" he said, pushing her toward the bedroom. "I busted some heads, and them K.C. pricks are gonna even the score, see? They know where you live and to get back at me, they're gonna come after you."

"I don't have nothing to do with that!" she protested fearfully. "What the hell do they want with me?"

"I just told you!" he said. "They'll take you somewhere, and about a dozen guys'll fuck you 'til your eyeballs bug out! And that's just the start."

"I didn't do nothing!" she insisted again.

"You didn't have to do nothing!" he yelled back at her. "But you're still in deep shit!"

"Oh God, Dwayne!"

Donna Sue went to the closet and got an old battered suitcase. Next she stumbled to the dresser and began pulling out underwear. Dwayne went back to the closet and pulled out some dresses and piled them in with the undies.

"They'll get wrinkled!" Donna Sue protested.

"That's the least of your problems," Dwayne said, closing the suitcase. He seized her arm and pulled her toward the door.

Donna Sue grabbed her purse off the table as he tugged her past it. When they went out into the hall, she turned and locked the door. With that done, Dwayne dragged her down the stairs and outside. Both rushed across the yard to the car, and Donna Sue got in as he threw her suitcase onto the backseat. Then he turned away from the curb and headed south toward Douglas.

Mrs. Greeley stood up and walked to the edge of the porch, watching them dart away. "Well! I never!" Then she smiled to herself. "I'll bet they're eloping."

Across the street, out of sight in a parked Pontiac, Billy Joe Clayton and Arlo Merriwell also observed the fleeing car. Clayton chuckled. "Now we know we got a snitch in the organization."

"Yeah," Merriwell agreed. "And we know who the son of a bitch is now."

―――

Donna Sue's mind was reeling with confusion, and the bewilderment increased when Dwayne pulled into the empty parking lot of the Harry Street Medical Arts Center. He went down to the end and pulled into a spot.

"Let's go!" he said. "Leave your suitcase."

They went to a door where Dwayne pressed out the required rhythmic pattern on the buzzer. A moment later it opened, and he dragged Donna Sue into the interior of an office. Rachel Brooks, startled and a little frightened, stepped back. "What in the hell is going on?"

"I need some help," Dwayne said, "bad!"

"Who's she?"

"My girlfriend," Dwayne said. Now he calmed down. "Rachel Brooks. Donna Sue Connors."

"Hi," Donna Sue said.

"Hi," Rachel replied. "Again! What in the hell is going on?"

Dwayne repeated, "I need some help."

"Okay," Rachel said.

"When I was over at Missus Davies' house, she said if I had any troubles that I was to let her know. She said she'd help me out."

"I know for a fact she's very grateful to you," Rachel said. "I'll call her, but you got to tell me more than that."

"The K.C. mob is pissed off about what I did to their guys over at the Riverview Hotel," Dwayne said. "They're planning on getting back at me by kidnapping Donna Sue. I need a place to stash her."

"Okay," Rachel said. "You two take a seat. I'll call Mrs. Davies and let her know."

Dwayne led Donna Sue over to the chairs by the wall, and they sat down. He looked at her, now trying to sound surer of himself. "Relax now, honey, things will be all right."

"Oh, God!" Donna Sue wailed.

Rachel called the mansion and eventually was able to talk to Mrs. Davies. She explained what had happened in a matter-of-fact tone, turning Dwayne's frantic version of events into simple statements. "Yes," Rachel said into the phone. "He's here right now with his girlfriend. All right." She looked at Dwayne. "Mrs. Davies wants to talk to you."

Dwayne got up and walked over to the phone, taking it from Rachel's hand. "Hello, Missus Davies."

"Hello, Mr. Wheeler," Mrs. Davies said. "Is it certain that your girlfriend is in danger?"

"It sure is," Dwayne said. "I learned it from the guy I told you about; the one on the inside working for me. He heard them making plans. He said I should get her hid as quick as I can." He hesitated, then said, "I was hoping you knew a good place where I could hide her."

"Indeed I do, Mr. Wheeler," she said. "You will drive her here."

"You mean at *your* house?"

"No place else," Mrs. Davies said. "And I advise you to get her here just as quickly as you can."

"I'll do that, thanks a lot. G'bye." He hung up the phone and looked at Rachel. "She wants Donna Sue to stay with her."

"I know," Rachel said. "I told you that you're on her sweet list. Mrs. Davies is good hearted toward those who have shown her kindness or done her favors."

"Well! This is going to turn out better than I thought," Dwayne said. He grabbed Donna Sue's hand, pulling the young woman to her feet. "Ever'thing's gonna be all right. Wait a minute."

Donna Sue, still stunned and confused, nodded with a slight smile.

Dwayne pulled the pistol from the shoulder holster and went to the door. He peered out into the parking lot for a moment, then nodded to Donna Sue. "Let's go!"

Once more they sprinted for the car.

———

RATHER THAN TAKE THE DIRECT ROUTE OFFERED by Hillside Avenue, Dwayne chose a more circuitous way by going east on Harry Street to Rock Road. From there he turned north going all the way up to Thirty-Seventh Street, turning back west toward Mrs. Davies mansion.

Donna Sue was quietly frightened at first, then as they rolled along, she began to regain a sense of calmness. "There's nothing but open country up here."

"Yeah," he acknowledged. "But it'll prob'ly be all built up someday."

"Where are you taking me?"

"To stay with a lady by the name of Missus Davies," Dwayne answered. "You'll like it there. She lives in a big house with a secretary, butler and chauffeur. And there's a big wall all around the place along with guards."

"Wow!" Donna Sue said. Then she frowned at him. "Just what is this fancy lady to you?"

"A client," he said.

"Wait a minute!" Donna Sue exclaimed. "What about my job? And the rent on the apartment?"

"I'll talk to your boss," Dwayne said. "And explain

ever'thing. Arnie can give me a call the next time he drops in for the receipts. So what's the rent on your apartment? Thirty a month, right?"

"Right."

"No problem," Dwayne said. "I'll go see the Greeleys and pay next month's in advance. I'll tell 'em you had to go out of town on a family emergency."

"Okay," Donna said. "That should work 'til this dies down." She was silent for several moments, looking at the countryside along Rock Road. "What's the story on Missus Davies? She must like you a lot."

"Yeah," Dwayne said. "She does, I guess. Missus Davies runs a call girl service."

"She's a madam!" Donna Sue shrieked, now more concerned about that situation than the chance of being kidnapped. "Where the hell are you taking me, Dwayne? To a whorehouse?"

"It ain't a whorehouse," Dwayne said. "She has a high class operation she runs out of her home and that office where Rachel works. Her girls entertain high society guys and others who are here in Wichita on business. All big shot rich guys."

"I hope she don't expect me to do any work for her," Donna Sue said sullenly.

"You're sure good looking enough."

"*Dwayne Wheeler!*"

Chapter 11

When Dwayne reached Mrs. Davies' estate, he found everything arranged for a quick entrance. The gate guards recognized both him and the car, and they motioned him through. He took the driveway toward the house, and when he reached the porch, the butler Carson wasted no time as he came down the steps and opened the door for Donna Sue. Dwayne let himself out the driver's side, and reached in the back to grab Donna Sue's suitcase.

"I'll take that, sir," Carson said as Dwayne walked up.

"Thanks," Dwayne said. He took Donna Sue's arm and they followed the butler into the house. They went all the way down the hall to the stairs, and ascended to the floor where Miss Caruthers' office was located. The secretary was waiting for them on the landing. "Good evening, Mr. Wheeler."

"Hi, Miss Caruthers," Dwayne said. "This is my girlfriend Donna Sue Connors."

Miss Caruthers displayed a slight smile.

Donna Sue felt shoddy and unkempt in front of the prim and neat woman. "I'm pleased to meet you."

"We've arranged a room for you, Miss Connors," Miss Caruthers said. "Please follow me."

The procession now consisted of Miss Caruthers in the lead with Dwayne and Donna Sue behind her. Carson brought up the rear, still holding the suitcase. When they reached a room at the opposite end of the hall, Miss Caruthers opened it, and stepped inside. Dwayne allowed Donna Sue to precede him. Carson came in and walked directly over to a window seat and set the suitcase on it.

"Is there anything else, Miss?" he asked.

"No, thank you, Carson," Miss Caruthers said.

Donna Sue, her mouth wide open, stared in wonder at the huge bedroom that was larger than her entire apartment. An enormous canopied bed occupied the east side of the room with bedside tables holding lamps and a telephone. A settee with end tables and two large easy chairs were on the west side of the chamber, and two large windows covered by heavy drapes occupied the north. Near there on the southwest corner of the room stood a chair and a writing desk with a small lamp.

Miss Caruthers walked to a door and opened it. "Here is your closet, Miss Connors. You may hang your things in there at your convenience.

Donna Sue gasped. "My God! It's another room!"

"It is a *walk-in* closet, Miss Connors," the secretary said. She went to another door, this one slightly ajar. She pushed it open. "The bathroom."

Donna Sue, consumed by curiosity, eagerly approached the entrance, then stopped and looked inside. The design was in two separate sections; the outside was a dressing room complete with a dresser sporting multi-drawers down both sides, a large lighted mirror and a cushioned bench. She walked through the front area into the bathroom proper. Her eyes opened wide at the sight of a toilet and sink with ornate plumbing.

"Are them faucets and pipes gold?" Donna Sue asked.

"Gold *plated*," Miss Caruthers replied.

Now Donna Sue turned to inspect a glassed-in combination bathtub and shower. Towels of various sizes and thicknesses were draped across a quartet of racks.

"Oh, Lord!" Donna Sue exclaimed. "I've died and gone to heaven."

"I am glad you are pleased with the arrangements," Miss Caruthers remarked in a slightly condescending tone of voice. "If you require anything you may ring the buzzers by the door. The top one will summon me, the middle Carson and the bottom a maid."

"A maid!" Donna Sue exclaimed. "I don't believe I've ever seen a maid."

"Do you have any questions, Miss Connors?"

"No, ma'am. Thank you so much."

"You will be called for meals," Miss Caruthers said. "You, Carson and the maid will eat together in the dinette just off the kitchen."

"All right," Donna said.

"Excuse me," Dwayne interjected. "Will I be able to visit Donna Sue here?"

Miss Caruthers nodded. "Mrs. Davies stated that you may call on her at any time. If you wish to phone, you'll find the number on the center of the telephone dial." With that, she walked from the room, shutting the door behind her.

Donna Sue rushed into Dwayne's arms. "I can't believe you brought me to a place like this. I thought I was going to be stuck away in a cheap motor lodge somewhere."

"Only the best for you, baby," Dwayne replied in his best Sam Spade style.

"I hate to unpack," Donna Sue said. "My stuff is gonna look so tacky in here."

"Listen, honey-bunch, I got to go," Dwayne said, glancing at his watch. "You settle in and I'll be in touch tomorrow or the next day." He walked over to note the number on the telephone.

"You call me if you can't come to visit," Donna Sue insisted. "I'm not so sure how I'm gonna fit in around here. I'll need to hear from you or I'll start being a little crazy."

"I will," he promised. He kissed her and walked to the door. He opened it and turned back. "Enjoy yourself."

"I think I'm too overwhelmed," she said.

The next morning, Dwayne went to the Jayhawker Restaurant to tell them about Donna Sue's absence. Art Manger, the owner, had come in to pick up the receipts from the previous day. When he saw Dwayne enter the eatery, he asked, "Where the hell is Donna Sue?"

"She got called away because of a family emergency," Dwayne replied. "I took her down to the bus station last evening."

"Aw, damn!" Art said. "How long is she gonna be gone?"

"It's hard to tell," Dwayne replied. "Prob'ly a couple of weeks at least."

Maisie Burnett turned in an order at the kitchen window, then joined them, giving Dwayne an angry glare. She turned her attention to the owner. "I can't handle the place by myself, Art."

"Shit!" the owner said. "I'm gonna have to go to an employment agency and get another girl to fill in."

"What about Sally?" Maisie asked.

Sally was Art's wife who had worked in the Jayhawker as a waitress until marrying the boss. She was a cute, plump girl fifteen years his junior, and she had him wrapped around her little finger from the moment that he fell for her. Now, much more than plump, she spent her time nibbling sweets and goading Art into taking her to the movies three or four times a week.

"Sally come back to work?" Art asked. "The last thing she wants to do is get behind this counter again."

"Tell her it's an emergency," Dwayne suggested.

"A hell of a lot of good that'll do," Art said, picking up the money and order slips. "The bank don't open 'til ten, so I'll have to put this in the office safe and run down to the employment agency. Man! This really screws things up."

When he went to the back, Maisie stepped up to Dwayne. "What is this crap? Donna Sue hasn't had nothing to do with her family in all the time I've known her. She's got a couple of sisters and a brother but I don't think she's seen 'em since the war."

"Well, maybe one of 'em wrote her a letter."

"Where'd she go, Dwayne?"

"I don't know."

"You said you took her to the bus station," Maisie said. "Where'd she buy a ticket to?"

"I can't remember."

"Bullshit!" Maisie exclaimed. "What did the sign say on the front of the bus she got on?"

"I didn't notice," he said. He was hungry but didn't plan on eating there. He was afraid Maisie might spit in his grilled cheese sandwich.

The waitress frowned. "You better not have done nothing to her, Dwayne Wheeler!"

"Oh, for Chrissake!"

He made a quick withdrawal, glancing over at the OK Barbershop as he walked down to the Ford to drive to Donna Sue's apartment house. Instead of going straight to his destination, he approached it from a roundabout way, making sure there were no cars with suspicious characters watching the area.

After parking and walking up to the front porch, he turned around to survey the immediate neighborhood from that vantage point. The .45 pistol was nestled comfortably in the concealed shoulder holster, and he was ready in case a bad situation developed. But the neighborhood was quiet with some kids playing and an old woman preparing her flowerbeds for the coming summer.

Dwayne walked into the hallway and stopped at the first door on the right. He knocked and waited. He could hear footsteps approaching, then the knob turned and Mr. Greeley stood there looking at him.

"Hi," Dwayne said. "I'm a friend of Donna Sue Connors, and I want to let you know that she's had a family emergency come up unexpectedly."

"Oh, goodness," Mr. Greeley said. "I'm so sorry to hear that."

Now Mrs. Greeley joined them. "What's going on, Eb?"

"This young man is a friend of Donna Sue's. He's just told me that she's had an emergency in her family."

"Oh, dear!" Mrs. Greeley said. "Is there anything we can do?"

"No, ma'am," Dwayne replied, reaching for his wallet. "She's gonna be gone for at least two weeks, and wanted me to pay you the next month's rent in case she can't get back in time."

"Donna Sue don't have to do that," Mr. Greeley said. "In fact, if she ends up a bit short, we would be happy to give her some extry time."

"Of course," Mrs. Greeley said.

Dwayne pulled thirty dollars out of his wallet and held the money out. "She's got no financial problems about this."

"Are you sure?" Mrs. Greeley asked. "Because she don't have to—"

"Thanks just the same," Dwayne interrupted. "But ever'thing's fine in the rent-paying department."

Mr. Greeley took the bills. "Well, if you hear from her and she needs anything a'tall, get ahold of us."

"We'll be happy to do what we can," Mrs. Greeley assured him.

"That's real nice of you folks," Dwayne said. "I'll be seeing you later."

He nodded a goodbye, then turned and walked through the front door, thinking that maybe the couple wasn't so bad after all; except where sex was concerned.

———

DONNA SUE STUDIED THE THREE CALL BUTTONS on the wall by the door to her room. When she had unpacked, she found her clothes hopelessly wrinkled and twisted; especially the ones that Dwayne had packed by throwing them in the suitcase. She needed an iron and ironing board, but wasn't quite sure who to buzz for the items. After several minutes she decided the very imposing Miss Caruthers and the high and mighty butler would not be the ones. She pressed the maid button and let it go.

There was no sound so she pressed it again; then again longer; and finally gave it four hard pushes. After staring at the device for a half a minute, she walked over to the settee and sat down to see what would happen.

A rap on the door sounded some three minutes later, and Donna Sue walked over and opened it. A short, skinny teenage girl in a black dress with a short white apron, stood there smiling. She had freckles and red hair with a conservative hairdo, and was made up tastefully with lipstick and rouge. The girl smiled shyly and curtsied. "Did you want something, Miss?" she asked in a deep southern accent.

"Oh, hi," Donna Sue said. "I need an iron and an ironing board, please."

"I'll fetch 'em for you, Miss."

Donna Sue watched as the girl hurried down the hall to a door and opened it. She withdrew an iron and ironing board, then came back to the room. She walked in and set up the board, plugged in the iron, and said, "I'm ready. What is it you want arned?"

"I can do that myself," Donna Sue said.

"No, Miss," the girl said. "That's my job." Then she added, "My name is Jewell."

"Hi, Jewell. My name is Donna Sue," she said. "And really, I can do it. I iron my things all the time."

"That's what I'm here for, Miss Donna Sue," Jewell said.

"All right, Jewell. It's that pile of clothes on the bed there."

Jewell walked over and sorted out the mound of clothing to suit herself, then came back with a blouse. She laid it out on the board, tested the heat of the iron, then went to work.

Donna Sue sat down on the settee and observed her

for a minute to see if the girl knew what she was doing. "I'm not used to having that done for me."

"I recollect that arning was one of the first things my mama taught me," Jewell said. Then she giggled. "Outside o' changing my little brother's diapers."

"My mother and I did the washing for other folks," Donna Sue said. "There was a lot of ironing involved in that, believe me."

"I bet so," Jewell said. "Are you a-coming to work for Missus Davies?"

At first Donna Sue was upset that the girl would think she was a prostitute, but she supposed that many of those women stayed in that room when they first arrived. She cleared her throat. "Uh...no. My boyfriend works for Missus Davies and I had to have a place to stay for awhile."

"Missus Davies is awful nice," Jewell said, pushing the iron expertly over the clothes. "When I come to Wichita from Mississippi with my boyfriend Proctor, we stayed in a hotel downtown while he looked for work."

"What kind of work was Proctor looking for?"

"He wanted to find a job at an airplane factory," Jewell explained. "Proctor figgered if'n he could learn to build airplanes, we could go back to Mississippi and he'd do it hisself and sell 'em."

It took a lot of effort for Donna Sue not to laugh out loud. She fought the impulse down to a smile, then asked, "How'd he do?"

"Proctor couldn't find nothing 'cause he cain't hardly read nor write, and we started running out o' money. Perty soon they wasn't nothing for us to eat and the hotel clerk was gittin' riled 'cause we hadn't paid no rent for awhile."

"It's always tough when the money runs short, isn't it?" Donna Sue remarked.

"Well, one night Proctor come up to the room with this fat ol' man who was kinda drunk," Jewell said. "He tole me the feller would give us five dollars cash money if'n I got into the bed with him. I din't want to, but Proctor said he was gonna smack me one if'n I din't. So I did. We got the money and went out fer something to eat."

Donna Sue leaned back into the settee knowing she was about to hear the true story of how Jewell came to that house.

"The next day Proctor brought back three fellers and we got enough money to pay the rent," Jewell said. She went over and got a skirt, coming back to the ironing board. "Then it got to be a reg'lar habit. But they din't pay five dollars, I had to do it for two or three. And some of 'em was rough and called me a bitch and bad stuff like 'at. One day I had to do seven o' them fellers and it was hard 'cause it made me so sore." She continued the ironing chore, talking easily about the ordeal. "Then one of them fellers turned out to be a cop. He arrested us both, and we got took to jail. I was put in the woman's side into a cell, and they was a really perty gal there all dressed up. She was in on the same charge as me. Prosty-too-shun. And she was mad 'cause she said the cops was supposed to be paid off in her case. I tole her about how Proctor was bringing men up to our hotel room, then she tole me that she went to men in nice hotels and they was gennelmen and paid her extry and that sometimes she went to parties where rich men was. They was nice stuff to drink and eat, and the men was real perlite when they ast a girl to go up to a bedroom with 'em." Jewell laughed. "I'll tell you, Donna Sue, that sounded a lot better than having Proctor drag in drunk fellers who jumped all over me."

"I imagine it was," Donna Sue said, growing fascinated.

"Anyhow, one of them lady guards come and took that perty gal out of my cell," Jewell continued. "I was sorry to see her go 'cause she was real nice, but about twenny minutes later, the lady guard come back and said somebody made my bail. I was took out of the cell and up to the front where that gal was with another women. D'you know who that woman was?"

"No," Donna Sue replied. "I don't have any idea."

"Well, it was Miss Caruthers," Jewell said with a giggle. "That gal had tole her all about me, and they got me out o' jail and all the charges dropped. They brung me out here and tole me I din't have to go back to Proctor no more and I din't have to put up with no men. They taught me how to be a maid. And here I am."

"That's quite a story," Donna Sue said. "Was Proctor the only boyfriend you ever had?"

"No, Miss Donna Sue," Jewell replied. "But he was the cutest. And the meanest, too, I reckon." She held up a blouse. "I kin put pleats in the back here. I'd be proud to do it, if'n that's what you want."

"Thank you, Jewell," Donna Sue said. "That would be lovely."

"It'll be time for us to eat perty quick," she said. "Me and the butler and the cook eat after Missus Davies and Miss Caruthers is served."

"Good," Donna Sue said. "I'm getting kind of hungry."

It was early evening, and Dwayne had stopped at a Kings-X hamburger house on West Douglas and picked up three boxes along with an extra large order of French fries. He went to his office and settled down at the desk to enjoy the meal. When he finished, he put the empty containers in the wastebasket and set it out in the hall for the janitor to get in the morning.

He dialed Mack Crofton's number and was glad when the bootlegger answered the call. "Mack, I want to thank you for the warning. I got Donna Sue to a safe spot."

"That's good, Dwayne," Mack said. "I haven't heard anything about the kidnapping, so maybe they didn't even try."

"Could be," Dwayne said. "Listen, Mack. I'd like to sit down and have a talk with you about things. I'm thinking maybe tomorrow evening out at a little café on Highway Fifty-Four east of town."

"Is that the Chatterbox?"

"Yeah," Dwayne said. "Can you make it at around eight o'clock?"

"No problem."

"See you then," Dwayne said. He hung up, thinking that things seemed to be grinding to a halt, and he wasn't any closer to finding out who had killed Stubb Durham. He had to figure a way to loosen things up and get some action rolling.

Chapter 12

When Donna Sue woke up the second morning of her stay in Mrs. Davies' house, she wasn't sure where she was for a few moments. The strange sights in the big bedroom surprised her, and she instinctively sat up in alarm. Then it all came back. The threat of kidnapping, the drive to Mrs. Davies' place, and being taken to this same room. She glanced at the small ornate clock on the bed table, noting it was a little past six. Normally she would be getting ready to go to work at that time.

She got up to pee, and stopped to look at herself in the dressing room mirror, thinking that even her nightgown looked cheap and tawdry in the luxurious surroundings. She walked over to the toilet and raised the lid. When she first used it, she had been astonished to find the seat actually had a thick, fuzzy cover. It was nice not to have to grimace against a cold one as she sat down.

With that taken care of, she went back into the bedroom and opened one of the drapes to look down at another unusual aspect of these temporary digs: a swimming pool. It was still early in the season, and no water was in it, but the sight was like something in a movie. An immense, beautifully manicured lawn ran from there to the wall. Beyond that she could see a wide expanse of the Kansas prairie stretching out to the horizon, the tall buffalo grass waving slowly back and forth in the gentle breeze.

A dark thought entered her mind as she thought of people living in a manner like this while others took in washing or waited tables, living from payday to payday. After a few moments of reflection on the unfairness of the world, the fugitive waitress turned to get her small makeup case and put on her face for the day.

———

Donna Sue was dressed, made up and ready for the day by seven. There was plenty of time before breakfast, and she had just started to make the bed when a rap at the door sounded. "Come in."

Jewell walked through the door, curtsied and said, "Good morning to you, Miss Donna Sue." She carried a table radio with her. "Miss Caruthers thought you might like to have this."

"Oh, that's just great!" Donna Sue exclaimed, glad to have something to help pass the days and nights. "By the way, Jewell, you don't have to call me *Miss* Donna Sue. Just my name will be fine."

"I been taught by Miss Caruthers to talk to guests like 'at," Jewell said. "If'n I don't I'd prob'ly git into trouble."

"Well then you don't have to curtsy."

"Same thing, Miss Donna Sue," Jewell said. "You ain't making your bed, are you?"

"I'm just starting."

"I'll do that," Jewell said, walking over. "I should have did it yesterday. And I'll straighten things up, too."

"I didn't know that was the way things were done around here," Donna Sue said. "I'm afraid I've already cleaned up the bathroom."

"That's okay. But I'll do it from now on."

"Sure," Donna Sue said. "I'm getting a little hungry."

Jewell began making the bed. "It won't be too long, then you and me can go downstairs for breakfast." She giggled. "I never seen anything like a dinette 'til I come here."

"By the way, where do Missus Davies and Miss Caruthers eat?"

"I carry up a big ol' tray to Missus Davies' sitting room just outside her bedroom," Jewell said. "Miss Caruthers eats with her there." She fluffed the pillows. "They sleep together."

"In the same bedroom?"

"In the same bed," Jewell said. "They's only one in Missus Davies bedroom. But it's even bigger'n this'un here."

Donna Sue was more than just a little taken aback by the knowledge. "That seems kind of strange, don't it?"

Jewell shrugged. "Oh, I don't know. Back home lots of us sleep in the same bed. They was eight of us kids divvied up 'twixt two beds. Our littlest brother slept with us girls. And we din't have no bathrooms neither. We had a outhouse."

Donna Sue, a city girl, had heard of outside privies before, but had never seen one. "Where did you take baths?"

"In the kitchen on Saturday nights," Jewell said. "We'd pour hot water in a tub we brang in from the back porch." She giggled again. "When it was us girls' turn,

Mama kept an eye on the winder to make sure our brothers din't try to peek in and see us nekkid."

Donna Sue grinned in spite of herself.

Jewell did some more straightening up, then said, "I reckon we can go downstairs to eat now."

DONNA SUE HAD FOUND THE EATING EXPERIENCE in Mrs. Davies' dinette quite pleasant. She also discovered that Carson the butler actually had a pleasing personality when he wasn't tending to business. The only problem was that his English accent made it difficult to understand him at times. "How have you found things so far, Miss Connors?" he asked.

"I'm as amazed as when I first got here," Donna Sue replied. "This is much more than I expected."

"Mrs. Davies was concerned about your comfort."

"I'm very comfortable, thank you."

The cook Mrs. Crawford also had a kindly disposition, and gave her a warm welcome to the table as everyone settled down. That morning the woman had prepared a sumptuous breakfast of scrambled eggs, ham, English muffins, and country-fried potatoes. The latter made Donna Sue think of Dwayne's early morning menu preferences.

After eating, Donna Sue went back to her room to listen to the radio for awhile. There were country music disk jockeys that alternated programs, the usual newscasts, and weather to keep her amused. At mid-morning, Jewell made another appearance with a rap on the door. "Miss Donna Sue, Miss Caruthers would like to see you. Foller me."

Jewell led her to the office down the hall, and gestured

for her to enter. Donna Sue walked in and saw Miss Caruthers sitting at her large desk. The lady smiled at her. "Please sit down, Miss Connors."

"Thank you."

Miss Caruthers seemed to be studying her for a moment, then she asked, "How are you settling in?"

"Real good," Donna Sue said. "Ever'thing's mighty elegant here."

"I'm glad it pleases you," Miss Caruthers said. "Mrs. Davies is looking forward to meeting you. Meanwhile, we'd like to know a little bit about you. I hope you don't mind if I ask you a few questions." She continued without waiting for an answer. "What sort of work do you do?"

"I'm a waitress," Donna Sue replied. "At the Jayhawker Restaurant downtown. Well, it ain't really a restaurant, it's a diner. But during the war I worked at Boeing. I was a welder. I got a Class A license, then after a year or so they made me a quality assurance inspector. I was making a whole lot more money than when I waited the counter."

Miss Caruthers' eyes opened wide. "That's quite an accomplishment for a woman. Why did you leave the job?"

"When the war ended, they laid off all us women. They didn't need us no more, but they kept the men on."

"Oh, dear," Miss Caruthers said. "Life isn't fair for the female sex, is it?"

"I was real upset, since some of the men weren't as good welders as us girls."

"That's too bad. So you went back to being a waitress. How do you like that job?"

Donna Sue frowned. "I don't like it at all. I had to quit school after the eighth grade to help my mother out. My dad left her and me and my brother and two sisters. So we did what we could. And now I'm doing the only other thing I know besides welding."

"Is there anything else you're interested in doing?" Miss Caruthers asked. "Something suitable for a woman?"

"Yes," Donna Sue replied. "I'd like to be a secretary. I could work for my boyfriend Dwayne like on the radio show he likes so much. It's about a detective and his secretary." She sighed. "But I don't even know how to type."

"Have you been involved with Mr. Wheeler long?"

"Not really," Donna Sue replied. "We been going together for a little while."

"Mrs. Davies holds him in high regard," Miss Caruthers said. "He has served her well in helping her in some difficult situations."

"I guess Dwayne is a good detective," Donna Sue said. "Sometimes he does things sort of bassackwards, but he comes out ahead in the end."

"Does he make much money in his profession?"

Donna Sue laughed lightly. "He'd do a lot better if he stopped betting on the horses."

"Does he drink much?"

Donna Sue was beginning to feel uncomfortable with the way the conversation was drifting. "No. Normal amount, I guess."

"Mmm," Miss Caruthers said. "You're a very attractive woman, Donna Sue."

"Thank you."

"It's too bad about little Jewell," Miss Caruthers said.

"She told me about her boyfriend and getting arrested and all."

"I'm afraid her looks limit her to the bottom of the oldest profession," Miss Caruthers said. "If she continued on the path she was following, the poor thing would end up turning tricks for a dollar and addicted to drugs while working for a street pimp who would treat her quite badly."

"Missus Davies seems to be most kindly to her."

"If you ever want to make your own life a lot better, let me know. You could end up with a nice apartment, beautiful clothes, and...well, you understand what I'm saying."

Now Donna Sue knew she was being offered a job as a call girl. She took a deep breath, steadied herself, and said. "I'll be all right."

"Of course you will," Miss Caruthers said. "And if you need to talk to me about anything, don't hesitate. You just march down here whenever you want to."

Donna Sue, sensing a dismissal, stood up. "Thank you, Miss Caruthers."

THE CHATTERBOX CAFÉ OUT ON HIGHWAY 54 was typical of the eating places for automobile travelers. It was set off by itself with a parking lot that offered easy egress and ingress to the two-lane highway that went by it. It was near dusk, and Dwayne had parked the Ford in the shadows at the side of the eatery and gone inside to order some coffee as he waited for Mack Crofton to show up for their meeting.

He chose a seat at the end of the counter that gave the best view of the door. He shifted his shoulder holster to a more comfortable position as he sipped the brew. The waitress was a rather heavy young woman with a noticeable moustache across her upper lip. If this caper had been one of Sam Spade's, she would have been voluptuous, beautiful and a big flirt wanting to lure him into bed.

He looked up as Mack came through the door. The

private detective got to his feet and went to a booth where the bootlegger joined him. The waitress came over with an expression on her face that indicated she knew her lack of attractiveness to men, and resented the hell out of it.

"Whatcha need?"

"A cheeseburger for me," Dwayne said. "And French fries. Large order. And an Orange Crush."

Mack said, "Just bring me an ice tea please."

As the waitress walked off, Dwayne gave his companion a look of concern. "Have you lost your appetite, Mack?" He studied him closer. "Y'know, I think you've dropped some weight."

"I ain't been eating good lately," Mack admitted. "When is this shit coming to an end?"

"Oh, man," Dwayne said brightly. "Things are really running along! That's why I wanted to talk to you face-to-face. What's happening at your end?"

"Well, there are lots of meetings and things like that," Mack said. "They're just about ready to make some big moves on the bookies. They sort of backed off where the bootleggers are concerned, because they don't want to rock the boat too much. If big trouble breaks out all of a sudden, it'll be bad for them. The bookies shouldn't be such a big deal."

"Has anyone mentioned Stubb Durham?"

Mack shook his head. "I ain't heard one word about him. It kind of sounds to me like a pissed-off bettor prob'ly did him in."

Dwayne was bitterly disappointed by the lack of meaningful information. "Well, I'll find out who shot him sooner than later, you can bet on that." He knew that was nothing but bullshit. He was at a dead end, and things were steadily getting worse where the K.C. mob was concerned. "Have you seen any cops around?"

"Nope," Mack said. "Harry Denton is showing up more and more, but he's the only local besides me and Arlo Merriwell."

The waitress walked up with the food and sat it down, giving Mack the cheeseburger and fries. As soon as she left Dwayne took the plate for himself. He leaned forward. "Think, Mack! Have any names been mentioned? That's real important. The more names I get, the faster I can solve this caper."

"I got to tell you God's truth, Dwayne. I ain't learning shit. Are you sure you can wrap this up real soon?"

"O'course, Mack, but you gotta keep in mind that there's certain legalities I got to watch out for. I can't make a case unless I tie up all ends so some slick lawyer can't get 'em off. The district attorney insists on it."

"Are you working with the D.A.?"

Dwayne looked around, then lowered his voice. "I ain't saying I am, and I ain't saying I ain't."

Mack, terribly unhappy, took a shallow drink from his ice tea.

The sun was almost below the horizon as Donna Sue gazed out the window. She had been thinking about Miss Caruthers' offer, but the thought of going to a hotel to meet strange men, then get naked in front of them and allow them to rut in her body was more than she could bear. It would be even worse than the times when her first husband came home after a couple of weeks on the road, and dragged her into the bedroom. He would throw her down on the bed, then raise her skirt and pull off her panties. After mounting her, he would begin humping away and order her take off her blouse and brassier.

Even the male customers in the Jayhawker trying to get her to go out with them were repulsive to her. Most weren't particularly attractive and she certainly didn't want to have sex with them. She remembered being disappointed when Dwayne didn't do any flirting when he came into the restaurant. He was really a good looking guy. Their meeting at Western Danceland had ended up being a blessing in her life.

A movement below the window caught her eye, and as she looked down she could make out two figures standing close together. It was Miss Caruthers and another woman. The two turned to each other, embraced, and exchanged a lingering sexy kiss. Donna Sue figured the stranger to be Mrs. Davies. From the way they were acting it was obvious they were either in love or lust with each other.

She could remember having a crush on a ninth grade girl when she was in the seventh grade at Roosevelt Junior High School. The object of her puzzling affection was from a well-to-do family and very pretty. Her hair was always made up, and she wore beautiful clothes and must have had dozens of outfits. Donna Sue would fantasize about being best friends with her, and going to her house to try on pretty dresses. Some of the daydreams involved kissing each other, and she had been very confused about her feelings. But eventually her romantic inclinations were turned toward a new cute boy who transferred into Roosevelt, and the other affection faded away.

And there had been some women at Boeing who dressed mannishly and wore their hair short. Everybody referred to them as "lesbos" and she could remember overhearing a male machinist talking to his buddies, saying,

"Them dykes make me nervous; I don't like being around women that like to eat pussy as much as I do." The remark elicited a lot of loud masculine laughter.

Donna Sue watched the two women as they released the embrace, then walked slowly around the swimming pool hand-in-hand.

DWAYNE LAID OUT SOME MONEY PLUS A TIP ON the table as he and Mack Crofton made ready to leave the café. They walked together toward the door with Mack in the lead. They had reached the outside and gone a few paces when a car came off the highway, and eased up to them.

The gunshots exploded the stillness of the evening and Dwayne, being a trained soldier, hit the ground while drawing his pistol. Mack caught a chestful of steel-jacketed slugs that staggered him backward to fall to the parking lot. As the car sped away, Dwayne leaped to his feet, chasing after it while firing hurriedly aimed shots. The back window shattered under the impact of his bullets as the vehicle disappeared down Highway 54.

Dwayne turned and trotted over to Mack, kneeling down to check him out. The bootlegger had the same look of death like the slain soldiers Dwayne used to see sprawled on the ground when his unit moved into areas of recent fighting during the war.

"Oh, God, Mack!" he said. "I am so fucking sorry!" He looked up to see customers from the café staring at him. They had run outside at the sound of the shots, and now stood in a huddled mass. The unattractive waitress, wide-eyed and slack jawed, gaped at him. Dwayne reached into his inside jacket pocket and pulled out the private investigator badge, holding it up. "I'm a detective," he yelled at them. "Call the sheriff's department! I'm going after the killers."

He raced to the Ford, started it up and sped out of the parking area.

Chapter 13

Dwayne had no intention of chasing after the shooters' vehicle. He was certain it had been stolen, thus would be abandoned, and the occupants picked up by another automobile. He wanted to put some distance between himself and the site of the shooting, even though he felt terrible about abandoning Mack Crofton's body. He continued west on Highway 54 until he reached a blacktop road headed north. He wheeled onto it and pressed down hard on the accelerator.

It was dark now and the only illumination out on the open prairie came from the Ford's headlights on the two-lane road. Now and then Dwayne could see the lights of a distant farmhouse, but there were no other signs of life. When he reached a spot where there was total darkness, he braked to a stop. After lighting a cigarette, he turned off the ignition and got out of the car. The silence in the area was close to overwhelming to a city boy, but Dwayne appreciated it as he sat on the left front fender with his feet on the bumper. It was time to settle down and concentrate on what was going on in the caper, not only at that moment but in the foreseeable future.

That evening's deadly incident was a setup, no doubt. Somebody had followed Mack to the place, then waited for him to emerge from the café. That would be the Kansas City pricks. They wouldn't have known Dwayne would be there, but being able to take some shots at the private detective bugging them had been an unexpected bonus. Except the bastards had missed.

Dwayne lit another cigarette on the remnants of the first one as his mental processes continued mulling over the situation. *What could Mack Crofton have done to make them want to take him out?* his mind pondered. Had they discovered he was a snitch? Wait a minute! Maybe the kidnapping of Donna Sue had been bullshit. The K.C. guys or one of their Wichita ass-kissers must have begun to consider the possibility that someone was working undercover on them. The most obvious suspect would be Mack. One way to find out was to tell him something that would cause some sort of reaction they could observe. When they told Mack about plans to snatch Donna Sue, it was in order to see what would happen. The minute Dwayne rushed her away from the apartment house proved that Mack had told him about the plot. And there must have been somebody from K.C. who had been in the neighborhood and watched it all. Probably from a parked car.

If that was the case, Dwayne could feel a little better. Billy Joe Clayton had set up Mack to be hit. Then a cold realization hit Dwayne hard. That meant the K.C. bunch would figure he knew one hell of a lot about them. Now they would be laying for him. And Dwayne also faced two other very bad possibilities. The cops were probably already working on getting his private detective license revoked. And no doubt some of them were in cahoots with the mob. And that would include his old pal Ben Forester. Maybe Ben had warned him away because he didn't want him to get bumped off. If Ben was told to take him out, there was a good chance he would refuse to do it. But Sergeant Gallagher and Lieutenant Cordell would have no objections at all.

Dwayne now lit a third cigarette. He had to face it. It was over. The caper was a lost cause. He had no idea who had killed Stubb Durham, and there was a strong certainty that he would suffer the same fate if he stayed in Wichita. And even if he survived, he would not be able to work as a private detective anymore. That part of his life was gone no matter what.

This was the worst day of his life since his mother died.

Dwayne, his throat raw from the cigarettes, threw the last one on the ground. He got back in the car and drove away. For awhile he wandered off onto dirt roads, but he eventually reached another blacktop that was State Highway 196. This led him to the small town of El Dorado. A motor lodge made up of frame cabins came into view, and he pulled off to rent one for the night.

It was time for some rest, then make some rather significant decisions about the rest of his life.

―――

DONNA SUE HAD JUST FINISHED BREAKFAST WITH her dining companions when Miss Caruthers appeared in the dinette door. "Donna Sue," she said. "Mrs. Davies would like to see you."

"I'm so glad. I really want to thank her for all the kind things she's done for me."

Miss Caruthers led her away from the dinette to the main part of the house. They went down the first floor corridor, then entered the room Mrs. Davies used for greeting visitors. She was seated on the sofa, and stood up. "Hello, Donna Sue. I'm pleased to finally meet you."

"Thank you," Donna Sue said, fascinated by the old fashion dress the lady wore. "I appreciate your consideration." She now recognized Mrs. Davies as the other woman kissing and caressing Miss Caruthers by the swimming pool.

Miss Caruthers said, "I'll leave you two to get acquainted."

She left the room, and Mrs. Davies indicated that Donna Sue should join her on the sofa. As soon as she was seated, the lady said, "I have a special regard for Mr. Wheeler."

"Miss Caruthers said he'd done some special things for you."

"That's right," Mrs. Davies said. "He proved to be both efficient and thorough. Would you care for some coffee?"

"No, thank you," Donna Sue said. "I just finished breakfast, so I'm fine for the time being."

"If I'd thought about it, I would have had you join Miss Caruthers and me for breakfast."

"Yes, ma'am."

"Miss Caruthers tells me you're a waitress at the moment, but you once had a rather important job at Boeing during the war."

"Yes, ma'am," Donna Sue said, always proud to discuss her aircraft career. "I was a welder and a quality control inspector."

"I see," Mrs. Davies acknowledged. "Miss Caruthers

also said that you were let go with the other women when the war ended. How unfair!"

"Yes it was."

"And you had to return to your job as a waitress. That must have been quite a loss in salary."

"Yes, ma'am. With overtime I was making close to ten times more at the plant."

"It's a shame when a young woman as attractive as you is forced to work beneath herself," Mrs. Davies said.

"To tell you the truth, I ain't really beneath myself. I don't have much education, so that's all I can do. Women don't have much choice anyhow. Even ones who've finished high school."

"I believe Miss Caruthers intimated that you could use your good looks and intelligence to earn much more money. Frankly, Donna Sue, with the right hairdo, makeup and clothing, you would be a beautiful woman."

"Oh, I doubt that."

"Believe me, I'm not exaggerating," Mrs. Davies said. "This is something in which I am quite experienced. You have the potential of moving up to a more than comfortable life; I am speaking of a luxurious existence."

"Yes, ma'am,"

"I have a number of women working for me who are earning between two and three hundred dollars a week."

Donna Sue, now very uneasy, only nodded.

"Some of them are even married," Mrs. Davies continued. "One of the girls has a husband who is attending Wichita University on the G.I. Bill. They are saving every dime that she makes to get established when he graduates. All the husbands appreciate the extra income."

Now Donna Sue was shocked. She had never heard of such a thing. "Well...I guess...I mean..." She cleared her throat. "You see, I want to be a secretary. If I was a secretary I could work for Dwayne in his office. But I can't type."

Mrs. Davies was silent for a moment, then she said, "Oh, yes, Miss Caruthers also mentioned that ambition. Would such a career make you happy?"

Donna Sue replied, "I'd really, *really* like to be a secretary."

"You seem to be quite fond of Mr. Wheeler. Are you two serious?"

"We're not sure right now," Donna Sue said. "Actually, we haven't discussed our feelings for each other too much. Well, we like to say sweet things to one another." She sighed and smiled. "But...to tell you the truth, I could fall in love with him."

"All right, Donna Sue," Mrs. Davies said, standing up. "Well, it was so very nice talking with you. I have business I must attend to, so please excuse me."

"Yes, ma'am."

Donna Sue walked from the room feeling a heavy sense of disquiet. She had read in magazines about girls and women being kidnapped and addicted to drugs, then sold into the white slave racket.

———

DWAYNE DIDN'T FEEL ANY BETTER IN THE morning when he awoke in the rustic cabin of the motor lodge. On the contrary, he felt worse. During last night's period of thinking things over, he realized he hadn't given Donna Sue a bit of consideration. When the new day dawned he knew he had to face the awful fact that there was still a chance she was in danger because the K.C. mob knew of her close association with him. They would figure she was also very well informed about them. He couldn't very well flee Wichita and leave her behind. If he did cut and run, those pricks would still want to harm her to show that nobody got away with standing up against them. A tough reputation had to be maintained in the underworld, no matter where the gang operated. And that included Wichita, Kansas.

He had to stick around and somehow get her out of town. That would mean going back to her apartment to get the rest of her things; and the bad guys knew her address and would be watching it. At least she was safe at Mrs. Davies' house for the time being. The best thing for him to do at the moment was to go underground locally and make some final plans, then put them into action.

Dwayne climbed out of the musty bedcovers, and dressed. He walked down to the lodge's bathhouse and answered nature's call. At least, like in the rooming house, there was a sink with a mirror in the room. He had brought in his satchel from the car the night before, and got out his toiletry kit.

When he was presentable, he went to the car to drive into El Dorado to get something to eat. He spotted a restaurant near the local theater, and pulled up to the curb. The locals were already out and about as he crossed the sidewalk to the eatery door. The place was clean and the fact that several townspeople were having breakfast meant the food had to be good.

Dwayne took a booth by the window so he could watch the street. A waitress came up with a cup and coffee pot, serving him without being asked. "Do you need a menu?"

"Uh, no," Dwayne said. "I'd like a couple of eggs over easy, link sausage, rye toast and an order of French fries."

"French fries?"

"Yeah."

"We can't give you French fries this time of day," she said. "All we have is hash browns."

God! he thought, *as if things ain't bad enough*.

―――

When Dwayne finished breakfast, he ordered another cup of coffee and lit a cigarette. He sipped from the cup in a mood of irritated contemplation. His mind was doing no more than asking questions without answering any. He suddenly missed the army. Too bad the convenience discharge wouldn't allow him to reenlist. Of course, if he came up with some phony documents and created a new I.D., he could reenter the service. Maybe it would be better to join the navy or—

That's it! his mind screamed at him.

Dwayne got to his feet and dropped a dollar on the table, and walked rapidly from the restaurant. When he got the car started, he backed up into the street, then headed down U.S. 77 to State 96. The place he searched for would be on a county road somewhere south of there.

―――

Back in the late 1930s, the bleakest period of Dwayne's life, there had been a glimmer in all that dark misery. It had been a ray of kindness from a very nice couple. Tommy and Margie Brady were both members of Wichita's Salvation Army contingent. They worked downtown near the hotel where Dwayne and his mother lived. The Salvation Army Center was where a free meal could be gotten every evening; and clothing was available for a very low price, and if some unfortunate was penniless, he could get it for free.

Tommy and Margie ran the place, and did so kindly but firmly. Any down-and-outer who showed no intention of giving up drink, could get a meal and a bed if he were sober. But if he was intoxicated, he either went back to the streets or the police were called. Tommy was a tough guy and could easily handle any disturbance, but the rules bade him follow a certain protocol that didn't include breaking somebody's nose.

However, most of those who sought help and succor at the center were suffering misfortune through no fault of their own in the Depression years. Tommy and Margie saw to it that they were treated with dignity and respect. That was the category that Dwayne and his mother fell into.

Tommy was originally from Brooklyn and served in the navy for several years during the 1920s. When Dwayne had thought of the navy back at the restaurant, it reminded him of Tommy. When Tommy was a sailor, he had won the Pacific Fleet middleweight boxing championship and held it for a respectable length of time. It was during those days when his ship was in San Francisco that he met Margie.

This occurred on one memorable evening he had been given shore leave and was headed for the roughest part of the waterfront for his three favorite pastimes; whoring, drinking and brawling. But as he swaggered toward his preferred hangouts, he came upon a Salvation Army band playing on a street corner. Normally he would have passed by without giving such a group as much as a second glance, but one of the young ladies who was playing a clarinet caught his eye. She wasn't particularly pretty; she wore black framed spectacles, her dull black hair was pulled back into a severe bun, and she was skinny as a starved sparrow. But through the lenses of her glasses, her eyes had a glow that almost made Tommy's Irish heart come to a complete stop. He dropped some money in the pot set in front of the band. Everyone, including the charming clarinet player, nodded their thanks to him and continued the performance. He started off toward his original destination, but went only another block before he returned.

A series of events occurred that evening after Tommy volunteered to help the band take their instruments back to the mission house. He began an acquaintanceship with Miss Margie Thompson the clarinetist, and visited the Salvation Army Center on every shore leave after that. As time passed, they eventually fell in love. It was under Margie's influence and affection that Tommy changed his wild ways and did not reenlist when his hitch in the navy was up. He proposed to Margie and she accepted. Almost immediately after the ceremony, he joined the Salvation Army, and eventually they were assigned to Wichita, Kansas.

―――

DWAYNE FOLLOWED A COUNTRY ROAD ON THE southeast side of the town of Augusta, checking mail boxes set out some short distances from various farm-houses. Each bore the names of the residents, and when he spotted one that read **THOMAS & MARGIE BRADY**, he whipped the Ford off the road and drove up a dirt track through the prairie toward a house and barn about three-quarters of a mile away. There were some bumps and ruts to negotiate before he pulled into the yard and turned off the engine.

The house was a frame two-story structure typical of rural residences. As Dwayne stepped up on the porch, he noted it was in excellent condition, and had been freshly painted. He knocked and waited. A full minute passed, then the door opened and an elderly gentleman stood behind the screen. The old guy was five-six with a husky build. His face was wrinkled but not enough to disguise the scars around his eyes or the fact that his nose that had been broken several times. He was definitely an ex-pug.

"Yeah?"

"Hi, Tommy. It's me. Dwayne Wheeler."

Tommy Brady was silent for only a moment, then that battered face showed a grin of pure delight. "For crying out loud!" he yelled, pushing the screen door open. "Get in here!"

Dwayne walked into a tidy living room festooned with photographs. Most were of Tommy and Margie together in Salvation Army scenes, but there were a couple of Tommy as a sailor. One portrayed him after a boxing match with his face showing the effects of the fight. He wore a pugilist's robe and he showed a wide, happy grin while holding a trophy being handed to him by an admiral.

"Where's Margie?" Dwayne asked.

"She went to her reward three years ago," Tommy replied.

"I'm sorry to hear that. She was really good people."

"That she was," Tommy said. "I'm living here alone now."

"I almost forgot you guys had a farm," Dwayne said. "You wrote me a letter about it when I first enlisted in the army. It sort of slipped my mind until this morning. All I could remember was that it was located someplace around Augusta. How'd you end up out here?"

"Margie inherited it when her father died," Tommy said. "That's when we decided to retire from the 'Army' and move out of Wichita. I was too old to be a farmer, so we rented a couple of sections of land out to local guys who grow crops there." He gestured to a chair. "Well, sit down, Dwayne. Can I get you a cup of coffee or something?"

"No, thanks," Dwayne said, taking a chair. "Actually, I'm here to ask a favor of you. I feel bad doing it because you've already done so much for me and my mom. And I really wouldn't bother you if it wasn't so important."

"Give me the details," Tommy said, also settling down.

Dwayne began relating the events of what he had titled the Payback Caper. He leaned forward in his intensity, going all the way from Stubb Durham's murder right up to sneaking Donna Sue off to Mrs. Davies' house. But he left out Mack Crofton's death. When he finished, he leaned back in the chair.

"So you're a private dick, eh?" Tommy remarked. "Well what a surprise. I figgered you'd stay in the army. I remember when you came over to our apartment that night and said you was going to enlist."

"I couldn't stay in," Dwayne admitted. He shrugged and grinned sheepishly. "There was a problem in Germany after the war. Black market stuff. They let me out on a convenience discharge."

Tommy, the old navy veteran, chuckled. "Discharged for the convenience of the government, eh? Oh, yeah, I know that drill."

"It's not much to be proud of," Dwayne said.

"Aw! Water under the bridge," Tommy said. "Well, what can I do for you?"

"I need a place to hide out until I can come up with some ideas. It'd be a big help if I could stay here."

"This makes a good place to lay low, awright. Sure! I

got an extra room upstairs. Get your stuff and make yourself to home."

"Thanks a million, Tommy," Dwayne said. "I can pay you. I've been pulling in quite a bit of cash money on this caper."

Tommy shook his head. "Margie wouldn't want you to."

―――

DONNA SUE HAD THE RADIO ON LOW, LISTENING to a KANS disk jockey playing the latest swing tunes as she gazed out the window. She had begun to find it relaxing to contemplate the countryside on the other side of the wall during quiet moments. The rustic view had a calming effect on her. Her reverie was interrupted by knocking. She went over and opened the door. Miss Caruthers, with a book under her arm, smiled at her and walked in with Jewell following. The little maid carried a typewriter in her skinny arms.

"Good morning," Donna Sue said.

"Mrs. Davies has something for you," Miss Caruthers said. "A typewriter and an instruction book on touch-typing. Shall we put them on the writing desk?"

"That'd be fine," Donna Sue replied, both surprised and curious.

Jewell walked over and set the machine down. After a grin and a curtsey, the little southern girl left the room. Miss Caruthers handed the book to Donna Sue. "There are lessons in here that can teach you to type."

They walked over to the desk, and Miss Caruthers indicated that Donna Sue was to sit down. She settled in front of the machine. "This is exciting!"

"All right, the first thing you must do is place your

hands in the correct position," Miss Caruthers instructed. "The fingers of your left hand will go from 'A' to 'F'."

Donna Sue complied. "What about my thumbs?"

"You'll use them for the space bar," Miss Caruthers said, tapping it. "You use that when you want space between words. Now. Put the fingers of your right hand on 'J' through the semi-colon and colon key."

"Why are they both on the same one?"

"You'll learn that when you reach the lessons on the shift key," Miss Caruthers explained. She opened one of the desk drawers and pulled out a sheet of white paper. After showing Donna Sue how to insert it in the machine, she turned to the book. "You'll notice that the first exercise consists of small words. It will take you time to learn all the keys' locations, but that will come automatically and easily like forming a new habit."

She directed her student through the exercise as Donna Sue laboriously typed out "what," "why," "when," and "where" with the fingers indicated in the instructions.

"Oh!" Donna Sue said looking at what she had placed on the paper. "I actually typed something!"

"As soon as you are certain you've mastered that lesson, go on to the next," Miss Caruthers said. She watched as Donna Sue repeated the fingering drill for a few minutes. Miss Caruthers walked to the door, then paused and glanced back at the young woman enthusiastically working away at the typewriter.

A secretary in the making.

Chapter 14

It was Monday morning, and Sergeant Ben Forester walked into the squad room of homicide in a fairly good mood. The only thing he had to do that day was turn in the final report on an open-and-shut domestic murder for the D.A. That would clear his workload, and perhaps grant him a breathing spell.

Sergeant Al Gallagher looked up at him from his desk. He showed a wry grin and said, "The lieutenant wants to see you."

"Oh, shit."

"I'm afraid so, ol' buddy," Gallagher said.

Ben crossed the room to Lieutenant Buford Cordell's office door. He rapped and waited for a reply. Cordell muttered something unintelligible and Ben took it as an invitation to enter. He walked in, stopping in front of the desk. "You want to see me?"

"Yeah," Cordell said, looking up from a stack of reports. "Sit down."

Ben complied, pulling a cigarette from the pack in his

shirt pocket. He grabbed the lighter off the desk, and lit up. "Is there anything special I gotta do?"

"You godamn right there is," Cordell said. He shoved a piece of paper across to the other policeman. "Get a load of that."

Ben noticed it was a Sheriff's Department incident report, involving a shooting out in the county on U.S. Highway 54. He perused the stilted writing describing the event, noting the times and places as well as statements from witnesses. When he finished, he handed the document back. "It's a hit plain and simple."

"It's a hit, yeah," Cordell agreed. "But it ain't plain and simple, Forester. You know the victim Mack Crofton, right?"

"A bootlegger," Ben said. "I've had contacts with him a few times over the years. He's actually a pretty mild, inoffensive guy."

"I don't give a damn about Crofton," Cordell said. "What's your take on the guy that was with him?"

Ben shrugged. "Prob'ly another bootlegger. The witnesses said the guy fired back at the shooters as they drove away from the scene. Then he got in his own car and took off."

"There's more than that in the report and you know it," Cordell snapped. "That guy showed a badge and identified himself as a detective. Not a *police* detective, just a detective. That's something a shamus would say, right? And the description the witnesses gave of him is a close resemblance to your pal Wheeler."

"Anything is possible," Ben said.

"I want you to go out and hunt down Wheeler and arrest the son of a bitch and bring him in here," Cordell said. "*Here*! That means *this* office."

"Yes, sir. On what charge?"

"As a material witness or a suspect or just for being ugly," Cordell said. "It don't matter, godamn it! Just drag his ass in here."

"I understand," Ben said. "I've got the final paperwork to turn in on that homicide up on North Market. The D.A. wants it in before noon today."

"Then take care of it," Cordell said. "I'm gonna put out an APB on Wheeler in hopes he'll stumble into a patrolman somewhere. But you're the only officer I got that I can put on a fulltime manhunt right now. When I can, I'll assign Gallagher to give you a hand. And I want results, understand?"

"Yes, sir," Ben said. He ground out the cigarette in Cordell's ashtray and left the office.

TOMMY BRADY BROUGHT THE SKILLET OVER TO the table and used a spatula to slide a hunk of scrambled eggs onto Dwayne's plate. Then he put the rest on his own. Dwayne looked at the serving for his breakfast that included biscuits and bacon. "Listen, Tommy, I really ought to pay you something for the food at least."

"Naw," Tommy said, sitting down. He tucked a napkin under his chin. "One thing I ain't hurting for is dough. I get plenty from the land rentals and the government gives me certain allowances for being a farmer even though I really ain't one. I think they call 'em subsidies. Anyhow they're from a fund left over after the war. I tried to turn the money down, but the local farm agent told me I couldn't. I *have* to take the payouts." He laughed. "I let the checks stack up for awhile, and the guy came out here all huffy and told me to cash 'em. I guess it's my patriotic duty to help the Feds keep their books balanced."

"Well how about this?" Dwayne said. "If you have any work you want done around here let me know."

"There ain't any," Tommy said. "I got a lady that comes out a couple of times a month to clean. She also does the laundry and ironing. I can do my own cooking, so I don't need no help."

"Then I'll clean the kitchen and do the dishes after meals."

Tommy laughed aloud. "Awright! *That* I'll agree to." He bowed his head and closed his eyes. "Lord, we thank you for the food we are about to eat and humbly beg your blessing on the two of us at this table. Amen."

Dwayne, caught by surprise, had almost begun to eat. Tommy didn't seem to have noticed and the meal began. They didn't talk much as the breakfast was consumed, except for casual comments about the weather and Tommy's prediction about the coming harvest of his renters.

When the meal was finished, Tommy sat back with a cup of coffee and kept Dwayne company while the younger man cleared the table and did the dishes. As Dwayne scrubbed the skillet, he said, "Tommy, I got to make a phone call to my girl to see if ever'thing's all right. To tell you the truth, I kind of worry about her even though I stashed her in a safe place."

"My telephone's on the wall there. Help yourself."

"That will be a toll call to Wichita, so it'll cost a dime for three minutes."

"We'll let the United States Government pay for it," Tommy replied. "At least part of those subsidy checks should go for something useful."

"Okay, thanks a lot," Dwayne said, pushing down on the steel wool to get the egg scum off the skillet. "By the way, I meant to tell you, you're looking fit. You seem to be enjoying good health. You don't move around like an old man."

"I got me a little gym down in the basement," Tommy said. "Got me a heavy bag, a speed bag, and some other exercise stuff. Feel free to use it while you're here."

"I'd be more interested in it to blow off steam than to build myself up," Dwayne said. "But I could use some exercise, believe me. It's been awhile."

When he finished the skillet, he set it back on the stove then turned to drying the dishes. After wiping down the table, the work was complete. Dwayne checked his watch. "I should be able to call now without waking up Donna Sue."

"I'll make myself scarce."

"You don't have to leave," Dwayne said.

"I always take a walk after breakfast anyhow," Tommy said, standing up. "Maybe I'll check the mailbox to see if there's any more checks in there."

Dwayne was actually glad his old friend had left the kitchen. Some of the ugly truths of the caper would be coming out in the conversation with Donna Sue. Luckily Tommy's phone was a regular one, rather than the type found in many farm houses in which everyone on the line could listen in. He dialed the operator, and gave her the number of the telephone in Donna Sue's room at Mrs. Davies' house.

"Hello." Donna Sue's voice was uplifting for Dwayne's spirits.

"Hey, honey bunch, it's me."

"Dwayne!" came back her happy reply. "It's been four days. How is everything going?"

"Not too good," he said. "I hate to say it, but this caper is now over and done with."

"Is it really that bad?"

"I'm afraid so," Dwayne said. "I have no idea who did in Stubb and that means the bookies are gonna stop paying me. They may even want some money back." He hesitated then said, "And I got shot at Friday night out east on Fifty-Four."

"That was on the radio news!"

"I'm not surprised," Dwayne said. "What'd they say?"

"That some guy had been killed," Donna Sue said. "I didn't connect you with it at all."

"That ain't the worst of it," he said. "It was Mack Crofton who was killed. No doubt the K.C. pricks figgered him for a snitch."

She was silent for a moment. "This is out of control. I'm really getting scared, Dwayne"

"Well...there's something else," he said.

"Oh my God! What more can there be?"

"The Wichita Police Department is gonna get my private investigator license pulled," he said.

"How in hell can they do that?" she asked.

"Because I lied on the application to the state," he explained. "I said I had an honorable discharge from the army. I didn't. I had what's called a convenience discharge. It's a quick, simple administrative way for the army to get rid of people they don't want. I never told you before, but I tried to get on the police force when I first got back to Wichita, and they turned me down because I didn't have an acceptable release from the service. That's why I ended up a private detective. And I had to lie to get that."

"Dwayne?"

"Yes."

"Why didn't the army want you?"

"There were lots of temptations in Germany right after the war ended," Dwayne said. "Things were topsy-turvy and out of control. Displaced persons from all over Europe were wondering around without papers, and the law enforcement was chaotic. I was in the military police and we did ever'thing necessary when it came to keeping the peace. Money didn't mean nothing. Soap and cigarettes were more valuable than cash. People were doing anything they could to—"

"I understand," Donna Sue interrupted. "What's this got to do with the army not wanting you?"

"I was about to get to that," Dwayne said. "There was what they call a black market. All kinds of deals could be made on scarce items. One of the officers in my comp'ny developed some connections that would take U.S. Government property into a pipeline to sell it. He offered me some of the action. I could make a lot of money, and I couldn't resist the proposal."

"Okay," she said. "You got caught, right?"

"I sure did," Dwayne said. "Anyhow it was the craziest thing, because they appointed this same officer as my defense counsel. They didn't know he was in the racket himself. He was a smart guy and he went off the record saying that if they charged me it would end up being a general court-martial. That would attract a lot of attention and cause embarrassment to the American military and civil government, not to mention pissing off people back in the States. So, to make a long story short, they said if I accepted a discharge from the service for the convenience of the government, they wouldn't charge me. I could get out of the army and go home Scot-free. I may not be smart, but I ain't stupid, so I jumped at the chance."

"Dwayne, what are you gonna do?" she asked.

"Right now I'm at a place where it's safe," Dwayne replied. "I think it's best that you don't know the location. Anyhow, it's a good chance to think things over and make plans."

"What about me?" Donna Sue asked. "I have a job I should get back to and I'm living with strangers. This can't go on much longer. Are you sure there isn't some way you can wrap up the Kansas City affair?"

"I lost out like I said," Dwayne admitted. "There's no way I can stop 'em. I even think Ben Forester is in on it with some more crooked cops. They beat me down, honey. I lost the war." He hesitated, then said, "You can't stay in Wichita."

"*What*!"

"You're still in danger and they'll be out to get you to keep their reputations as badasses."

"You mean they want to *kill* me?"

"I'm sorry. It's my fault."

"Dwayne, you got to figure something out!"

"I know, sweetie," he said. "Give me some time. I'll be in touch."

———

IT WAS EARLY AFTERNOON BEFORE SERGEANT BEN Forester finished his business with the D.A. The case they were wrapping up involved a man shooting his wife after learning she was having an affair. The incident occurred during a drunken party at their house and there had been about a dozen witnesses who watched the episode play out in front of their eyes. An assistant D.A. drew up a partial list of the partiers who Ben deemed to have been the most sober and reliable onlookers. These would be the ones subpoenaed as prosecution witnesses at the trial. The cuckolded husband had already entered a plea of not guilty by reason of temporary insanity.

With that taken care of, Ben was able to turn his attention to Lieutenant Cordell's assignment to find Dwayne Wheeler. He decided to begin by going to Dwayne's rooming house. He drove from downtown to the intersection of Estelle and Douglas, turning north to go the short distance to the residence. When Ben parked, he spent a few moments looking up and down the street to see if he could spot either Dwayne's Pontiac or Elmer Pettibone's Ford. Not seeing either one of them, he got out of the car and walked up to the front porch. He rang the bell and waited.

It took a couple of minutes before a rather stout middle-aged lady opened the door. She was wearing an apron and carrying a mop, looking very busy. "We got no vacancies at the moment."

"I'm not looking for a room," Ben replied, showing his badge. "I'm looking for Dwayne Wheeler."

"What's he done?" the lady asked.

"Nothing that I know of," Ben replied. "It's a routine matter that needs to be cleared up. Is he here?"

"I don't think so," the lady said. She introduced herself. "I'm Missus Busch the landlady."

"I'm Sergeant Forester, ma'am," he said. "Would you mind letting me have a look at his room?" He actually should have produced a search warrant, but most Wichita folks weren't that interested in protocol. If they saw no harm in the request, there was no refusal.

"I guess it's okay," she replied, opening the screen door. "Come on in. I'll take you upstairs."

He entered the house and followed her up to the second floor. When they reached Dwayne's room, she pulled a set of keys out of her apron. Within a moment she had the door open. "Help yourself."

"Thank you, ma'am."

Ben walked in, not surprised that the place was a bit on the messy side. The bed was sloppily made by having the sheets and blankets simply pulled up, and the floor needed a vacuuming. He walked over to the sink, noting the open tube of Pepsodent toothpaste and a toothbrush on the left side of the faucets. A sliver of soap was in an indentation on the right side. He opened the mirror and saw a packet of aspirin, a safety razor, some brushless shaving cream and a bottle of Wildroot Hair Cream. Ben grinned at that. Wildroot was the sponsor of Dwayne's favorite detective radio program *Sam Spade*.

Mrs. Busch spoke from the doorway. "I have things to attend to. When you leave, close the door. It'll lock automatic. You can let yourself out."

"Yes, ma'am."

Ben left the sink area and ambled over to the dresser. He opened the top drawer. Two manila envelopes, three recently laundered and starched shirts, socks, handkerchiefs, and some miscellaneous magazines and back copies of the *Racing Form* were visible.

Ben took out the first envelope and opened it, turning it upside down. Photographs of various sizes fell out on the top of the dresser. He went through them, noting they were family photos that seemed to go back to Dwayne's early childhood. There were snapshots of him and his parents that covered several years. In a couple he was on a tricycle with his mother standing beside him; others were taken during family outings to Riverside Park along with miscellaneous scenes in their yard. Ben studied young Dwayne's boyish happiness, and thought about the sadness that would soon encroach on the kid's life.

An eleven by fourteen studio portrait of the three of them was among the collection. Dwayne appeared to be around five or six years of age at the time. He sat in front of his parents who had the usual stiff posed smiles so common in such likenesses. However, the boy Dwayne seemed to be having fun having his picture taken, and he had the wide grin of a kid enjoying himself. The elder Wheeler was a balding man wearing spectacles and Mrs. Wheeler was a pleasant looking young woman, not altogether unattractive. Ben could remember meeting her one time after he had arrested Dwayne for shoplifting toy soldiers at the downtown Kress Variety Store at Broadway and Douglas. She must have aged fast since the portrait, because he recalled her looking drab and tired. Or perhaps the virulent cancer had already begun to attack her.

He replaced the photos, and turned his attention to the other envelope. Inside he found a mimeographed set of military orders authorizing that Staff Sergeant Dwayne Wheeler of the 337th Military Police Battalion be given a discharge from the United States Army for the convenience of the government.

The rest of the contents were snapshots of army scenes. There were several of Dwayne and his buddies, some with Dwayne in the company of what appeared to be European women, and one showed Dwayne in a Class B uniform with a leather Sam Browne belt holding a holster and magazine pouch. He wore bloused boots and the white cover of the Military Police over his service cap. Beneath all that were several photographs of dead German soldiers lying where they had fallen. Ben could tell the bodies had been searched for documents by the way the clothing had been disarranged. No doubt Dwayne and his fellow MPs had been involved in that activity before taking the pictures.

Ben put it all back in the envelope and returned it to its original spot. The second drawer in the dresser had underwear, gloves, a scarf, stocking cap, ear muffs and other miscellaneous items. From there Ben went to the closet, noting the suits hanging there. A search of the space revealed nothing, so he walked to the middle of the room and slowly turned around looking for something he might have missed. Wherever Dwayne had gotten off to, he certainly hadn't taken much with him.

Ben went to the door, pulled it shut, then walked down the hall to the stairs.

Chapter 15

Ernie Bascombe looked up from his haircutting, surprised at the unexpected appearance of Sergeant Ben Forester in the OK Barbershop. The barber, following his customary manner of greeting visitors while engaged in tonsorial activities, waved his scissors at the policeman. "How're you doing, Ben? Are you gonna have a haircut?"

"Not today," Ben replied. He walked toward the back of the shop where the three bookies, Longshot Jackson, Ollie Krask and Rory Talbert sat close to the phones. The trio eyed him with a slight suspicion born of numerous unpleasantness with enforcers of the law.

Longshot regarded him in a semi-friendly way. "Looking for tip on a good horse, Ben?"

Ben shook his head. "I'm just wandering around. What's up?"

Talbert wasn't as much at ease as Longshot. He had an ingrained dislike of anyone with authority that went all the way back to his youth. He spoke coldly, saying,

"Nothing special going on around here. Unless somebody stirs something up. Like a cop."

"Relax," Ben said, controlling a desire to punch the wiseass in the chops. "If any bets are called in I'm deaf, okay?"

Ollie held a half-eaten chocolate cupcake in one beefy hand. "So how's it been going with you, Ben?"

"Oh, so-so," he replied. "I've been cooped up in the squad room lately, so I thought I'd get out and stretch my legs." He knew damn well the bookies weren't buying that. He feigned looking around, then asked, "What do you hear from Dwayne Wheeler?"

"Dwayne?" Longshot asked, assuming his usual role as bookie spokesman when visitors were around. He appeared thoughtful for a moment. "Y'know, I don't think I've seen Dwayne in a coon's age." He glanced at the other two bookies. "What about you guys?"

"Same here," Ollie said.

Rory was more direct. "What do you want with Dwayne?"

"He's an old friend," Ben said. "You know that. I just want to say 'howdy do', that's all."

Longshot grinned. "And I'm sure Dwayne would like to see you, too, Ben."

Rory, who was still visibly upset at the unexpected appearance of the detective, suddenly blurted, "How's come you cops ain't doing shit about finding out who killed Stubb Durham?"

"How do you know we ain't?"

"Ever'body knows it," Rory said. "You guys don't give a shit about a murdered bookie."

Longshot laughed nervously. "Aw! Now we know that ain't true. It's just a tough case, right, Ben?"

"I don't know," Ben said. "Why don't you ask Dwayne the next time you see him?"

"Why would Dwayne know anything?" Longshot asked.

Ben looked him in the eye. "Don't bullshit an old bullshitter. You guys hired him to look into the shooting. He's been nosing around town asking questions. He's even visited the widow a time or two."

Longshot and Ollie displayed expressions of utmost innocence and ignorance. Rory, on the other hand, said, "So what?"

Ben ignored the surly bookie. "The next time he calls you, tell him to get in contact with me. It's important."

"Why sure, Ben," Longshot said.

Ollie smiled. "We'd be glad to."

Rory Talbert only glowered at the detective.

Ben turned and walked slowly back through the shop, going out the door. He crossed the street to the Jayhawker Restaurant and walked in. He recognized Maisie Burnett, but not the other waitress. He sat down and ordered a cup of coffee from Maisie. When she served him, he glanced around the diner. "Where's Donna Sue?"

"She's got a family emergency," Maisie said. She turned to the other waitress. "Hey, Janet, come here a minute."

"Sure," Janet said, walking up.

"This is Ben Forester," Maisie said. "He's a cop that comes in here once in awhile. He's a fairly nice one though." She looked at Ben. "This is Janet Dugan. She's taking Donna Sue's place while she's gone."

"Hi, Janet," Ben said. "How d'you like working here?"

"It's a job," Janet replied. She was a tall brunette of

some thirty years with a bold look in her eye. "How about something besides the coffee?"

Ben winked at her. "What do you have in mind?"

Janet laughed. "Nothing I'm gonna tell a cop."

Ben turned his attention back to Maisie. "I'm sorry to hear about Donna Sue's situation. What seems to be the trouble?"

"I don't know," Maisie said. "Dwayne came in here and told Art that she'd be out of town for a few days." She leaned toward him with a knowing look in her eyes. "It sounded suspicious to me."

"Why's that?"

"Because I know for a fact that Donna Sue ain't been in contact with her family for a hell of a long time," Maisie said. "I even told Janet that this job might turn out to be permanent for her."

"Whoop-dee-do!" Janet remarked sarcastically. "I have found the pot at the end of the rain barrel."

Maisie chuckled derisively. "That's rain*bow*. Ain't you never seen the *Wizard of Oz*? The song Judy Garland sang in it was *Somewhere Over the Rainbow*, not the rain barrel."

"It was a long time ago when I seen it," Janet said defensively.

"When did Dwayne come in here?" Ben asked, not wanting the two women to get involved in an inane conversation about an eight-year-old movie.

"Last week," Maisie answered. "Wednesday or Thursday I think."

"Did Dwayne say he was going with her?"

Maisie shook her head. "He said he put her on a bus. When I asked where, he said he didn't remember."

"Has he been here since?"

"No. And I wouldn't be surprised if he done something bad to her," Maisie said. "Them private detectives are as bad as the crooks they chase. I seen that in the movies a lot. Dwayne's a sneaky guy and I think he's up to no good most of the time." Her eyes suddenly opened wide. "Say! Is that why you're looking for him?"

"No," Ben said. "I've known the guy since he was a kid. I just wanted to see how he's doing."

"If he drops by, I'll tell Dwayne you're asking after him."

"Okay," Ben said. "Well, I gotta run, ladies. I'll see you later."

"Sure," Janet said. "Come back when you want more'n a cup of coffee."

He winked at her again, and left the restaurant.

DONNA SUE WAS IN MISS CARUTHERS' OFFICE, sitting in front of the typewriter table with her hands in her lap. She watched as the secretary counted the words on the piece of paper in front of her on the desk. When she finished, Miss Caruthers smiled. "This is hard to believe! You've typed thirty-five words a minute on this test."

"Is that good?" Donna Sue asked.

"It is astoundingly good," Miss Caruthers said. "You've barely started the lessons and you've already mastered the fingering system. There wasn't a single error. All you need to do is put in some serious and regular practice and you'll be up to eighty or ninety words a minute in a matter of weeks."

"Would that be good enough to become a secretary?"

"I'm afraid not, Donna Sue. In order to work in a business office in that capacity you need to know shorthand, filing and other administrative skills. But you could certainly work in the steno pool."

"What's that?"

"Those are girls who are good typists, but aren't qualified for secretarial positions," Miss Caruthers explained. "Well, some are, but they're only in the pool temporarily until a proper job opens up for them."

"Do you have a secretarial book I could study like the typing one I been using?" Donna Sue asked eagerly.

Miss Caruthers shook her head. "You would have to go to business college to learn those more difficult subjects. It would take two or three years. In your case probably two, provided you had a knack for shorthand. But in order to get into business college you need a high school diploma."

"I can't go back to school."

"You could take a test for an educational certificate," Miss Caruthers said. "If you pass you'll be recognized as a high school graduate."

"I don't know how I'd pass it," Donna Sue said.

"You might surprise yourself," Miss Caruthers said. "And even if you fail, there is a program where you could take studies in the evening. I personally know a woman who did exactly that, and she ended up as an executive secretary in a big company in Chicago."

"Is an executive secretary more than a regular secretary?"

"Certainly, Donna Sue," Miss Caruthers said. "They work for high-ranking officers of corporations. And they earn top pay for women. Almost as much as a man when he enters the work force of a business."

"Sounds better'n being a waitress," Donna Sue said.

"There's another advantage to consider," Miss Caruthers said. "Since you're an attractive woman, even if you worked in the steno pool, you might catch the attention of a man earning a big salary. The fellow might not be young and handsome, but he'd be an excellent provider. There've been plenty of girls who married like that and ended up living in quite comfortable circumstances. And others who were content to be put up in fancy apartments with plenty of gifts and spending money. The smart ones saved as much as they could and never had to work again."

"It's like I mentioned to you before," Donna Sue said. "I want to be a secretary for Dwayne. I would be a lot of help in his business. I told Missus Davies about wanting to work for him. Dwayne and me would be like the Sam Spade radio show."

Miss Caruthers sat in silence for several moments, staring at the younger woman. "Donna Sue, I really think I should have a long talk with you."

IT WAS LATE AFTERNOON WHEN DETECTIVE Sergeant Al Gallagher sat waiting in his unmarked police car parked at the curb in the warehouse district. He had been looking for Ben Forester and had just spotted him approaching. Gallagher waved. "Ben! Over here."

Ben picked up his pace and approached the car. When he reached the vehicle, he slid in the front beside the other detective. Gallagher gave him a close look. "The lieutenant has assigned me to work with you until we catch Wheeler. How's it been going?"

"Not good at all," Ben said. "This has been a wasted day."

"Nothing on the shamus, eh?" Gallagher asked.

"He's dropped from sight," Ben remarked, lighting a cigarette. "I've talked to bookies, the waitresses where his girlfriend works, a couple of bootleggers and miscellaneous acquaintances of the guy. No one has seen him."

"We got to get our hands on the son of a bitch and pull him in," Gallagher said. "We either get him off the street, or he's gonna throw a monkey wrench in the works where the Kansas City guys are concerned."

Ben gave Gallagher a hard look. "I want you to understand something, Al. I don't want Dwayne to get hurt."

"Don't go soft on me, Ben," Gallagher snapped. "Anyhow, there's not a damn thing you can do to protect him under the circumstances. And it's as sure as shit stinks that he was the guy that was with that bootlegger who got shot up out on Highway Fifty-Four. That means he's penetrated the operation, and that's something that ain't gonna be tolerated by the K.C. boys or us."

"Okay," Ben relented. "But there may be something that'll save his ass. When I went to the restaurant I was hoping to talk to his girlfriend to see if she could help me."

"Donna Sue, right?" Gallagher said. "Good looking with a nice ass and big tits."

"That's the one. One of the gals there told me that he came in and said she had left town because of an emergency in her family. But the waitress said she knew for sure that Donna Sue didn't have a family, or if she did, she didn't have any contact with 'em. That was last week, and nobody's seen her or him since. I'm beginning to think they've both cut and run. Dwayne is smart. He knows when it's time to get out of town."

"You're prob'ly right," Gallagher said. "And for your pal's sake I hope you are. But Lieutenant Cordell ain't gonna let up on finding him. We're on a permanent assignment, ol' buddy."

"Well, I'm going back to the station and report in,"

Ben said, opening the car door. "If I got to keep looking, then that's what I'll do."

"Well, I'll be looking, too," Gallagher remarked. "And you better hope you find Wheeler before I do. I'll give that shamus son of a bitch something he'll never forget."

Ben got out of the car and walked back toward his own. He also had some problems to deal with at home. Ben had two daughters; one was a senior at North High and the older had married a no account drugstore cowboy who evidently was a good dancer. He remembered she seemed surprised when this attribute didn't make him an excellent husband and father. Now the marriage was on the rocks, and not only was she moving back home, but she'd be bringing a three-month old baby with her.

And Ben had just begun the work of turning her old bedroom into a den.

THE SHADOWS ACROSS THE FARMYARD HAD grown noticeably long as the prairie sunset eased through its crimson-colored process. Dwayne and Tommy Brady had finished supper, and the dishes were washed and put away. Now the two had settled down at the kitchen table, ready to pass a quiet evening.

"Not much on the radio on Monday nights," Dwayne remarked.

"Sometimes the *Lux Radio Theater* is good," Tommy opined, mentioning a program that broadcast movies as radio scripts.

"I never cared much for it," Dwayne said. "When it comes to movies I prefer to *watch* 'em not *listen* to 'em."

Tommy got up and went to the pantry. He came back with a bottle of bourbon and two glasses. "Here we go."

"What's this?" Dwayne asked surprised.

"I used to be quite a drinker back when I was in the navy," Tommy said, setting the liquor down. "I gave it all up during my Salvation Army days. I really turned myself to Jesus and became a Christian. It was with Margie's help, of course. But since she passed away, I've started taking a nip or two in the evenings. I don't figure it a sin." He poured out two drinks and sat down. "One of my land renters gets it for me from his bootlegger."

Dwayne took his libation and raised it. "Here's to better days."

Tommy responded to the toast and took a sip. "I'm beginning to appreciate your comp'ny, Dwayne. I didn't realize how lonesome I had got 'til you moved in."

"Well, I won't be here long," Dwayne said. He paused, took a drink, paused again, then spoke. "I've really fucked up bad, Tommy. Oops! Pardon the bad language."

"As long as you don't take the Lord's name in vain," Tommy said, leaning back in his chair. "You ain't got the law on you, do you?"

"Only crooked cops," Dwayne said. "And also a bunch of K.C. pricks who are moving into Wichita."

Tommy topped off their drinks. "You awready told me about that when you first got here."

"I didn't tell you the worst part," Dwayne said. "I got a guy killed. He was a bootlegger by the name of Mack Crofton. I'd been nosing around and found out he'd been invited to go in with the Kansas City guys. He didn't want to do it, but I talked him into it so's he could be a snitch for me. I told him I had big connections with the cops and it was only a matter of time before we busted things up for the bad guys. It was all bullshit." He sighed. "At least he was a lifelong bachelor and didn't have any close family."

"Wait a minute," Tommy said. "Was he the guy that was killed out at that café? I heard about it on the radio."

"Yeah," Dwayne said. "I was with him, and cut and run after the shooting." He drained his glass. "I'm whipped, Tommy. When I told you I needed time to figure out what to do, it wasn't to keep the caper going. I gotta come up with a way to get my ass out of here. And I'm gonna take Donna Sue with me."

"D'you love her?" Tommy asked in his direct way.

"I don't know," Dwayne said. "But I'll tell you true; I'd take bullets for her."

"What about her?" Tommy inquired. "Would she go with you?"

"She's *got* to," Dwayne said. "She's right at the top of the Kansas City shit list; not because of what she's done, but because of what I've done. They'll use her to set an example for anyone else that crosses 'em."

"Yeah. She's in a bad way awright."

"All this came about from my bullshitting," Dwayne said grimly. "And that includes the bookies who are paying me to find Stubb's killer. I gave 'em the idea I was closing in on the guy that did it and that I'd be solving the case any day. Hell! The truth is that I don't have the slightest idea who the shooter is, or where to begin digging for him." He raised his voice. "It's all lies. And a good guy is dead because of it."

"Calm down, Dwayne," Tommy said. "You didn't do nothing wrong on purpose. What we gotta do is figure out a plan of action for you, okay?"

"I do have some money," Dwayne said. "Close to a couple of hunnerd bucks right now after spending some of what I got. But part of that is a retainer from another client. And she's the one hiding Donna Sue. If I keep it I'll be stealing from her. I just couldn't do that."

"Okay, okay," Tommy said. "This isn't the time to start getting excited. Your situation is more serious than I first thought and it's a little late in the day to give it the attention it deserves. Let's start talking about something else. We can deal with what you gotta do tomorrow in the light of day."

"You're right."

Both men fell into silence for close to ten minutes, imbibing slowly in the quiet of the kitchen. It was fully dark now, and they sat in what was both a moody and natural gloom. It was Tommy who broke the silence.

"I guess you miss your ma a lot, huh?"

"Yeah," Dwayne said. "It was a funny thing, but the two times I visited the widow of the bookie that was shot, the old feelings came back. I guess it was because she was suddenly alone in the world like what happened to me."

"I really feel my loss when it comes to Margie," Tommy said. "Sometimes in the middle of the night I'll wake up, and she'll slip into my mind. The next thing I know, the grief comes back as strong as when she first passed away."

"Yeah," Dwayne said. "The same thing happens to me sometimes."

"Those are the times I know I ain't gonna sleep," Tommy continued. "So I get up and go downstairs to the living room. I get out our photo albums and look through 'em real slow. Somehow the memories that are stirred up bring nice thoughts to me and I find it comforting. That's when I know she's watching me. Then I say a little prayer to God and thank him for letting me have her as long as I did."

"I never looked at things that way," Dwayne said. "I got some snapshots of mom. There's not too many; maybe a couple of dozen."

"Then when you're feeling real sad, you should get 'em out," Tommy counseled him. "I'll bet anything they'll make you realize just how good things was in those days. It'll make you feel there was some worth to your life after all. Your mom will find it comforting when she's looking down at you."

"I suppose you believe in life after death, huh?"

"Yeah, I do," Tommy said.

"You're a real Christian, ain't you, Tommy?"

"Yes, Dwayne. I am."

"I've tried to be, but I just can't do it," Dwayne said. "Something gets in the way. I can't make a lick of sense out of religion. It seems to me that there might be a God, but he ain't as powerful as the Bible says."

"I don't understand what you mean."

"Well," Dwayne said, "I don't think he can control the weather like when he was supposed to be have made it rain for forty days and nights. Surely he ain't responsible for tornados that come along and tear hell out of ever'thing. It's for sure he can't stop 'em."

"He's all powerful, Dwayne," Tommy said.

"There's too many bad things in nature that's cruel, like animals eating other animals, good people getting bad sick and dying, and starvation from famines," Dwayne said. "Sorry, Tommy, I can't buy religion."

Tommy shrugged. "You never know when grace will come over you. Maybe it never will." He smiled at his companion. "I'll pray for you, Dwayne."

"I don't think God figgers I'm worth the trouble of getting out of this mess I got myself into. But I'd appreciate you praying for a little support to be sent me from upstairs."

Tommy poured two more drinks.

"And you're sure this ain't a sin, huh?" Dwayne asked.

"It don't seem so to me," Tommy replied. "We ain't exactly out on a tear with starving wives and kids at home."

Dwayne was silent for a moment. "I'm responsible for another man's death that I caused by telling him lies."

"I said I'd pray for you."

Chapter 16

It was almost ten o'clock when Tommy came down for breakfast the next morning. He found Dwayne already seated at the table with a pot of coffee perked on the stove. The former sailor joined him. "You must've woke up hungry."

"Not really," Dwayne replied. "I reached a decision about how I'm gonna handle this screwed up situation I'm in."

"That seems like a good reason to talk," Tommy said. "Why don't I just put some bread in the toaster and we'll chow down on that along with butter and jam."

"Sounds fine to me," Dwayne said. He went to the cupboard for a couple of plates and a pair of table knives.

Tommy fetched a loaf out of the breadbox and grabbed the butter dish and a jar of strawberry jam from the refrigerator. He brought it all to the table, and waited for Dwayne to join him. As soon as his guest sat down, Tommy said grace, and inserted a couple of pieces of bread in the toaster. He glanced at Dwayne. "So what'd you decide?"

"Well, I figgered up the deal with the bookies, and we're quits," Dwayne said. "I've worked off the amount of dough they gave me and won't be needing more. The money I owe to Missus Davies is something else. I suppose I could ask her to carry me 'til I earned enough to pay her back the extra on the advance. Actually, that's exactly what I'm gonna tell her I'll do. I got no other choice in the matter. I need all the money I got so me and Donna Sue can do some traveling. I'm going to have to take the Ford back and get my Pontiac, and that jalopy is questionable at the best of times. I'll prob'ly end up having to have some repairs before we get too far down the road."

The toast popped up and Tommy gave a piece to Dwayne and kept one for himself. "Where are you heading for?"

"I'm thinking about Georgia," Dwayne replied, spreading the butter. "I was stationed at Fort Benning for about a year and a half before I went overseas. It's the only place outside of Wichita I've ever lived. I know the area pretty good around Columbus including a couple of bars where I used to hang out. Maybe I could get a job as a bartender in one. And there's plenty of restaurants where Donna Sue could work. The army has a lot of soldiers at Benning. At least it would give us a good start and we could begin saving money for future plans."

"It all sounds sensible to me," Tommy said. "And I tell you what. I can give you a loan. Take your time in paying me back."

"Oh, no!" Dwayne said. "You've done way too much for me as it is."

"Then I'll write you a letter to the local Salvation Army there. If things get real tough, they could help you out."

"Getting helped by the Salvation Army has developed as sort of a habit with me, ain't it?"

Tommy grinned at him. "You could do a lot worse."

The two consumed their light breakfast with small talk that was directed away from Dwayne's present predicament. Both figured more discussion in the matter would muddy the waters. Dwayne's clean-up chore was simple and quick after they finished. He turned to Tommy. "Well, I'll get things rolling with the bookies." He checked his watch. "They'll be at the barbershop now taking bets for the east coast tracks so it's a good time call 'em."

"I'll pour us each one more cup of coffee," Tommy offered.

Dwayne put in the toll call, and when Longshot Jackson answered, he said. "Hey. It's me. Dwayne."

"Hey, Dwayne," came back the bookie's voice. "We got a call for you from Pete Driscoll. He wants to talk to you."

Pete was a fence and a royal pain-in-the-ass. The guy always had something for sale; ranging from refrigerators to jewelry with a plethora of items in between. All were stolen goods of course. Pete seemed to be in a permanent mood of good cheer; and showed an enthusiastic enjoyment for his larcenous lifestyle. However, Dwayne had very little respect for people who dealt in loot that was somebody else's property. The buyers were as bad as the thieves as far as he was concerned.

Dwayne asked, "What's he want to sell me?"

"He didn't say nothing about selling anything," Longshot said. "But he was kind of excited and worried-like. He says it's really important and to make sure we got the word to you to phone him."

"Hey, thanks," Dwayne said. "I'll give him a call now.

And I'm gonna need to talk to you today. You'll be around, right?"

"I'll be here all day," Longshot said.

Dwayne hung up. He was puzzled. This was an unusual situation. Pete's life was simple enough. He bought out-of-town items from as far away as Los Angeles and Chicago to be sold in Wichita. And he purchased locally stolen goods from burglars to be shipped to the out-of-state fencing operations. Dwayne couldn't figure out why the guy would be so anxious to talk to him. He had always refused to buy a single item from him. Then Dwayne had an idea. Along with Pete's other sins he was a loan shark. Dwayne only borrowed from him occasionally because of the high interest the happy little weasel charged. But since he was leaving town, and Pete didn't know about it, he could probably float a six or seven hundred dollar loan. That way he could pay back Mrs. Davies, and have enough money left over for the trip to Georgia. He could then settle the debt later with Pete at his own leisure. That would include the exorbitant interest, too. To Dwayne's way of thinking a deal was a deal, but he would refuse to cough up any penalty payments.

Dwayne put in a call to the fence. It wasn't Pete who answered. His helper Charlie got the phone. Dwayne couldn't remember the guy's last name, and he had only seen him a couple of times. When Dwayne told him he was responding to a call from Pete, Charlie showed a bit of uncommon eagerness. "Yeah! Pete wants to talk to you. He told me that if you called, I was to get him right away."

"Okay, Charlie," Dwayne said. "So get him right away."

In less than a minute, Pete Driscoll was on the phone, and his voice had more of a strain in it than the usual zest.

"Dwayne, I got to see you. And I mean just as soon as you can make it."

"What's going on, Pete?"

"I can't talk right now," Pete said. "We're unloading a truck and there's a bunch of guys around here. Pick a place and I can be there in an hour."

Dwayne was now concerned. This was an extremely strange occurrence. Pete always had his own way of handling his emergencies and he was well set up to take care of himself. Maybe he needed to hire a private detective for something unusual or sensitive. It could be a chance for some quick cash along with a loan.

"Okay," Dwayne said. "Let me think...uh, yeah! Drive to the intersection of Pawnee and Hillside. Go just south of there about a half block. You'll find a small shopping center. We can meet in the parking lot."

"Good," Pete said. "I'll be there in an hour."

Tommy sat nursing his final cup of coffee. "It sounds like something's up."

"Yeah," Dwayne replied. "Listen, Tommy, I hate like hell to bother you yet one more time, but could I borrow your car?"

"Sure," Tommy replied. "It's out in the barn. There's plenty of gas in it, too."

"What are you driving now days?"

"It's a cream-colored two door Oldsmobile sedan," Tommy informed him. "I bought it with some of them farm funds I keep getting. Nineteen-forty-one model."

"Good contrast there," Dwayne said. "If anybody's looking for me, they'll expect to see me in a black Ford."

———

Dwayne drove straight from the farm toward Cessna Aircraft's location. After a south turn off Kellogg onto Rock Road, he went down to the plant at Pawnee Avenue. It was a short distance to Hillside where the shopping center was located. Dwayne pulled into the site, going to a parking spot that offered a quick exit if necessary. He always liked to arrive early for a rendezvous to have the place scoped out before anything went down.

A cigarette would have been nice while he was waiting, but Dwayne didn't smoke in Tommy's house because he figured the nice old guy wouldn't appreciate the smell of stale tobacco smoke, and it would be the same for his automobile. Dwayne could have gotten out of the car to smoke, but if Pete Driscoll were late, he would be standing out in the open long enough for somebody to spot him. There was always a possibility this rendezvous was a set-up.

Dwayne had a twenty minute wait before Pete showed up. The suspicious P.I. gave the area another quick study, then got out of the Olds and waved to the fence. Pete drove his big Chrysler up and parked. Dwayne quickly got in and lit a cigarette.

"Man!" Pete said. "I am really glad to see you."

"What's going on?"

Pete hesitated, grabbing the steering wheel with both hands. He kept his gaze straight out the windshield as he spoke. "I was with Stubb Durham that night he got shot."

The words struck Dwayne's auditory nerves like the crack of a rifle shot. "What'd you say?"

Pete snapped his eyes to Dwayne. "Are you deaf? I said I was with Stubb Durham when he got shot."

Dwayne recovered with a feeling that this was too damn good to be true. "Have you talked to the cops?"

"Hell no I didn't talk to those bastards," Pete said. "It

ain't like I don't want justice for poor ol' Stubb, but you know I can't have anything to do with the law. It don't help me none to get their attention. Ever'time they get a chance they like to shake me down. I got to move my operation two or three times a year."

"Okay," Dwayne said, feeling his heart pounding. If he was ten or twenty years older he'd probably be having a heart attack. He fought down the emotional surge that was near dizzying. "Okay. Okay. Did you see who done it?"

"I sure as shit did," Pete said. "It was Arlo Merriwell."

Dwayne swallowed hard and cleared his throat. "Okay, Pete. Give me the details."

"Yeah," Pete said. "I had some jewelry that came in from out of town. Really nice pieces that I was gonna cut up for resale. Y'know you can't put whole necklaces and bracelets and stuff like that out there on the market the way they're stole, 'cause it's too easy to identify 'em, and—"

"I know!" Dwayne snapped. "Get on with the story."

"Sure. So Stubb had come over to my place to pick up some money I owed him on a bet." He paused. "I owed a couple of 'C' notes on a real bad pick I'd made. There was this fucking nag at Delmar in California that I think is still out there on the track trying to find the finish line."

"Godamn it, Pete!" Dwayne swore. "Just stick to the fucking details on the shooting. Can you do that?"

"Sorry," Pete said. "Anyhow, Stubb took a look at the jewelry and offered to exchange what I owed him for a piece. I was agreeable, so he said we could go over in his car to his house and show the stuff to his wife. She could pick out what she wanted. I said okay. So we got in the car and drove over. I wasn't worried about the cops or nothing since it was after midnight."

Now Pete was talking, so Dwayne let him go about his own way of relating what happened that very early morning.

"So we pulled up to the curb and got out of the car. I dropped the box of jewelry and bent over t0 pick it up while Pete was walking up toward the house. A couple of the pieces fell out and I had to hunt for 'em in the dark. They was wrapped in tissue paper, and I wanted to make sure I didn't miss anything. Anyhow, I guess Stubb hadn't noticed I wasn't with him. The next thing I knew I heard the pop of a pistol with a silencer. I looked up and seen Arlo Merriwell standing at the side of house, aiming a pistol at Stubb who was now down on his knees. Arlo shot twice more, then ran off down the street. He never noticed me at the car. Thank God for that good luck, huh? If he'd've seen me, there'd been two dead bodies."

"And you're sure it was Arlo?"

"I could see the son of a bitch plain as day in the light from Stubb's living room window," Pete said. "I took off running in the opposite direction of Arlo. You can understand I didn't want to get involved in the killing at that stage of the game. That's when the cops are looking for a quick arrest, and I'm one guy they like to haul in ever' chance they get."

"Sure, Pete," Dwayne said. "And you're now willing to testify against Arlo?"

"Yeah," Pete replied. "That's exactly what I want to do. But I want you to handle things for me, okay? I got a lawyer, but you're a better bet to take care of the preliminaries. I know you're pals with Sergeant Forester, so you can go see him on my behalf. I'm gonna lay low, but you can get ahold of me through Charlie. I got a packed bag in my trunk, so I ain't going back home. When you figure the time is best for me to sing, you can come get me."

"That's real white of you, Pete," Dwayne said sincerely. "Arlo could have gotten away with this if it wasn't for you."

"I always liked Stubb," Pete said. "That's why I did all my betting with him. We used to play cards at some of the floating games around town." He took a deep, calming breath. "I feel better now. How much money d'you want to represent me in this?"

"I'm gonna have to tread real careful," Dwayne said. "How's about a couple of hunnerd?"

"A hunnerd and fifty," Pete said.

"Done."

"Man!" Pete said. "I feel a lot better now. This has really been bothering me."

"Did you know I was investigating Stubb's murder?" Dwayne asked.

"When did this start?"

"Right after it happened," Dwayne said. "Some bookies hired me to look into it 'cause they weren't happy with the way the cops were handling things."

"Well, I don't get out and about much," Pete said. "In my line of business it's dangerous." He lit a cigarette. "But I heard talk about some guys from Kansas City being in town. Do you know anything about it?"

"Sure," Dwayne said. He didn't want to spook Pete with the knowledge that by fingering Arlo, he might well have that mob coming after him. "It's no big deal. I think they're interested in the call girl action here in Wichita." He laughed. "That's a headache for the cops to deal with."

"A friend of mine has a pawnshop up in K.C.," Pete said. "Now and then I run stuff by him that can't be identified. He's good for quick cash. But all in all, I don't care for any of that bunch."

"I don't blame you," Dwayne said, not really interested. "So, listen, Pete. The best thing you can do is not to talk to anybody about this at all. Get lost like you're planning to do, and just sit back and let me handle the situation. When the time is right, I'll bring you in to talk to Ben. Okay?"

"You got it, pal. That's when I'll bring my mouthpiece into the picture."

Dwayne got out of the car and returned to Tommy's Olds for the drive back to the farm.

―――

THE FIRST THING DWAYNE DID WHEN HE returned was to inform Tommy that things had completely turned around. Tommy was slightly stupefied. "D'you mean all this happened in the short time since you left this morning?"

"Right," Dwayne said. "One of my informants picked up some important information that filled in some big holes. I'm ready to keep the caper going, and I'll have it wrapped up by the end of this week."

"See?" Tommy said. "I told you to have faith."

"Maybe you got something there after all," Dwayne said with a wink.

"I'm gonna pick up some groceries," Tommy said. "Are you gonna stick around?"

"I will if it's okay with you," Dwayne replied. "Like I said, I've got those loose ends to wrap up, and I'll need to stay out of sight as much as I can. Your car will come in handy."

"Fine with me," Tommy said. "D'you want me to pick up anything special for you at the grocery store?"

"No," Dwayne replied. He reached in his pocket and

pulled out the bills that Pete had given him. "Here's twenty bucks for the grub."

"I awready told you I didn't want any money," Tommy said.

"C'mon!" Dwayne chided gently. "I'm starting to feel like a leech."

"Okay," Tommy said, relenting. "I'll get some steaks."

After Tommy left, Dwayne called Donna Sue. When she answered, he said, "It's me, baby."

"Hi, Dwayne."

"Remember what I told you?"

"How could I forget?" she countered. "You got me scared shitless. When are we leaving Wichita?"

"We're not," Dwayne said. "I solved the caper, baby."

"Stop talking like that godamn Sam Spade!" Donna Sue snapped. "I can't understand all that malarkey."

"What I mean is that I've wrapped things up," Dwayne said. "I got a positive I.D. on the guy who killed Stubb Durham. I got the witness hid away, see? When the time is right, I'm gonna produce him and this town is gonna explode."

"Dwayne, I'm confused," Donna Sue said. "You were talking nothing but gloom and doom just a little while ago, and now you're on top of the world."

"You haven't said anything to Missus Davies about us cutting and running, have you?"

"No," Donna Sue replied. "I didn't think you wanted me to."

"Right. But now you can let her know that I've solved the case, and the only thing I got left to do is scope out the K.C. pricks to get a final bearing on them. Then I can turn my case over to the F.B.I."

"Why the F.B.I.?"

"Because I can't trust the Wichita cops," Dwayne said. "And that includes the Kansas Highway Patrol. If certain people find out what I know, there wouldn't be any place this side of hell where we could run off to. So I got to handle things real careful like until all the bad guys are in custody."

"Now it sounds like things are more dangerous than ever," Donna Sue complained. "You be careful, Dwayne!"

"I know what I'm doing, baby. Not to worry, huh?"

"I'm gonna worry plenty!"

"Listen, sweetie, you don't seem to appreciate how great things have suddenly started humming along. This could triple my business. I could get a bigger office in a fancy building."

Donna Sue's voice brightened. "And I could be your secretary and type up the reports on your capers for the clients."

"You don't know how to type, honey."

"Dwayne Wheeler, you don't know as much as you think you do!"

"Whatever, baby," Dwayne said. "I'll be talking to you later. Bye."

Chapter 17

Detective Sergeants Ben Forester and Al Gallagher were two of the busiest cops on the Wichita Police Department. Their boss Lieutenant Buford Cordell had furiously bawled them out after efforts to locate Dwayne Wheeler ended up an absolute zero. Now both were exempt from all other cases, and Gallagher was teamed up full time with Ben, and would stay that way until the successful conclusion of their assignment.

The workloads of the other detectives in homicide increased dramatically and they resented the situation; especially since they had no idea what Forester and Gallagher were actually doing. The other cops knew the pair was not working murder cases, but no inquiries or protests regarding the matter were made to the fuming Lieutenant Cordell by his frustrated subordinates.

THE TWO DETACHED SERGEANTS WERE STARTING out fresh after normal duty hours on that Tuesday evening, following some rather loud verbal orders by the lieutenant to turn Wichita and Sedgwick County upside down until they found the rock Wheeler was hiding under. When they dug him out, they were to give Cordell a call and he would tell them where to take the private detective, and it would definitely *not* be back to Wichita Police Headquarters as per previous orders. Some very special plans were in effect for Dwayne Wheeler, esquire.

The first port of call for Ben and Gallagher was the Riverview Hotel. They arrived in the lobby at seven o'clock and went straight to the registration desk to summon the house dick. The clerk went through a door behind him to the main office and came back with Harry Gaston.

Gaston was a retired Wichita cop whose heyday had been twenty-five years earlier at the height of Amendment XVIII to the United States Constitution. This was the document behind that period of American history known as Prohibition. The unpopular piece of legislation, titled "Liquor Prohibition Amendment," stated that the manufacture, sale, or transportation of intoxicating liquor within the United States of America was illegal and punishable by heavy fines and/or long prison terms.

Denver, like other policemen of his ilk along with criminal elements all over the country, profited greatly from this legalized idiocy. The amendment brought millions of dollars into the coffers of newly organized crime syndicates whose members had been only minor criminals and thugs before prohibition was enacted. They immediately turned all their criminal attention to supplying the forbidden intoxicating liquor to a thirsty nation. Underground saloons, called speakeasies, quickly appeared in all the populated areas of the nation.

Underpaid cops suddenly found themselves tempted

by large payments of untraceable cash to look the other way and keep the bootlegging gangsters informed of pending police raids. Even after Amendment XVIII was repealed December 5, 1933, certain places in the United States held elections and voted their areas to remain dry. Kansas was one of these.

Denver, who never rose above the rank of patrolman, had taken advantage of the Prohibition milieu, and was able to salt away enough money to assure himself a very comfortable retirement. He took the job as house detective at the hotel because of boredom rather than financial need.

Denver exchanged quick greetings with Ben and Gallagher, giving them a knowing grin. "I bet you two are pretty curious about the latest happenings here at the Riverview, ain't you?"

"That we are," Gallagher said. "Particularly where a certain shamus by the name of Dwayne Wheeler is concerned."

"Y'know something, fellers," Denver said. "I been waiting for you."

"Unload on us, Harry," Ben said.

"There was a ruckus here last Monday night," Denver informed them. "I was expecting trouble because of the way the bellboys was acting when hookers showed up. I couldn't quite figger out what was going on 'til I noticed I didn't recognize any of the girls. They was new. I thought that was real odd. And our head bellboy was real upset and fretful."

"Okay," Ben said. "Would that be Jimmy Thompson?"

"No one else but," Denver said. "So I kept an eye on things, then I saw Jimmy head for the rear exit that opens up on the alley. That's where the girls come in. We make 'em keep a low profile, and they're supposed to hurry over to the elevators for the trips upstairs to their johns. Anyhow, I was real curious about what was going on, and I went back there and found a good place to keep an eye on things without being noticed. The next thing I know is that Wheeler and some guy show up and meet with Jimmy. Then they settle down to wait."

"Who was the other guy?" Gallagher asked.

Denver shrugged. "I didn't recognize him. O'course I been off the force for awhile so there's plenty of bad guys on the streets now days that wasn't there when I was a cop."

"What'd he look like?" Ben inquired.

"Muscular guy, close to six feet and maybe a hunnerd and eighty to ninety pounds," Denver said. "I didn't get at his face, but he seemed to be in his twenties or thirties. Anyhow, him and Wheeler are hanging around out there, then some time passes and two bozos show up with a woman. Then the shit hits the fan. Wheeler and this guy cut loose on the pair and in a blink of an eye, the victims are down and hurt bad. Even in the dim light coming in from the alley I could see they had been hit fast and hard with brass knuckles. Then Wheeler says something to the girl, and she's scared shitless. She takes off down the alley, and Jimmy heads back for the lobby. Wheeler and his buddy get into the shadows on the side of the door. A minute later the whore comes back with a third guy who helps the two poor dumb bastards to their feet. They walk down the alley, prob'ly to a car, and when Wheeler and the other guy figure they're gone for good, they cut out and leave the scene."

"And you didn't recognize the guy who was with Wheeler, eh?" Gallagher asked.

Denver shook his head.

"Okay," Ben said. "We're going out to the site of the assault. Do us a favor, Harry. Get Jimmy Thompson and tell him to meet us there."

"Will do," Denver said. "Good luck."

Ben and Gallagher went toward the rear of the lobby and walked through the door leading to the alley. They went outside and could see bloodstains on the cement. Ben let out a soft whistle. "Those two guys were really fucked up."

"Yeah," Gallagher agreed. "Y'know what I think? I think the guy with Wheeler was from out of town. I bet that shamus is in cahoots with somebody that don't like the K.C. mob. Could be another group wanting to make Wichita their new home."

"Well, we don't want nobody else but Schomp and his boys moving into Wichita, do we?"

"We sure don't," Gallagher said. "We've put too much work in setting this thing up."

They were interrupted by the appearance of a very reluctant Jimmy Thompson. The bellboy looked at them with a sullen expression on his face.

Gallagher grinned at him. "How're you doing, Jimmy?"

Jimmy made no reply. He had a special abhorrence for Gallagher. A year before some hooker had rolled a customer in his room after slipping the guy a Mickey Finn. She got away with close to two thousand dollars. The detective accused Jimmy of being in on the crime and took him down to the police station for questioning. Gallagher's usual method of interviewing suspects included punches and slamming the prisoner up against interrogation room walls. Jimmy got the full treatment until the session was broken up by the hooker's arrest. When Jimmy's name was brought up, she was quick to clear him of any complicity in the robbery. He was turned loose without any sort of apology.

Ben, knowing he could get more cooperation out of the hotel bellboy than Gallagher, stepped forward. "We hear there was quite a ruckus out here last Monday evening."

"I wouldn't know nothing about it," Jimmy said.

"C'mon, Jimmy," Ben said. "You been fingered by a witness. Don't worry, we're not interested in you. We know Dwayne Wheeler was one of the musclemen. What we don't know, is the name of his pal. Care to clue us in?"

"You know introductions ain't made during times like those," Jimmy said.

"I guess not," Ben allowed. He knew they would get nowhere with the bellboy. "Thanks for your time."

Jimmy spun on his heel and rushed back into the hotel.

Gallagher checked his watch. "It's too late to get anything done now. That chickenshit Cordell is out of his mind if he thinks we can run around all night digging up information."

"You're right," Ben said. "Let's go over to the Snodgrass building tomorrow. How about picking me up around nine in the morning?" Lieutenant Cordell had authorized them only one car, and it was Gallagher's.

"Sure," Gallagher said. "What's with the Snodgrass Building?"

"Dwayne's office," Ben replied. "And we can have a word with his landlord. There's always a chance that he saw something."

―――

It was about a quarter after nine the next morning when Ben Forester and Al Gallagher pulled up in front of the Snodgrass Building. They went through the squeaky revolving door and checked the battered wall directory at the entrance for the location of Dwayne's office. After finding the room number they went up the stairs, and walked down the hall checking the doors. They both grinned at the stenciled sign Dwayne had made to identify his agency, and a twist of the handle showed the office was locked. They retraced their steps back to the first floor. The building's owner Twig Clanton looked up startled when Gallagher walked into his office without knocking. Ben sauntered in behind his partner. Then both displayed their badges.

Clanton rose from his chair. "And what can I do for you?"

"Have you seen Dwayne Wheeler around?" Gallagher asked.

Clanton shrugged. "Not for a couple of weeks. Or ten days." He was used to police and others searching for his shadowy renters. "I don't pay much attention to any of my tenants unless they're behind in their rent."

"Then you must really have a close relationship with the shamus Wheeler," Gallagher said.

"I'm pretty sure he's up to date right now," Clanton said.

"Have you seen him around here in the comp'ny of another guy?" Ben asked. "He'd be six feet, one hunnerd eighty-five pounds and husky. Prob'ly a tough looking customer."

Clanton shook his head. "I can tell you for sure that lately when I've seen Dwayne he's been alone."

"We'd like to look at his office," Gallagher said.

Clanton unlocked his desk drawer and pulled out a

large ring of keys. "C'mon," he said, leading the way out into the hall. The three men went up to the second floor, and Clanton unlocked the door, pushing it open. "Do me a favor," he requested. "Let me know when you leave so's I can lock it back up."

"Sure," Gallagher said. He walked into the office and stopped. "Jesus! What a dump."

"Something just dawned on me," Ben said. "In all the time Dwayne's been a private eye I've never been up here."

"As you can see," Gallagher said. "You ain't missed much." He walked over to the desk and pulled out the drawers. All were empty except for the center one that had some odds and ends such as chewing gum, pencils, paperclips and lighter fluid. Then the cop noticed some carbon copies of typed papers to the rear. He pulled them out and leafed through them.

"What'd you find?"

"Evidently he gets reports of his cases typed up," Gallagher said, studying the documents. "He seems to have done a few jobs for A.J. Kessler."

"The midget bail bondsman?"

"Yeah," Gallagher said. "Damn! It looks like Wheeler has pulled in some sweet amounts of dough for the work."

"And you can bet it all went to picking the wrong horses," Ben said. He walked around the nearly bare room, looked out the window, then turned back to his partner. "I suggest we call on Kessler. Maybe he's seen Dwayne with that mysterious ass kicker he's hanging out with."

"Never ignore a lead," Gallagher said, tossing the reports to the floor.

Ben frowned. "Now why'd you do that?"

"The next time he comes in here, he'll know he's had

visitors," Gallagher said. "Maybe that'll knock some of the overconfidence out of the son of a bitch."

They went downstairs and Ben took a couple of quick seconds to go down the hall and tell Clanton they were leaving. Then they went to Gallagher's car and headed east on Douglas to Main Street where Gallagher turned right. They rode down a couple of blocks past the police station to a small cement block building. A large sign in gold on a blue background was painted across the top front of the simple structure, reading: **A.J. KESSLER BAIL BONDS**. There were no windows on either side of the front door, which was a structural design that Ben figured gave the customers a little privacy from public view while arranging to get a family member or friend released from jail.

The detectives left the car and walked across the sidewalk. This time Ben led the way in. Gallagher followed and looked with distaste at the cluttered interior. There were two desks, a safe, and a long table; all cluttered with papers. Two doors were located at each end of the room.

A young woman who appeared to be in her late teens or early twenties sat at one of the desks. A.J. Kessler sat at the other. He looked up from sorting through a stack of bond vouchers. Even though A.J. was sitting down, it was obvious that he was a little person because his arms were disproportionately short. He recognized the visitors as cops he had seen from time to time.

"I'm Sergeant Forester and this is Sergeant Gallagher."

"Yeah," A.J. said. "I've seen you two guys around. What can I do for you?"

"We need some information on Dwayne Wheeler," Gallagher said.

"Okay," A.J. said. He slid off the chair to the floor. "Let's go into my private office." The bail bondsman was a little shorter than four and a half feet in height, and he had thick black hair that matched the handlebar moustache under his nose. He went through the door and sat down at yet another desk. The cops followed him into the room.

"Have a seat," A.J. invited.

After the two detectives had settled down, Ben asked, "When's the last time you saw Dwayne?"

"Oh, it's prob'ly been a month or two," A.J. said. He knew enough not to ask questions. Those cops were going to give him only the information they wanted to anyway.

"He's done work for you from time to time, right?" Ben said.

"Sure," A.J. said. "He's helped me hunt down runners. It's all legal since he's a private detective."

"Have you seen his license?" Gallagher asked.

A.J. shook his head.

Gallagher continued, "What would you say if I told you his license wasn't any good?"

"Nothing," A.J. said. "In fact I don't give a rat's ass if his license is valid or not."

"That's got nothing to do with why we're here," Ben said.

"Then why'd your buddy bring it up?" A.J. inquired in a tone of irritation. There was a strong hint of audacity in his eyes, and the bail bondsman looked directly at Gallagher with a challenging gaze.

"I might bring up a lot of shit before we're out of here," Gallagher said. "We got some questions, so you answer 'em."

"I'm not being uncooperative," the little man said. "And don't you be such an asshole."

Gallagher leaned forward to speak, but Ben reached out and stopped him, before continuing the interview.

"We would also like to know if you've seen him in the company of another man. He's a husky guy about six feet high and a hunnerd and eighty-five or so."

A.J. shook his head. "The only time I've talked with Dwayne or seen him, he's been alone. And that's generally when we're teamed up to take a bail jumper into custody."

Gallagher asked, "How's come you use Wheeler to help you?"

"Dwayne is smart and he's tough," A.J. replied. "And he knows Wichita better'n anybody else I know."

Gallagher smirked. "And you need a tough guy to get between you and your fugitive, right?"

From somewhere on his person, A.J. produced a telescoping metal baton in a sudden flash of movement. He flicked it, and its length doubled from twelve inches to twenty-four. Another lightning quick movement brought it down on the desk with a resounding whack. "You want a taste of this?"

Gallagher got to his feet. "You just try it, you little shit!"

A.J. next pulled a small Beretta semi-automatic pistol from his shoulder holster. He was careful to keep it pointed toward the ceiling. "I got this baby, too."

Now Ben was standing up, positioning himself between the antagonists. "Come on, you two!"

"Don't start this 'you two' crap," A.J. said. "This shit heel is asking for it." He slid off his chair, keeping a sharp eye on Gallagher. He opened the door. "Both you get the hell out of here," he ordered. "And don't come back here without a warrant. I won't even give you the time of day without one."

The detectives went through the door and passed the girl at the desk who looked at them wide-eyed. Gallagher winked at her, and followed Ben out to the car. When they got in, Gallagher asked, "D'you think he's doing that young broad?" Then he answered his own question. "Prob'ly not. Somebody'd have to pick him up and put him on her."

"Oh, Jesus Christ, Al!" Ben said angrily. "You really know how to fuck up an interview, don't you?"

"I didn't do nothing," Gallagher protested.

"C'mon! Let's go down to the warehouse district and talk to Elmer Pettibone."

Gallagher started the car, then whipped it around to go back up to Douglas.

———

ELMER PETTIBONE ADMITTED THE POLICEMEN TO his office, and all three sat down. Ben, who had made Gallagher promise to stay quiet or at least show a little restraint, opened the conversation with a blunt statement. "We're looking for Dwayne Wheeler."

"I haven't seen him for a couple of weeks," Elmer replied.

"You ought to be worried," Gallagher interjected. "He's driving your car around town."

"He's got my permission," Elmer replied in a matter-of-fact tone. "His own is broke down, so he left it here and I lent him the Ford."

"How's come you're so generous and kind?" Ben asked.

"Dwayne's a good friend of mine," Elmer said. "He left his old coupe parked out in my garage."

"D'you mind if we look at it?" Gallagher asked.

"I got no problem with that," Elmer replied. He got up and went to a door at the rear of the office. He opened it and stepped into the garage, pointing. "It's down at the far end. And if you find anything that interests you, remember the car belongs to Dwayne." He went back in his office.

Ben and Gallagher walked down to the old Pontiac. Gallagher laughed. "If there's any evidence that Wheeler is a nickel-and-dimer, that car is proof."

The two set about looking inside the vehicle. Although it was old and dingy, there was no trash or other miscellaneous items inside. The glove compartment was completely empty. The policemen walked back toward the office and entered without knocking.

Elmer was sitting with his feet on his desk. "Anything else I can do for you?"

"Have you seen a guy hanging around with Dwayne?" Ben asked. "About six feet, husky and maybe a hunnerd and eighty pounds."

Elmer shook his head. "Nope. By the way, have you guys heard the rumor that strangers are moving into Wichita?"

"What kind of strangers?" Gallagher asked.

"The type that stick their noses into other people's business," Elmer said.

Ben shrugged. "That's news to me." He looked at Gallagher. "What about you, Al? Have you picked up on anything like that?"

"Not a word," Gallagher replied. He looked pointedly at Elmer. "Who told you about any strangers?"

"I can't remember."

"Let me tell you something, Pettibone," Gallagher said. "You try being cute and you'll find yourself taken to the station, understand?"

"Don't get smart with me, Gallagher," Elmer said

coolly. "I got a lawyer. You take my ass to jail and I'll be out of there within an hour."

"I got my eye on you, Pettibone," Gallagher remarked.

"C'mon, Al," Ben said. "Let's go."

The two detectives left the bootlegger's office.

Chapter 18

Donna Sue had been spending close to ten hours a day on her typing lessons. Her devotion to the task had reached a level bordering on outright mania as she sat in front of the machine. She had even missed meals as she advanced past the fingering exercises, completely mastering them in such a short time that Miss Caruthers was amazed. Donna Sue had even typed a fifty-word-a-minute exercise that was graded by the professional secretary.

The next learning series consisted of typing up business letters in different formats. She found the results of these drills extremely satisfying, and she could imagine doing such tasks for Dwayne in his office, or even in a big important company for some executive officer. After doing a half dozen of the pseudo-communications, Donna Sue turned all her thoughts to being Dwayne's secretary. She even typed up the letterhead she would use for his correspondence.

Dwayne Wheeler

Private Detective
The Snodgrass building
Suite 205
000 West Douglas Avenue
Wichita, Kansas

Donna Sue couldn't remember the street address, so she used three zeros, knowing that each letter and number took up the same amount of space. And she thought the word "suite" was much more dignified and sophisticated than "room." That was something she had picked up in the examples of her lessons.

Now she was in the part of the book that taught her how to use the tab key for another thing beside paragraph indentures. She would type lists of figures, making sure each set of numbers was perfectly aligned with the other in its column, then hit the tab to go to the next. Donna Sue liked the looks of those results, too, thinking they seemed quite scientific and business like. She could remember seeing similar pages in the welding manual that Boeing had provided her during the war. These were tables she referred to during her quality control activities.

Her work was interrupted by a familiar rapping on her door. "Come in, Jewell," she called out.

Jewell walked into the room and curtsied. "Hi, Miss Donna Sue. Miss Caruthers tole me to tell you that Missus Davies can see you now."

"Okay," Donna Sue said. She had requested a meeting with the lady of the house through Miss Caruthers. When Miss Caruthers inquired as to the reason, Donna Sue told her it was a message from Dwayne for Mrs. Davies and she could only divulge it to her. Miss Caruthers insisted on knowing the full details, but Donna Sue remembered

Dwayne saying she was to speak to no one but Mrs. Davies, and she politely refused.

Jewell spoke up again. "I'm supposed to take you to Miss Caruthers first."

Donna Sue left her typing and walked with Jewell down the hall. When they reached the door to Miss Caruthers' office, Jewell stopped and curtsied again. Donna Sue entered the secretary's bailiwick to find her waiting.

"Hello, Donna Sue. Mrs. Davies is able to see you now. Please come with me."

They walked side by side out of the office and down the hall to the stairs. When they reached the first floor, they went into Mrs. Davies' reception room. The lady was sitting on the sofa. "Sit down, Donna Sue."

"Thank you," Donna Sue replied. She noticed that Miss Caruthers remained in the room. "I'm sorry, but Dwayne told me I wasn't supposed to speak to nobody but Missus Davies."

Mrs. Davies looked at Miss Caruthers. "And we shall honor Mr. Wheeler's request." She waited until the secretary had withdrawn, then she turned to Donna Sue. "Now what was it that Mr. Wheeler wanted you to tell me?"

Donna Sue brightened and she smiled. "He says to tell you that he's solved the murder case. And he said all he has left to do with the Kansas City people is complete his investigation and wrap up loose ends. He expects to come and get me by the end of the week."

Mrs. Davies, plainly pleased by the news, also smiled. "It sounds like Mr. Wheeler has performed in his usual efficient manner. Is he going to turn everything over to the police?"

"Oh! I almost forgot. He's going to the F.B.I. because there's crooked cops in the middle of all this."

Mrs. Davies was thoughtful for a moment. The fact the Federal Bureau of Investigation would be called in disturbed her a bit. "Isn't there at least one trustworthy element within the Wichita Police Department he can turn to?"

"I guess not," Donna Sue said. "Dwayne always knows best about those things."

"I'm certain that he does," Mrs. Davies said. She had faith in Dwayne Wheeler's decisions. In fact, calling in outside law enforcement might actually be better where she was concerned. The Federal Government had no real interest in call girls unless they were being transported over state lines. And her operation was strictly local. Also, if the bookmakers and bootleggers would survive any investigative incursions by the Feds, she would be safe, too. Some pressure might be expected, but she had loyal clients from the upper echelons of Wichita's male population. And there were more than just a few who would be happy to see that she got safely through any legal probing. That would be not only for her sake, but for their own sakes as well. Any exposure of her business could lead to very embarrassing disclosures about their particular recreational activities and interests. A divorce was financially devastating for any man, but was particularly brutal to wealthy Lotharios. Any who faced a betrayed wife's rage could expect to pay an inordinate amount of alimony for a very long time. Perhaps even to the end of their days on earth.

"I really want to thank you for your kindness to me," Donna Sue said. "I'm sure you'll be glad to see me go."

"On the contrary, Donna Sue. You are a very

charming young lady. And Miss Caruthers tells me you have developed into a very competent typist."

"Yes, ma'am," Donna Sue said. "My next step will be business college. Oh! I got to get me one of them high school certificates first. Then I'll go to business college and learn shorthand and other things."

"I'm sure you will succeed in attaining your goals."

Donna Sue stood up. "If you'll excuse me, I think I'll get back to my typing lessons."

"Of course, Donna Sue. And thank you for relaying Mr. Wheeler's report to me."

"You're welcome," Donna Sue said. Then a thought occurred to her. "If you want, I could type it up for you."

Mrs. Davies smiled and shook her head. "That won't be necessary. An oral account is quite sufficient."

MAISIE BURNETT LOOKED UP IN SURPRISE WHEN Ben Forester and Al Gallagher walked into the Jayhawker Restaurant. As they sat down she brought them cups of coffee. "Have you caught Dwayne Wheeler yet?" she asked.

"Nope," Ben replied. "Him and Donna Sue have walked off the face of the earth. You haven't heard anything from her, have you? A letter or a phone call or something?"

"Not a word," Maisie said. "And I still think he murdered her."

Gallagher's eyes opened wide. "What makes you think that?"

Maisie, who was always uncomfortable around him, replied, "I just figger he did. I don't believe a word of what he said about her. She didn't have no family emergency and have to go somewhere. She had a brother and a couple of sisters, but she never had nothing to do with 'em."

"Well, Maisie," Ben interrupted. "We can't arrest him on your suspicions. And we don't know where he is anyhow."

"He's on the lam," Maisie said.

"Okay," Ben said. He turned to Gallagher with a wink. "Let's put an APB out on Dwayne Wheeler."

"Good idea," Gallagher said, winking back. "But I think Lieutenant Cordell has already done that."

"What's a APB?" Maisie asked.

"That's an all-points bulletin," Ben answered. "That means ever' cop in the whole world will be looking for him."

"Then put out a APB," Maisie urged them. "And make him tell where he buried Donna Sue."

"We're on it," Gallagher promised.

Janet Dugan joined them after turning in an order for the restaurant's only other customer. She gave Ben a bold look. "Glad to see you back."

"According to Maisie you have a permanent job here," Ben said. "She's sure Donna Sue's boyfriend has killed her and hid the body."

"Then you'll always know where to find me, won't you?"

Gallagher looked at Ben in surprise. "Is there something going on I don't know about?"

"Yeah," Ben said. "Me and Janet are having a hot passionate love affair."

"You bet," Janet said, laughing.

"Well," Ben said. "Actually I came in here for another less important reason." He looked at Maisie. "Has Dwayne ever shown up at the Jayhawker in the company of another guy? A buddy maybe? We heard he's been hanging around with somebody."

Maisie shook her head. "He's always alone when he comes in here."

"Well, has there been any guys coming in lately that are about six feet tall?" Gallagher asked. "And husky looking with a mean look about 'em?"

The two waitresses looked at each other then shrugged.

Ben pulled out his badge wallet and took out two business cards. He handed one each to Maisie and Janet. "If you remember anything you heard being said or see anything that might shed some light on Dwayne and Donna Sue, you call this number. It's homicide, and if I ain't there, they can get ahold of me. Okay?"

"It don't matter how small it is," Gallagher emphasized. "Sometimes just a bit of information can lead to a big clue."

The moods of the two young women plummeted. Ben's request, that included the word 'homicide,' deflated their collective good humor. Maybe Donna Sue had really been murdered.

"Yeah," said Maisie. "We'll call all right."

The two cops finished their coffee. "Okay, girls. We'll be seeing you," Ben said.

He and Gallagher walked out of the restaurant leaving the waitresses gazing worriedly at each other. When the cops got back to the car, they didn't drive off right away.

"Shitty day," Ben pronounced.

"Yeah," Gallagher agreed. They were silent for almost a full minute, then he asked, "Did your daughter move back in?"

"Yeah," Ben said sullenly.

"That pretty much fucked up your plans for a den, huh?"

"Oh, God," Ben moaned. "I really had some good ideas for her old room. A nice easy chair, magazine rack, and a radio to listen to ball games. It would have been a perfect place to do crossword puzzles."

"Yeah," Gallagher said. "You're one of them brainy guys that like that shit."

"It doesn't make much difference now," Ben said. "The only thing moving in there is gonna be a crib."

"Well, the kid's your grandson, right? So he's family."

"This ain't my idea of being a grandpa," Ben said. "Her and the dipshit she married were supposed to come over on Sundays, spend a couple of hours, then get the hell back to their own place."

"As I recall you warned her about the guy."

"Yeah," Ben said. "What I should've done was to praise the shit out of the son of a bitch. Once she'd figgered I liked him, she would have broken their engagement."

Gallagher chuckled. "Ain't that the truth? I'm glad me and Doris didn't have any kids. It would've made the divorce ten times worse."

"You're lucky she ran off with another guy," Ben said.

"Yeah," Gallagher agreed. "No alimony. That was a big break; believe me!"

"Well, let's get back to the station."

Gallagher turned on the ignition and stepped down on the starter. "The lieutenant is gonna be pissed."

"No shit," Ben murmured.

There were only two other detectives in homicide when Ben and Gallagher walked into the squad room. They went directly back to Lieutenant Buford Cordell's office, and rapped on the door. As usual there was a husky unintelligible reply, and Ben led the way in. Cordell looked at them as they sat down. His curiosity was expressed by his eyes.

"Nothing," Gallagher said. "We got nothing."

"Not quite," Ben countered. "We found an eye witness to Wheeler and another guy beating up those two guys of Schomp's who brought the whore to the Riverview Hotel."

This news awoke Cordell's deeper interest. "What witness?"

"Harry Gaston, the house dick," Ben said. "He figured some strange things were going on from the way the bellboys were acting."

"Right," Gallagher chimed in. "And he didn't recognize any of the hookers that began showing up that night."

"I remember Harry when he was on the force," Cordell said. "He's the kind of guy we should bring in on this operation. Did he say what Wheeler and his partner beat those poor bastards with?"

"Brass knuckles," Ben replied. "Those guys were knocked down pretty fast according to Harry."

"God!" Cordell exclaimed with a humorless grin. "I seen one of 'em. He looked like he'd been in an ax fight without an ax."

"He just about was," Gallagher said.

"Well, I think Schomp made the wise choice by backing off the call girl racket," Cordell said. "The last thing we need is getting a lot of attention before things are firmed up enough to have a handle on everything."

"Y'know," Ben said. "I been thinking. D'you suppose that Dwayne is fronting for another out-of-town mob? Maybe from Dallas or Saint Louis?"

"That thought has just now occurred to me," Cordell said. "We might have some serious competition."

"That'd really put Schomp in deep shit," Gallagher observed. "He'd be trying to take over Wichita and would end up in the same trouble he had in Kansas City."

"Maybe another Mafia gang has decided to move on Wichita," Ben suggested.

"Could be," Cordell mused. "If one of them Wop mobs got control over the country from Dallas all the way up through Oklahoma City, Tulsa, Wichita and then Kansas City, they'd have a big money-making operation going."

"I wonder how come they never tried it before," Gallagher pondered.

Ben replied, "That's 'cause back in the big eastern cities they think the middle of the country is all farms and hick towns. If they found out about all the oil, cattle, farming and manufacturing money that's circulating out here, they'd want a big piece of it. They'd even start setting up crooked labor unions like they got in New York and Chicago."

"I don't know," Gallagher said. "The Mafia can fuck over other criminals, but dealing with the public can be another matter altogether. Wichitans wouldn't take a lot of shit off a bunch of greaseballs. Especially some businessman whose workers were being unionized."

Ben chuckled. "I can just see some hood going into the Uptown Billiard Parlor and trying to shake down Delmar Watson."

Gallagher laughed, too. "They'd have to scrape the Guinea off the sidewalk. Them guys ain't gunfighters.

Shooting another guy in the back of his head while he's eating a plate of spaghetti in a restaurant ain't exactly Wyatt Earp or Bat Masterson."

"Well," Cordell said, "at any rate, we got to be real careful at this point. As cops we all know that Wichita's rackets are disorganized and pretty much operated in an easy going style."

"*Laissez-faire*," Ben remarked.

"What the hell does that mean?" Gallagher asked.

"It means not interfering," Ben explained. "Letting things pass. Keeping it simple and easy. Operating like—"

"Okay!" Gallagher snapped. "I get it."

"You see," Ben said. "You do crossword puzzles and you learn a lot."

"I don't give a shit what you call it," Cordell said. "What it all adds up to, is that the local vices aren't able to defend themselves from takeovers like Al said a minute ago."

"And right now, neither can Schomp," Ben reminded him.

"We gotta find Wheeler," Cordell growled. He looked at Ben. "You've known the guy since he was a snot-nosed kid. Don't you have any idea where he might be laying low? And don't forget his girlfriend is missing, too."

"He evidently has connections I don't know about," Ben said. "That's why I think he might be working for another mob."

"Shit house mouse!" Gallagher exclaimed in exasperation. "We're gonna end up in the middle of a gang war."

"Let's relax," Ben counseled, lighting a cigarette. "It's hard to figure out what's really going on. This whole mess with Dwayne started when that bookie Stubb Durham was killed."

"I know who did it," Cordell said. "It had to be Billy

Joe Clayton. From what I heard, not only did Durham turn down an offer to join the takeover, he said he was going to warn the other bookies about it."

"But why'd they knock off Mack Crofton?" Gallagher asked.

"They weren't sure they could trust him," Cordell said. "I never told you guys about this, but Schomp got a call from Wichita awhile back, and it was somebody who claimed to be Harry Denton. But it wasn't Harry. Whoever it was, learned about the Wops. That set ever'body on edge. There was a snitch somewhere. So Clayton came up with the idea of telling Crofton that they were going to kidnap Wheeler's girl, then him and Arlo Merriwell staked out her place. Sure enough Wheeler showed up and took her away. So they decided to take Crofton out. They followed him over to that café on Fifty-Four. They think it was Wheeler who was with him, but nobody's sure."

"Let me tell you something," Gallagher said in a cold voice. "Wheeler is going to show his face sooner or later. And when he does...well, he'll end up in the Big Arkansas River."

Ben felt sincerely sorry. "He really got himself in it big time, didn't he?"

DONNA SUE FINISHED THE SELF-IMPOSED TYPING test and pulled the paper out of the typewriter. She counted the number of words she had typed and deducted the two errors. It left her with a score of sixty-two words a minute. She smiled to herself and reached over and turned the lamp off. It had been a long day at the keyboard and she felt a tightness in her shoulders. She had just stood up when a knock on the door sounded. "Come in."

Miss Caruthers opened the door and stepped into the room. "Mrs. Davies tells me you'll be leaving us very soon, Donna Sue."

"Yes," Donna Sue said. "And before I go I want to thank you for all the help you've given me on learning to type."

"You're certainly welcome," Miss Caruthers said. She walked over to the window and stared out at the growing dusk. "You are an extremely intelligent woman, Donna Sue. It's a shame you didn't have more advantages and opportunities as a girl."

"That's the way it goes sometimes," she said. "My dad just left one day, and I really didn't have many choices. I was the oldest of us four kids." She joined her at the window. "I just wish I could have kept that job at Boeing."

"I came in here to tell you that when you leave, you can take that typewriter with you, if you wish," Miss Caruthers informed her. "And the typing lessons book as well."

"Please tell Missus Davies I appreciate the kindness."

"Actually, it's my machine and book. I really don't have much use for them anymore."

"Thank you very much," Donna Sue said. "You've been so nice to me."

Miss Caruthers turned toward her, then stepped forward and put her arms around her. "I hope you will always think of me as a friend."

"Oh, I will Miss Caruthers!"

"Donna Sue, you are one of the most remarkable women I've ever known," Miss Caruthers said. Then she kissed her gently on the cheek and stepped back. "My first name is Kathryn." Then she added, "Kathy."

"I'll always remember you in the best way...Kathy."

The secretary smiled sweetly at her, then turned and quietly left the room. For an instant Donna Sue experienced the same feelings of that junior high crush she'd had on the pretty ninth grade girl; then the emotions ebbed away.

Chapter 19

Dwayne and Tommy Brady sat down for a late supper in the farmhouse kitchen. There was about twenty minutes left of the murky daylight, and both men were hungry. Earlier that day, Tommy had gone into Augusta and picked up a couple of T-bone steaks weighing close to twelve ounces each. There were baked potatoes, boiled carrots and whole wheat bread to go with the meat. When they sat down to eat, Dwayne bowed his head and waited for Tommy to say grace.

Tommy looked at him. "Why don't you say the blessing tonight?"

"I don't know any prayers, Tommy. I'd just mess it up."

"Go on," Tommy urged him. "God don't care if you don't say nothing fancy."

"I hate to say this, Tommy, but I feel silly. I'm sorry."

"It ain't a hard thing, Dwayne. Just thank God for the food."

Dwayne hesitated, then said, "Thank you for this food, God."

"Amen," said Tommy.

"Amen," said Dwayne. "Pass the potatoes, please."

The meal started at that point and within moments both men had their plates filled. "So," Tommy said after taking a bite of steak. "What're you gonna be doing next on this caper?" He had picked up the Sam Spade terminology over the few days that Dwayne had been staying with him.

"It's time to wrap this thing up," Dwayne said. "Tomorrow evening, I'm going to the Riverview Hotel and check things out. My final plans will depend on what I find out over there."

"Won't that be kind of dangerous?"

Dwayne shook his head. "I'm gonna disguise myself. I got some theater stuff in my valise. I'll put on a moustache and I also got some spectacles with plain glass in 'em. The rims are the black kind like the comic guy Harold Lloyd used to wear. Nobody will know it's yours truly."

"That ought to do the job," Tommy allowed.

"There's more to it," Dwayne said. "I've got a Stetson hat, too. I'll wear that and pass myself off as a cattleman who's come to town to do business with the stockyards. I got my jacket with the rodeo pockets that I wear out to Western Danceland. That'll add to the look. It don't matter what the pants are like."

"What about cowboy boots?" Tommy asked. "All them guys wear 'em, y'know."

"I didn't think of that," Dwayne said.

"There's a pair in the attic that Margie's older brother used to have before he moved away," Tommy said. "I think they're in pretty good shape and shouldn't look too bad if you brushed 'em off."

"I hope they fit," Dwayne said.

"We'll see."

A couple of minutes later they were well into the meal, shoveling food into their mouths with a minimum of conversation as hungry men are wont to do. When the main course was consumed and the plates wiped with pieces of bread, Tommy fetched a quart of chocolate revel ice cream from the refrigerator freezer. Each dished himself a generous helping of the dessert, and finally that was gone, too.

"Wow!" Dwayne said, leaning back in his chair. "Now in the army that's what we called good chow."

"Same in the navy," Tommy said.

They sank into silence again, then Dwayne, after a satisfying belch, forced himself to get up and tend to the cleanup chore. In the four days he'd been at the farm, Dwayne had developed a marked efficiency at clearing the table and washing the dishes. Within fifteen minutes the silverware and dishes were washed, dried and put away, and the table wiped clean. Dwayne turned to Tommy. "How's about a look at them cowboy boots?"

"I'm too full to move," Tommy said. "Go up in the attic on the backstairs. I think they're wrapped in an old towel and on that shelf next to the west wall."

Dwayne followed the directions, and went to the full attic that ran the entire length and width of the house. He had to bend over since the slant of the roof lowered the overhead, but he located the shelf and saw a large bath towel wrapped around something. He grabbed it and stepped back to the center of the room where he could stand up straight. He unrolled the covering and saw a pair of cowboy boots. They weren't real fancy, but they obviously hadn't been worn too much. He left the attic and took his newfound prize back to the kitchen.

"You got 'em, huh?" Tommy asked.

"Yeah," Dwayne said. He sat down and pulled off his shoes, then slipped his feet into the boots. After taking a few tentative steps toward the kitchen door and back, he sat down again. "They're a little tight, but I think they'll do."

"Go outside and walk around the farmyard," Tommy said. "That way you can check 'em out better and maybe they'll loosen up some." He waited as Dwayne left the house and went outside. Five minutes later, he returned.

"They're tight," Dwayne said with a slight grimace. "But I can use 'em." He grinned. "I hope I don't have to do any running."

"You can always take 'em off," Tommy pointed out.

"Yeah," Dwayne said. "But I sure hope nothing happens that'll make me have to haul ass in my stocking feet."

Dwayne and Tommy slept in the next morning, and spent the day in idle talk and walks around the farm as well as enjoying a couple of strolls down the road between meals. Early that evening, while Tommy had gone over to visit his renter, Dwayne dialed the Riverview Hotel and asked for Jimmy Thompson. When the bellboy answered, Dwayne identified himself.

"Where the hell have you been?" Jimmy asked.

"Getting things organized for the big finale," Dwayne replied. "Has anything special been going on over there?"

"Hell yes!" Jimmy exclaimed. "Them two cops Forester and Gallagher came looking for you."

"Well, they're a coupla guys that're gonna get what they got coming to 'em before this is over with."

"And something is happening now," Jimmy said. "The police lieutenant Cordell has been going in and out of Denton's office several times during the day with Merriwell that asshole of a bookie."

"Are you sure it was Merriwell?" Dwayne asked. "I didn't know you knew him."

"I remember the son of a bitch from before he got kicked out of the OK Barbershop," Jimmy said. "Anyhow people have been visiting Denton's office all day. I found that out from the elevator operator."

Now Dwayne knew that a gathering of the Kansas City and Wichita conspirators was about to be called to order. "Listen, Jimmy. I'm coming over there, and I'll be dressed up in a disguise."

"You mean like the Lone Ranger?"

"Aw, hell no!" Dwayne snapped. "I ain't gonna wear a mask. I'm gonna make myself up like a rancher, see? And I'm gonna get a room so's I can keep an eye on things. I'll get in touch with you, but in the meantime I need you to make a special note of people who are visiting Harry Denton. Can you do that?"

"Yeah," Jimmy answered, "except when I have to carry guests' suitcases for 'em, and run errands. But I'll do my best."

"I can't ask any more'n that," Dwayne said. "I'll be there in about an hour."

He hung up and went into his room, getting the satchel from under the bed. He pulled out the Stetson and the theatrical makeup kit. He used the large mirror on the dresser to apply his disguise. He first dabbed the sticky gum to his upper lip, and carefully placed the moustache under his nose. When he was satisfied with that, he put on the hat and the glasses, turning his head left and right to study the effect. He liked how he looked, thinking that glasses made it even better.

The next item of business was to change his clothes, and he turned back to the contents of the valise. He slipped into a necktie and clean shirt, then changed into a pair of slacks. The cowboy boots came next, then he put on his shoulder holster with the Colt semi-automatic pistol, and slipped into the rodeo jacket. Another look in the mirror affirmed he was well disguised. After he got his wallet and badge, he was ready to roll.

He could hear Tommy's car pulling up, so he stood by the bedroom door and waited for his host to come into the house. As soon as Tommy came through the door, Dwayne stepped out from the bedroom and gave a western greeting. "Howdy, partner."

Tommy grinned at the sight. "Now ain't you something else?"

"How do I look?"

"You look differ'nt," Tommy said. "I'll give you that."

"That's just what I'm going for," Dwayne said. "You don't mind loaning me the car again, do you? I'll need it 'til tomorrow afternoon prob'ly."

"Help yourself," Tommy said, tossing him the keys. "I wasn't going anywhere anyway."

Dwayne went back into the bedroom and closed the valise after putting in his toiletries. The battered piece of luggage would make him appear as if he were a traveling man on the road. He returned to the living room, beaming a smile at Tommy. "I reckon I'll be moseying along."

"Well, 'Happy Trails,' as Roy Rogers sings in his song," Tommy said with a grin and a wave.

It was almost seven thirty when Dwayne walked into the lobby of the Riverview Hotel. He went up to the front desk where the evening clerk was on duty. "Howdy," Dwayne said. "I need me a room."

"Yes, sir," the clerk said. He looked carefully at the new arrival. "I believe you've stayed here before, sir. You look familiar."

"Oh, I sure have," Dwayne said. "I got business at the stockyards, y'see. I'm gonna be shipping a herd of cattle up here to Wichita from the Texas Panhandle. I was thinking of Kansas City or Chicago, but I got to tell you I'm kind of fond of Wichita, so I decided to deal with my friends here."

"Well, we're happy to have you back, sir. I take it you'd like a single room."

"That'd fill the bill," Dwayne said, signing the register.

The clerk turned the book around and looked at the signature. "Ah, I recognize your name, Mr. Starrett."

Dwayne almost chuckled. He'd chosen the pseudonym because his favorite movie cowboy was Charles Starrett.

The clerk continued, "I'll put you in room two-oh-five. It'll give you a nice view of the river."

"I appreciate that."

"Do you need help with your bag?" the clerk asked, handing him the key.

"Naw, I'm traveling light," Dwayne said. "By the way, is that bellboy Jimmy Thompson still working here?"

"Yes he is."

"Would you send him up to my room?" Dwayne asked. "Him and me got along real well the last few times I was here. We got an understanding." He winked at the clerk. "Y'know what I mean?"

"Yes, sir."

Dwayne walked carefully toward the elevators in the tight boots. Over by the door leading to the alley, the house detective Harry Gaston watched him. He waited until Dwayne stepped into the elevator and the door closed, then he walked to the front desk, going around it to the office. Denver stepped inside, then pulled a business card from his pocket. It was the one given him by Sergeant Ben Forester. The sergeant's home phone was written on the back. Denver dialed the number, and when Ben answered, he said, "This is Denver at the Riverview. Dwayne Wheeler just checked in dressed up like a cowboy or something. I can get the room number if you want it."

"I'll be down there in a jiffy," Ben said. "You can give it to me then." He hung up, then put in a call to Al Gallagher at his apartment.

Dwayne answered the knock on his room door and opened it to see Jimmy Thompson. The bellboy started to speak, then stopped to stare at Dwayne's appearance. "So you're a cattle guy like you told me, right?"

"Exactly," Dwayne said. "I'm supposed to be a rancher by the name of Starrett. I told the clerk I'm up here from Texas to make a cattle sale to the Wichita Stockyards."

"I guess it'll work," Jimmy said.

"So what's been going on?"

"There's prob'ly about eight guys up in Denton's office now," Jimmy said. "They've ordered room service and I sent out for some liquor. Say! Y'know, there's a shortage of bootleg hooch that's getting worse."

"That'll be taken care of real quick," Dwayne said,

"just as soon as those guys up in that office are thrown in jail."

"Take your time," Jimmy said. "They're big tippers."

"Enjoy it while you can," Dwayne said. "Listen. I'm going up the stairs to the top floor and find a place where I can make a surveillance on Denton's office. I'll be in touch later."

"You ain't gonna need a lookout then?"

"Nobody will recognize me," Dwayne said. "So I can work all right alone."

"That's good," Jimmy said with a tone of relief in his voice. "I gotta tell you, Dwayne, some of them guys look pretty tough to me. Good luck."

Dwayne waited five minutes after Jimmy left the room before he donned the Stetson, and stepped out into the hall. He walked gingerly in the tight boots to the door leading to the stairs, and quickly slipped inside. Then he began the climb to the eighth floor. When he reached the landing, he paused long enough to open the door a crack to see if the hall was empty. There was no one in sight, and he boldly strode from the stairwell and sauntered down the hall toward Denton's office.

With the Stetson pulled down low, Dwayne eased up to the door and stopped. The sound of masculine conversation and glasses clinking were easy to discern. He thought he recognized Merriwell's voice a couple of times in the conversations. The sound of the elevator caught his attention, and Dwayne hurried past the office to the shadows at the end of the hall. He stepped around the corner, and when the elevator doors opened, he leaned out just enough to see who had arrived. Lieutenant Buford Cordell and no less a personage than Billy Joe Clayton exited the conveyance and made their way to the door. They knocked on it, and were allowed to enter.

Hail, hail, Dwayne thought, *the gang's all here!*

Now was the time to make his initial contact with the F.B.I. and reveal all he'd found out. He started for the elevator, but someone suddenly grabbed him by the jacket collar and violently pulled him back. Dwayne twisted around just in time to catch Sergeant Al Gallagher's fist straight to the nose. He felt his olfactory organ crunch under the impact as a shower of blood spurted and dribbled down his chin.

Gallagher laughed. "Now ain't you a sight? What are you dressed up for? A Gene Autry movie?"

A combination wave of pain and dizziness swept over Dwayne and his knees buckled. He would have fallen, but Gallagher grabbed his tie and held him up. Now Dwayne was choking, but he managed to get his feet under himself and stand.

"We're taking us a little trip down to the basement, shamus," Gallagher said. He dragged the dazed private detective down to the freight elevator. He had come up to the eighth floor on it, and the gate was still open. He shoved Dwayne into it so hard that he fell to the wooden floor. "Stay there, or you'll get a hard kick to the jaw," Gallagher threatened.

The heavy elevator began descending in a rocking motion. Dwayne tried to clear his head as he saw the shaft walls and doors ease past, looking as if they were rising while he was motionless. When they reached the bottom, Gallagher slid the gate up and opened the door. "C'mon, shamus. You can walk."

Dwayne stumbled out into what was the building basement that was divided into cages holding cleaning supplies, bedding and other hotel items. Gallagher took him by the arm and steered him roughly toward a door.

The cop opened it and shoved Dwayne through. Ben Forester looked at him. "Sit down."

Dwayne obeyed, noting they were in a small store room with a deep sink. Ben went over to a paper towel dispenser and pulled some out. He wetted them and handed the sodden mess to Dwayne. "Put that on your nose."

Cold fear now swept over Dwayne, and he knew he was in an extremely sticky situation. Ben Forester might be an old friend, but the guy had gotten himself into a desperate situation where he had too much to lose if Dwayne succeeded in his investigative plans. The dampened towels felt good on his nose and eyes as his mind raced for a solution to this predicament.

"Godamn it, Dwayne," Ben said. "I told you and told you to butt out of this shit."

Gallagher laughed. "Did you really think you wouldn't be recognized? The only thing that getup is good for is when you're around people who don't know you in the first place."

Even Ben chuckled. "You'd've been better off if you'd put a paper sack over your head."

A knock on the door startled Dwayne, but both Ben and Gallagher's lack of surprise showed the two had been expecting a caller. When Ben opened the door, a well-groomed man in a suit stepped through it. He looked at the injured private eye. "So this is Wheeler, huh?"

"The one and only," Gallagher said.

"Yeah," Ben said. "The guy who's been a stumbling block to us for the last month."

The stranger took note of the blood and towels. "What happened to him?"

"He attacked me," Gallagher said. "He slammed my fist with his nose."

The stranger pulled up a chair and sat down, looking straight at Dwayne. "Wheeler, you have no idea how pissed off we are at you."

Dwayne, frantically trying to come up with a plan of how to smash through the three and escape the room, remained silent.

"I might as well introduce you two," Ben said. "Dwayne, this is Steve Williams of the F.B.I."

Dwayne's eyes opened wide.

Williams glared at him. "We've been trying to set up R.K. Schomp for a fall along with all his mob and their Wichita pals. But you kept blundering in the way."

Finally Dwayne was able to speak, but all he could say was, "What the fuck?"

Gallagher butted in. "And Mack Crofton's murder was a particular pain-in-the-ass. It brought the Sheriff's Department into the picture and me and Ben had a hell of a time keeping them from digging in too deep."

Ben nodded. "And when you told me you'd found out about the Mafia, I just knew you were going to turn this thing into a Chinese cluster fuck."

"How'd you find out about that, shamus?" Gallagher asked.

"I searched Denton's office and found a note telling him to call Schomp," Dwayne explained. "I took the memo with me and called him the next morning, saying I was Denton."

"Ah!" Ben said. "So you were the mysterious caller?"

"Yeah," Dwayne said. "Schomp wasn't there, but one of his guys was. He told me about the Eye-talians and the deal Schomp made with 'em."

"That was a real coup, Dwayne," Ben said.

"Maybe so, shamus," Gallagher allowed. "But you ended up being the turd in the punch bowl."

Dwayne snuffed and wiped his nose again. "So even you're undercover, are you, Gallagher?"

"That's right, shamus," the sergeant replied. "Now you know why you was pulled in that night and given a hard time. Trouble is, you was too stupid to figger how important it was for you to butt out. And I couldn't tell you nothing. It was like you added two and two and came up with five."

"Are you guys gonna have my license revoked?"

"Naw," Ben said. "But I got to tell you, Dwayne, there was a moment or two when I was really tempted."

"Well," Dwayne said, shifting in the chair. "I'd say you guys was at a dead end."

"Thanks to you," Williams snapped

Now Dwayne chuckled. "Well, do you three wise acres want to know something? Something that will brighten your day?"

Gallagher smirked. "Now what in the fuck could you know that would please us so much, you fuck ass shamus you!"

"I know who killed Stubb Durham," Dwayne said.

"Bullshit!" Gallagher snarled.

"And I got a witness to the murder," Dwayne added.

Now the three lawmen exchanged glances among themselves. Ben said, "Dwayne doesn't bullshit. If he says he's made the killer, you can bet your bottom dollar he's made the killer."

"Wait a minute!" Williams said. "So he's solved a local killing. What good does that do us?"

"The killer," Dwayne said in a superior tone, "is one of Schomp's men. A Wichita guy."

Now Ben, Gallagher and Williams were practically in his face. "Who did it?"

"Piss up a rope," Dwayne said with a big smile.

Ben turned to Gallagher and Williams. "If we can pull the guy in on this, you can bet he'll roll over to avoid the gallows. He'd snitch on the whole Kansas City mob with times, dates, places, and—"

Williams interrupted, looking at Dwayne. "Start talking, Wheeler."

"Okay," Dwayne said. "It was Arlo Merriwell."

"*Son of a bitch!*" Gallagher yelled.

Williams controlled his enthusiasm. "This is rather significant."

Ben looked at Dwayne. "So who's your witness?"

"Uh uh," Dwayne said. "No dice. I ain't saying nothing about the guy until we come to some agreements that I'm gonna insist on."

Williams frowned. "Such as?"

"I'm gonna be in on all the action," Dwayne said. "All the arrests, the interrogations, and even hearings and trials. I put in a lot of work on this, and I want credit for what I accomplished."

Williams nodded. "I can arrange that through the Bureau."

"And I want to be put in a safe place with a guard until this thing is wrapped up just in case something weird happens," Dwayne continued. "And that includes my girlfriend Donna Sue Connors. I have her stashed someplace that's prob'ly okay, but I don't want to take any chances."

Williams nodded again. "We have a safehouse over on Nineteenth Street in Riverside.

"Anything else?" Gallagher asked.

"Yeah," Dwayne said. He groaned and got to his feet. After a deep breath, he drove the heel of his hand at an upward angle into Gallagher's nose. The sergeant's head snapped back and he hit the wall hard, bouncing off and falling to his knees. Dwayne started punching his face, getting in a half dozen quick, sharp blows until Ben pulled him away.

Gallagher fell to the floor, and lay unmoving.

"Okay," Dwayne said. "Now let's all settle down and we'll discuss the rest of my demands."

Chapter 20

Dwayne drove the Ford slowly down Thirty-Seventh Street toward Mrs. Davies' house. It was Friday morning after the big scene at the hotel, and he had returned Tommy Brady's Oldsmobile to him, and spent the final night with his old friend. There first thing he had done when he woke up that day was call Donna Sue to tell her to pack up.

When he arrived at the gate to the property, the guards were expecting him. They both gave him friendly waves as he drove through the barrier and up to the house. Carson the butler was waiting for him on the porch. When Dwayne got out of the car and joined him, Carson politely ignored the tape on the visitor's nose. "We are most sorry to be losing Miss Connors," he said. "We've all grown rather fond of her."

"Yeah," Dwayne said. "She's a nice kid all right."

He was led through the foyer of the house to the waiting room. Donna Sue was sitting on the couch, and when she saw him, she rushed into his arms, then came to a stop. "What happened to your nose?"

"Nothing to worry about," Dwayne said. "Just part of the caper."

"Did those Kansas City guys beat you up again?"

Dwayne rolled his eyes. "This has got nothing to do with those son of a bitches."

"Then are things winding down like you said?"

He grinned at her. "Sam Spade would be proud of me. Are you ready to leave?"

"I have everything here," she replied.

"What's in that case?" he asked noticing something she had not brought with her from the apartment.

"It's a typewriter," Donna Sue said. "Miss Caruthers gave it to me. I learned to use it, too. I can do sixty-two words a minute."

"Is that good?"

"Better than average," Donna Sue said.

Carson picked up her luggage. "Mrs. Davies and Miss Caruthers send their regrets. They are unable to be here to say goodbye to Miss Connors."

They were interrupted by Jewell the little southern maid. She curtsied as she entered the room, then hurried over to Donna Sue and threw her arms around her. "I am gonna miss you so, Miss Donna Sue!"

"I'll miss you, too, Jewell," Donna Sue said. She pointed to Dwayne. "This is Dwayne Wheeler my boyfriend."

Jewell curtsied to him. "How do, Mr. Dwayne."

"Hi," Dwayne said, not quite sure what the girl meant by dipping down then straightening up. He turned his attention back to Donna Sue. "We've got to go. This is gonna be a busy day."

Carson led the two out the front door with Jewell following. Dwayne opened the trunk of the car, and the butler put the bags inside. He closed the lid. "I am sure I shall be seeing you again from time to time, Mr. Wheeler."

"Prob'ly," Dwayne said. "Thanks for all your courtesy."

He and Donna Sue got into the car, and she turned to wave goodbye to Carson and Jewell. Dwayne drove slowly toward the gate, exchanging nods with the guards as he steered out onto the street.

"Oh, dear," Donna Sue sighed. "I'm gonna miss that luxurious bedroom and the bathroom. Especially the fuzzy covering on the toilet seat."

Dwayne laughed. "That must have been nice."

"It was warm and snug first thing in the morning," Donna Sue said. "But I guess it'll be good to get back to my little apartment."

"We ain't going back to your apartment yet," Dwayne said. "Or the Jayhawker either. I'm stashing you someplace else."

"Oh, Dwayne!" she pouted. "Why couldn't I have just stayed with Missus Davies and Miss Caruthers?"

"Because we're going to an F.B.I. safehouse," Dwayne said.

"What's a safehouse?"

"It's a place where witnesses, agents and other people stay when they got to lay low."

"Wasn't Missus Davies' house safe?" Donna Sue asked.

"The advantage of the F.B.I.'s place is that we can stay together while I'm wrapping up this caper," Dwayne said. "It's really convenient and close to the action." He turned and winked at her. "And we'll sleep in the same room."

"Really?"

"Yeah," Dwayne replied. "And I'm horny."

"You're always horny," Donna Sue pointed out.

"Well, maybe if we're sleeping together for a few nights, I won't be."

"Will the safehouse be as nice as Missus Davies' place?"

"Who cares?" Dwayne remarked. "We can sleep together like a man and woman should." He frowned. "You don't seem too excited about that."

"Well, sure I am, honey," Donna Sue said. "It's just that you're throwing a lot at me all of a sudden."

He turned south and drove along the Big Arkansas River to Nineteenth Street, and made a right. After going a couple of blocks, he pulled into a driveway beside a two-story house, driving all the way to the back where a paved parking area was located. He pulled up beside a Pontiac sedan.

"There ain't a butler here," he said. "So I'll do the toting."

After he got the bags out, they walked up on the back porch. Dwayne knocked on the door and it was opened by a slim man wearing a shoulder holster. "Hi, Dwayne. Williams just called and said he'd be by about one o'clock."

"Thanks, John," Dwayne said. "This is Donna Sue. Honey, this is John Mikowski. He's part of the security detail that watches over this place."

Dwayne led the way up a flight of stairs to the second floor. They went down a couple of doors to a small bedroom. After throwing the bags on the bed, he gestured at the accommodations. "Simple and comfortable. This one has its own bathroom so we don't have to go down the hall."

"What's behind them other doors out there?"

"Other bedrooms," Dwayne said. "But nobody's

using 'em. We're the only tenants right now. There's a couple of F.B.I. guys but they stay downstairs."

Donna Sue sat down on the bed. "Now tell me exactly what's going on."

"Sure, baby," he said, settling beside her. "We'll be busting that K.C. mob wide open over the weekend. We're gonna start arrests this afternoon. That's what Agent Williams is coming by to get me for. And guess what? My old buddy Ben Forester and that no good son of a bitch Al Gallagher are working for the F.B.I., too. They're undercover, and I didn't even know about it. But that ain't the really big news."

She looked at him expectantly.

"I found out who killed Stubb Durham and I got a witness," Dwayne said. "And that's my ace in the hole. I let the F.B.I. and Wichita Police know I found out who did it. But I ain't told 'em who the witness is, see? I made a deal with 'em to let me in on the round-up, and give me public credit. It'll be really good for my business."

"Yeah!" Donna Sue said. She kissed him on the cheek. "And if you want your caper report typed up, I can do it for you. You don't have to go to the steno service you usually use."

"Hey!" Dwayne said with a laugh. "I'm *really* like Sam Spade now." He slipped his arm around her shoulder and drew her close to him, placing his lips on hers in a lingering kiss. "And I get to sleep with *my* secretary." He slipped his hand into her blouse, working his fingers beneath her brassiere.

"No, Dwayne," she said, pushing him away. "We're not gonna do it in the daylight when people we don't know are in the house. We'll wait 'til dark this evening."

"God!" Dwayne moaned. "Why couldn't all this have happened in the winter with shorter days?"

Dwayne rode in the F.B.I car, sitting in the front beside Steve Williams who was driving. Ben Forester and Al Gallagher sat in the back. Gallagher, like Dwayne, had tape across his battered nose. Although the two men spoke to each other, there was no friendliness in their demeanor, and a simmering tension existed between them. Their hatred for each other was so intense that Ben knew there would be more confrontations in the future.

The F.B.I. car was traveling east on Douglas Avenue, and when they crossed Hillside, Williams pulled up and parked in front of the Uptown Billiard Parlor. He pointed to a car across the street. "That's a couple of my agents. They tailed Merriwell here and confirmed he's not departed the premises." He turned and looked at Ben and Gallagher. "Okay. I can't make an arrest for that local murder. So you guys are going to have to take Merriwell in. Once we have him at the police station, we'll start the interrogation. You do the initial questioning, and I'll step in when we get to the takeover. That'll be the Federal side of the case."

Gallagher glared at the back of Dwayne's head. "You better really have a witness, shamus."

Dwayne scowled up at the cop's reflection in the rearview mirror. "O'course I got a witness! D'you think I'd go this far on pure bullshit?"

"Yeah," Gallagher said. "I think you would."

"Eat me, asshole!"

They all got out of the car, and Ben and Gallagher led the way into the pool hall. Dwayne and Williams brought up the rear. When the quartet entered, Delmar Watson looked up from reading the *Racing Form* at his usual place behind the counter. He recognized the two Wichita policemen and Dwayne, but not Williams. He started to speak, but noticed they were all looking at Arlo Merriwell who was shooting a solitary game of rotation at the front table.

Merriwell was about to make a shot, then stood still with his cue poised as he realized someone was watching him. He turned to look at the new arrivals, and straightened up without saying a word.

"Put the cue on the table," Ben told him. "And step over to the wall."

"What the fuck is this about?" Merriwell asked.

"Do what you're told, ass face," Gallagher said, moving around the opposite side of the table to get behind him.

Ben announced, "You're under arrest."

"What for?" Merriwell snapped.

"First degree murder," Ben replied.

"C'mon!" Merriwell said. "This is bullshit. So who did I first degree murder?"

"Turn around and face the wall," Ben ordered, ignoring the question. "And put your hands behind you."

Merriwell hesitated.

"Don't be stupid," Gallagher said. "There's four of us. You try any funny business and we'll beat the shit out of you just for the fun of it. Believe me, you don't want to add physical hurt to what you'll be going through."

Merriwell gave in and obeyed. Ben snapped cuffs on his wrists, and grabbed his arm, leading him out of the pool hall. Delmar watched the procession leave, and spoke to Dwayne as he was passing by. "What the hell's going on?"

"You better start looking for a new resident bookie," Dwayne said, going out the door.

MERRIWELL SAT IN THE INTERROGATION ROOM chair, the bright light shining in his face. Ben and Gallagher stood to his direct front, looking down at him. "Okay," Ben said. "Here's what's going on. You're being charged with first degree murder of Stubb Durham. Now you can save us all a lot of time and trouble if you keep the bullshit down to nothing, and own up to it."

Merriwell laughed. "Are you crazy? I never killed Stubb. Hell, I knew Stubb. He was a bookie like me. Why would I kill him?"

"Because he wouldn't join the Kansas City mob's takeover," Gallagher said.

Merriwell was confused, and the presence of the stranger didn't ease his mind. "Listen, godamn it, you two are the last guys that should be talking about any takeovers. You're up to your own ears in some pretty deep shit."

Now Steve Williams stepped into the light. Ben nodded to him. "This is an F.B.I. agent, Arlo. We've been working undercover with the Feds on busting up Schomp's gang. And that includes the Wichita shitheels who joined up with him and his dickheads."

Now the bookie was completely bamboozled. "This don't make any sense. And what's this shit about me killing Stubb got to do with it?"

"Listen, Arlo," Ben said. "Even though Gallagher and I were in on some of the meetings and strategy sessions, we had no idea that you had bumped off the guy. You and the K.C. bunch were keeping that to yourselves because when push came to shove, we were cops. You guys kept a lot of stuff from us."

"So what makes you think I was the one who bumped off Stubb?"

"There's a witness," Gallagher said.

"Bullshit," Merriwell said with a nervous laugh. "Fucking preposterous, that what this is."

Now Dwayne joined the others in the light. "You were seen shooting Stubb, then going over to where he was kneeling and putting two more bullets into him."

"Who saw me?"

"Pete Driscoll," Dwayne said.

Ben and Gallagher exchanged looks of surprise mixed with pleasure.

"He and Stubb had gone over to Stubb's house to show Missus Durham some jewelry," Dwayne said. "Pete dropped the box and bent over to pick it up while Stubb walked up toward the house. When Pete straightened up, he saw you shoot Stubb, then go up and finish the job. And he's willing to testify to the facts."

"Okay, Arlo," Ben said. "We're gonna leave you for a bit. You got a lot to think over. You're facing the very real possibility of getting taken up to Lansing and being hung for murder. However, there's a way that might save your life, and we'll be back to discuss it."

The three men left the room and went out into the hall. Ben closed the door and locked it. Gallagher checked his watch, then nodded to Ben. "I'll take care of that other matter, and be back within fifteen minutes."

He walked down the hall to the stairs, going up to the second floor. He went directly to the homicide squad room, and entered. The three men sitting at desks looked up at him with curiosity. Gallagher ignored them, going straight back to Lieutenant Buford Cordell's office. He entered without knocking.

Cordell gave him a furious glare. "Where the fuck

have you been? Is Forester with you? I got things for you two to do."

Gallagher didn't sit down. "Two quick bits of information for you, Lieutenant. The first is that we've been working undercover with the F.B.I. on this Kansas City takeover bullshit. And the second is that you are going to be arrested and charged in the case. That will include state and Federal indictments."

Cordell's mouth dropped open. He started to stand up, but sank back into his chair.

"We just brought in Arlo Merriwell," Gallagher continued. "We're charging him with Stubb Durham's murder. Somehow that shamus Wheeler figured things out and had a witness. We just laid it all out for Merriwell, and he's cooling his heels in interrogation. What we'll offer him is a chance for a life sentence instead of the gallows, providing he rolls over on everybody. There's an F.B.I. agent downstairs with us to start building up the U.S. Government's case."

Cordell's eyes went from Gallagher's face to the desktop.

Gallagher continued, "Ben and I decided to let you in on the news before a warrant for your arrest is issued. Since we've all been on the department together for a long time, we owed you that much. But that's the end of any consideration we'll be showing you. I'm going back down now and we'll talk to Merriwell. If he wants to cooperate, we'll get a steno and take down a preliminary statement. If he doesn't want to come clean, you're still in deep shit. Me and Ben will be testifying against you. But you can bet your ass that Merriwell is gonna do ever'thing he can to keep that noose off his neck. It's all over, Lieutenant." He turned and went to the door, opening it and walking back through the squad room.

When Gallagher got back downstairs, Ben looked over at him. Gallagher did no more than nod to him in an affirmative manner. Ben looked at Dwayne and Williams. "I don't see any sense in waiting any longer."

He opened the door to the interrogation room and they walked in. Merriwell was staring at the floor, his face pale with beads of sweat on his forehead. He looked up at his inquisitors. "How do I know I can trust you?"

"Are you willing to give us the full story?" Ben asked. "When this comes to trial, me and Gallagher will be testifying on our part in this thing. And you know how we weren't privy to the real inside information on Schomp's big plan. So you'll have to fill in some pretty big holes."

"And if I do, I don't get hung?"

"That's right," Ben said. "I can get a state attorney from Kansas and a steno here to take your statement. The state attorney general can guarantee a deal with you. The arrangement has already been made between Kansas and the United States."

"I'd like to talk with a lawyer," Merriwell said.

"You don't need a lawyer," Gallagher snapped. "And if you start turning into a wiseass with talk about a mouthpiece, we'll call the whole thing off."

"I want something in writing," Merriwell insisted.

"That will come with the steno," Williams interjected.

COFFEE AND SANDWICHES HAD BEEN BROUGHT IN along with cigarettes for Merriwell. Everyone settled down to wait, with very little conversation among them. It was seven p.m. before a Kansas state attorney appeared on the scene with a court stenographer. The first thing the prosecutor did was hand a piece of paper to Merriwell. It was a promise that if he revealed all about the Kansas City takeover conspiracy, the state attorney's office would ask the judge to forego the death penalty for a term of life in prison.

Merriwell nodded his agreement and was given a pen to sign the document. The deputy state attorney countersigned it, and the deal was struck. As soon as everyone was settled, Detective Sergeant Ben Forester began the interrogation.

"We already know the answer to this one," Ben said. "But for the record, what was the motive for R.K. Schomp wanting to move into Wichita?"

"He was being run out of Kansas City by Eye-talian gangsters," Merriwell said. "He made a deal with 'em to give him time to get organized in Wichita. They agreed to it, because they didn't want any gang war or nothing to draw attention to them moving in up north."

"When me and Sergeant Gallagher were present at various get-togethers, it appeared to us that you had been given a high-ranking position in the conspiracy. Is this true?"

"Yeah," Merriwell said. "I showed Schomp I was on the ball. The plan was that I would be taking Billy Joe Clayton's place within a year."

"What was to happen to Clayton?" Ben asked.

"He'd be given a lower job in the organization," Merriwell replied. "But he would still have a good deal going for him."

"Okay," Ben said. "Now start at the beginning of how you joined the Kansas City bunch."

Merriwell told how things started rolling after he was first approached by Billy Joe Clayton to join the takeover. The idea was that Merriwell would talk the other bookmakers into going into the organization with him. Eventually, the locals would be squeezed out altogether, and all the hometown betting action would belong to Merriwell. The first guy that Merriwell contacted was Stubb Durham.

"I couldn't talk the guy into nothing," Merriwell said. "He flat-out refused to go along with things. He said he'd warn the other bookies, so Schomp decided to have him hit. They made me do the job to prove my loyalty. I had to kill him. I swear to God! Or they would've knocked *me* off."

"Okay," Ben said. "And what about the bootleggers?"

"The first thing Schomp did was go down to the suppliers in Dallas," Merriwell explained. "His brother was a big shot in that operation. The two Schomps came up with a scheme where Dallas wouldn't send no more booze up to Wichita. The Schomp brothers paid plenty for that, believe me. Clayton says that the Schomps coughed up seventy-five big ones to get a promise of ninety days of no deliveries."

"I see," Ben said. "Now how did Harry Denton fit into all this?"

"Harry Denton is an old pal of the Schomps," Merriwell said. "He had been into narcotics distribution for a long time when he first came to Wichita back during the war. He worked out of the port of New Orleans, using the Kansas City mob as distributors. The guy had lots of dough and set up a phony real estate office in Wichita as a cover. The Eye-talians made their own deal with Denton and cut the K.C. mob into it as middlemen. That was advantageous to ever'body."

"Now what about the bootlegging operation?"

"We first approached Elmer Pettibone, but he wanted nothing to do with it like Stubb," Merriwell said. "Schomp wasn't too worried about that because him and his brother had already bought off the Dallas distributors. I told 'em they should talk to Mack Crofton since he had a good business going and was kind of a pussy. They followed my advice and he agreed to join up."

"And how'd that work out?" Ben asked.

"Okay at first, but after awhile we got suspicious of him. There had been a phone call from Wichita up to Schomp from somebody who evidently knew something of the operation. Clayton figgered there was a snitch in the organization, and we were all uneasy about Crofton. We knew that him and Dwayne Wheeler was friends, so we decided to say something about kidnapping Wheeler's girlfriend at a meeting when Crofton was there. Then we watched the broad's apartment house. Sure enough Wheeler shows up right away and sneaks her away to a hideout."

"And you went after Crofton then?"

"It was later when we followed him out to a café on Highway Fifty-Four," Merriwell said. "When he came out, the hit was made. But it wasn't me. It was Billy Joe Clayton. Anyhow there was another guy with Crofton who looked a hell of a lot like Wheeler. He shot at us and hit our rear window. And we didn't see Wheeler around no more."

Dwayne stepped in front of Ben. "It sounds like Mack was marked for death pretty early on."

Merriwell nodded. "Yeah. If he'd done like Stubb and refused to go along with the plan right off the bat, he'd have been done in anyway."

Dwayne felt a flood of relief. Even if Mack had refused to act as a snitch for him, he would have died just the same. "Y'know something, Arlo, I'm sorry as hell you're rolling over. I'd love to go up to Lansing and attend your necktie party."

"Fuck you, Wheeler!"

"Okay," Williams interjected. "That's enough of the bullshit." He turned his eyes on Merriwell. "Now here's what we're gonna do. It's time to give some attention to the Federal side of this situation. So you start from the first time Clayton recruited you, then go day by day right up until we walked into the Uptown Billiard Parlor and arrested you. We want times, dates, places, and the names of those involved."

Merriwell began speaking in a slow precise way, his extraordinary memory kicking in as the little steno's pencil flew across her shorthand notebook.

CHAPTER 21

The next day after Arlo Merriwell began spilling his guts to keep from being hanged, Dwayne Wheeler, Detective Sergeants Ben Forester and Al Gallagher accompanied F.B.I. Agent Steve Williams to serve a Federal warrant for Lieutenant Buford Cordell's arrest. They entered the Wichita Police Department by the back door, walking past the interrogation rooms and up the stairs to the homicide squad.

When they walked in, the officers at their desks looked up. The mood among the cops was one of confusion and uncertainty. The word of a state attorney complete with a stenographer showing up in the station had caused waves of consternation to spread throughout the entire department. And the fact that a known minor bookie was being held in isolation was reason for even more bafflement among the law enforcement officers. A few local cops had some special deals going on around the city that would not look well in the light of day.

"What the hell's going on?" an investigator named

Croker asked. He was more than a little disturbed by the presence of Dwayne Wheeler.

"It'll all be explained later," Ben replied.

"Bullshit!" the detective said. "You let us know now."

"Can it, Croker!" Gallagher barked at him. "This thing is bigger'n you know."

They started back for Cordell's office, but Croker interrupted them. "The lieutenant hasn't come in yet."

"He's got to be at home," Ben said to Williams. "He wouldn't cut and run."

"In that case," Williams said, "let's call on him at his residence."

The group walked from the squad room, watched with suspicion by the detectives. One reached in a desk drawer and took out a flask filled with bootleg scotch. He treated himself to a deep swallow. Croker walked over to him and took the liquor. He put it to his lips and almost finished it off. The owner grabbed it back. "Hey! You guzzle your own hooch, godamn it!"

"Shut up," Croker said. "I may be sending out for a case before all this crap winds down."

Meanwhile, Williams led Dwayne and the two sergeants to his car. They sped down the alley toward Williams Street and turned north. Dwayne relaxed in the back seat, gazing unseeing out the window as he thought about the two lovemaking sessions he and Donna Sue had enjoyed at the safehouse the night before.

This was actually the first time they had spent an entire night together and fallen asleep in the same bed. After they made love quietly because of Donna Sue's nervousness at being in the house with strangers, Dwayne felt a great deal of comfort in listening to her steady, soft breathing as she slumbered beside him. During the occupation of Germany when he was in the army, he spent plenty of nights with his German girlfriend, but somehow this was completely different. He had reached out and laid his hand on Donna Sue's, feeling a mellow sort of contentment he had never experienced before in his life.

He drifted off gradually, slipping into a dreamless period of dozing. Just as dawn was lighting the room, he had awakened to put his arm around her, finding that she, too, was stirring. They didn't speak, but turned to each to begin making love in a gently spontaneous way. The session ended with further kisses and caresses that expressed more affection than lust. Donna Sue responded enthusiastically to Dwayne's lovemaking, clinging to him and softly moaning her pleasure.

It took twenty minutes to reach Lieutenant Buford Cordell's home that was between Central and Third Street on Chautauqua. Most of the residents of the area had lived there for decades, and Cordell had inherited his home from his parents. Williams swung up into the driveway, going almost to the garage that was separated from the residence as was common in all older houses. The four men got out and walked back to the sidewalk leading to the front porch.

"Wait a minute," Ben said.

"What's the matter?" Williams asked impatiently.

"How about letting me and Al handle this?"

Williams shook his head. "I have a Federal warrant in my pocket, and it's up to me to serve it."

Gallagher interjected, "That don't make any differ-'nce. I can guarantee you the lieutenant won't resist."

"The soon-to-be *ex-lieutenant* isn't going to get any special treatment," Williams stated. "And that includes getting arrested and handcuffed by Federal law enforcement."

Gallagher started to protest. "Yeah, but this is—"

"Knock it off!" Williams interrupted. "I'm giving you guys a break by letting you come along. If you give me a ration of crap I won't do it again. I should really have a couple of F.B.I. agents with me."

Ben and Gallagher knew they had to back down. This was the U.S. Government's side of the operation and they had no authority whatsoever beyond providing assistance. Williams led the way to the front door and pressed the buzzer. The door opened and Cordell's wife Mildred answered. She was plainly puzzled by the sight of the four men. "Hello, Ben. Al. If you're looking for Buford, he's out in his workshop behind the garage."

"Thank you," Williams said tersely.

Dwayne felt as much an outsider as Williams. He was well aware of the tight connections between cops, and Ben and Gallagher's discomfiture was obvious from their conduct. He purposely lagged a couple of paces behind as they all walked past the garage to the workshop door. Williams knocked on it, then pushed it open and entered.

Buford Cordell was slumped over in an old tattered easy chair, appearing as if he had dozed off. Williams walked up to him and started to inform him he was under arrest. Then the agent reached out and placed his first two fingers on the side of Cordell's neck. There was no pulse. "He's dead."

Ben and Gallagher walked over to their lieutenant and gave him a close look. Dwayne noticed an empty bottle lying tipped over on the workbench with the cap nearby. He looked at the label. "Sleeping pills," he announced.

"Shit!" Ben said. He took another look at the dead man. "Listen, Williams, me and Al are going into the house to tell Mildred. You stay the fuck out of it. Understand?"

Williams nodded. "I got no problem with that. In fact, I think it's a good idea under the circumstances."

The two detective sergeants left the workshop and went to the back door, letting themselves into the kitchen. "Mildred," Ben called out.

She came in from the front of the house, then stopped abruptly. "What's wrong?"

"Buford's dead," Ben said. "We just found him in his chair out there."

"Oh, God, no!" she wailed.

Ben walked over and helped her sit down. "I'm really sorry." He hesitated then said, "It was prob'ly a heart attack."

"That's the way it looks to me, too," Gallagher said.

"I don't think he was feeling well when he got up this morning," she said weakly. "He said he wasn't going to work, and I could hear him giving himself an enema." She stood up. "I got to see him."

"Sure," Ben said.

He and Gallagher flanked her as they left the house and went to the workshop. When they entered, Dwayne and Williams stepped to one side. Now Mildred began weeping aloud and she went up to her dead husband, putting her hands on each side of his face. "Oh, Buford!"

"Is there somebody we can call to come over?" Ben asked.

"Yes," she said. "My sister lives a couple of blocks away. And my daughter...oh, this is terrible. So unexpected."

Ben gently took her arm. "Let's go back into the house, Mildred." He glanced at Williams. "We'll call the coroner. The law requires an investigation in sudden deaths like this. I'll take charge of it."

Dwayne stayed with Williams in the workshop. Cordell had a calm expression on his face, though his eyes were half opened. His head was bent forward and his mouth was slack. Williams looked around to see if something obvious like a suicide note was visible but there was nothing that attracted his attention. The two went outside to avoid disturbing anything.

Within five minutes Ben and Gallagher were back. "I'm going to secure this as a crime scene," Ben said.

"I looked for a note but couldn't see anything," Williams said. "He didn't try to hide the fact that his death was anything but self-inflicted."

"Yeah," Ben said. "He prob'ly didn't leave anything in writing 'cause he'd have to confess his association with the Kansas City mob."

"His wife said he gave himself an enema," Gallagher said. "I guess he didn't want to shit all over hisself when he croaked."

Williams nodded. "And he had the decency not to blow his brains out all over the place. I've known of sick bastards that have done that in their homes. It leaves a mess so bad that the carpeting even has to be torn up and tossed out not to mention the blood and brains on the walls."

"C'mon," Ben said to Gallagher. "Let's go inside and get started." He looked at Williams. "Me and Al will catch a ride back to the station when the investigative team from the department shows up."

Williams tapped Dwayne on the arm. "I'm headed back to the safehouse. I've dispatched agents to pick up Schomp, Clayton and Denton. We expect they can eventually lead us to the others in the group. At any rate, they'll be bringing them to the safehouse. You're cleared to observe the interrogations and make any meaningful comments you might have on the results."

"Let's go," Dwayne said.

WHEN WILLIAMS DROVE THE CAR INTO THE parking area behind the safehouse, Dwayne noticed there were a couple of extra vehicles. He figured them to have been used for picking up the rest of the fugitives. He and Williams went inside and were met by the agent John Mikowski.

Mikowski was apologetic as he said, "We didn't apprehend any of the three wanted men. They've all fled the Wichita area, and so have their subordinates. But one arrest has been made."

Williams was confused. "Who the hell was it?"

"None other than Miranda Denton," Mikowski informed him. "She's married to Harry Denton the so-called real estate tycoon."

The lady had been taken to a special corner room of the house, and when Dwayne and Williams approached the area, they could hear her angry voice going nonstop. They stepped inside to see she was being watched by an agent named Art Vinton. The lady snapped her eyes toward the newcomers, treating the pair with an angry glare of pure indignation and rage.

"And just who the hell are you?" she shrilled.

"I'm Agent Williams," he said. "I'm in charge of this investigation."

"Well, *Agent Williams*, you are in deep, deep trouble," Mrs. Denton said. She was an attractive, slim and athletic blond who appeared to be in her mid-thirties. She was dressed in a white sleeveless tennis outfit with the appropriate footgear.

Vinton explained her appearance, saying, "We picked her up at the Prairie Wind Golf and Tennis Club when we couldn't find her husband at home. She was pointed out to us on the courts by one of the waiters."

Mrs. Denton literally snarled, "And when I find out who the miserable weasel was I'll see that he loses his job."

Dwayne looked at her with an instant intense dislike. She reminded him of women he had seen from time to time as a youngster, who gave him insolent looks and brusque demands in the days when he worked as a busboy in restaurants or a janitor's helper in apartment buildings.

"You'd better calm down, Mrs. Denton," Williams said firmly. "You are in the middle of an extremely serious situation. As of now, your husband is a Federal fugitive with a warrant for his arrest."

"Preposterous!" she said. "On what charges?"

"Racketeering and narcotics violations," Williams said.

Mrs. Denton's face paled and her eyes opened wide. "This is a big mistake! A great big stupid mistake!"

Williams, an experienced interrogator, picked up a sudden lessening in her original defiance. He sensed fear in the woman. "Mrs. Denton, you would be doing yourself a big favor by cooperating with us."

She was quiet for a few moments, then shrugged.

Agent John Mikowski came into the room and handed Williams a note, then went back to his post at the front of the house. Williams read the message carefully, hiding a grin. He glanced down at Mrs. Denton, and said, "Your husband has looted your checking accounts. As of this moment, you don't have any money in the bank."

"He wouldn't do that," she said.

"I have no objection to you calling the bank to verify the facts," Williams said.

"How can I?" she asked angrily. "My purse with my address book is back at the club."

"We have a phone book you can use," Williams said. He nodded to Agent Vinton. The man left the room and returned within moments with a telephone and a Bell directory for Wichita. He handed the book to the woman, then plugged the phone into a wall outlet.

Mrs. Denton went through the pages and found the number. She took the phone from Williams and dialed. "I would like to speak to Mr. Jarvis. This is Mrs. Harry Denton..." A half minute passed, then she spoke again. "Hello, Mr. Jarvis, this is Mrs. Denton...what...I see...are they still there?...But are they allowed to look into the safe deposit box?...A warrant...yes, thank you." She hung up and Williams took the phone back.

"Do you have any questions, Mrs. Denton?"

At first she was silent in a morose way. When she finally chose to speak, she did so in an undertone. "That son of a bitch."

"Are you ready to answer some questions, Mrs. Denton?"

She looked up at him. "I can do much better than that. I will admit that I was aware of Harry's activities. And I was also aware that someday this world of ours could be shattered, and I wanted to protect myself. I have some information that you will find most interesting. Names of people...things I've observed...it's all there hidden in my dresser at the house. And I will testify to all I know in court. I can do that, you see, because Harry and I aren't really married."

"We've known that for some time," Williams said.

"Your name is Phyllis Barkin and Harry Denton is an alias for Daniel Meyers."

"Well, then," Phyllis Barkin said, "since he's left me high and dry, I'm ready to make a deal." Then she mumbled, "As if I have a fucking choice."

Dwayne, who had been standing by a window, listening, walked toward the door. "I guess I'm finished here."

"Yeah," Williams said. "At least for the time being. There's still going to be a lot of activity before this is wrapped up."

Dwayne left the interrogation area and went upstairs. He could hear some tapping in the hallway as he approached the room he shared with Donna Sue. When he opened the door, he saw her sitting in front of a typewriter. She turned around. "Hey, honey. One of those nice F.B.I. guys brought me up a typing stand."

"Wow!" Dwayne exclaimed. "You really do know how to type."

"I told you so," Donna Sue said smugly. "And when you're ready to dictate your caper like Sam Spade, you just let me know."

"It's Saturday," Dwayne said. "We can do it tomorrow. All I need is a report on Stubb's killing to turn in to Longshot and Ollie. We can do it in your apartment."

Donna Sue smiled in happy surprise. "Are we leaving here?"

"Yeah," Dwayne said. "This caper is all wrapped up except for the shouting." He looked at her stuff scattered around the room. "Get packed, baby. I've got to turn in that Ford to Elmer Pettibone and get my Pontiac. I'll be back here in less than an hour to pick you up."

"Can't you keep the Ford, Dwayne?"

"I wish I could, but Elmer needs it for deliveries. His

Dallas suppliers will be back in business by Monday week."

Donna Sue sat beside Dwayne in the old coupe as he drove down from Riverside toward her apartment house. Both were quiet, any exuberance sobered by the finality of the past month's frantic activities. The sudden cessation of danger and uncertainty had created an emotional vacuum for both of them.

They rolled into Donna Sue's neighborhood as she sat with her precious typewriter in her lap. "Dwayne, I feel like we're starting a new phase of our lives."

"How's that?"

"Okay," she said. "Let me tell you my plans. Listen up. I'm going to get me a typing certificate. Then I'm going looking for a job in a steno pool somewhere. After I do that, I'm going to take a test to get me a high school certificate."

He chuckled. "You're gonna be the most certified gal in town."

"And once I do that, I'll go to business college and learn shorthand, filing and all that secretarial stuff."

"What's the end result of all this activity?"

"I'll be your secretary," Donna Sue said. "Didn't you say that this caper was gonna pay off big time for you? You'll be able to get a bigger office and more clients. You'll need a secretary to answer the phone and take messages and type up your reports."

"Yeah!" he said in happy agreement. "And know what else? I'll prob'ly hire some more private eyes to work for me. Yeah! They're called operatives, y'know? I'll prob'ly stay in my office and direct ever'thing like an army general."

"See? It's just like I said. A new stage in our lives is really starting."

They pulled up in front of the apartment house and Dwayne braked to a stop. He looked at Donna Sue. "This entire caper isn't finished yet, so you'll have to stick to your cover story for awhile. So tell your landlord and landlady you were with your family, okay? All this will be coming out in the papers and on the radio, and a lot of folks in Wichita are gonna be real surprised."

"Let's go in, Dwayne," Donna Sue said. "I still have time today for some typing practice."

"Practice, hell!" Dwayne exclaimed. "You're gonna type up my caper report."

It was Monday morning, and Dwayne and Donna Sue walked hand-in-hand from his car up to the front door of the Jayhawker Restaurant. She wore her waitress uniform, and he carried a manila envelope in his hand. When they entered the diner, the owner Art Manger was behind the counter with a cook's apron around his waist, waiting on customers. "Thank God!" he yelled out, not only seeing Donna Sue, but noting she was ready for work.

Donna Sue frowned in puzzlement. "What in the world is going on?" she asked.

Maisie looked over from turning in an order at the kitchen window. "That waitress Janet hasn't been here since last Wednesday. I think she left town with her latest boyfriend, and Art had to come in and take over her job."

Donna Sue headed toward the back to get her apron. "Well that problem is solved."

Dwayne sat down at the counter and looked up to see Arnie Dawkins' face peering at him from the kitchen. Arnie grinned, asking, "Are you ready for the usual, Dwayne?"

"You betcha!" Dwayne said.

Donna Sue reappeared ready for work. "Okay, Art. Take a break."

The owner gave a look of thanks heavenward, and headed back into the kitchen, taking off the apron. For the next forty minutes both Donna Sue and Maisie worked frantically, handling the breakfast crowd as Arnie labored over the grill. Donna Sue grabbed Dwayne's breakfast off the window shelf and served him, then turned her attention back to the regular customers. The number of diners gradually thinned out until only a couple of coffee drinkers were left.

"Whew!" Maisie said. Then she turned her head toward the kitchen and spoke loud enough for Art to hear. "It's good to have some competent help for a change."

Art yelled back, "I heard that, Miss Smarty-Pants!"

Maisie grinned and looked over at Donna Sue. "So? Is ever'thing okay with your family? I hope it wasn't a serious illness."

Dwayne interrupted, saying, "Her Aunt Tillie got a tit caught in the wringer."

"Shut up, Dwayne!" Maisie snapped.

"Everything turned out all right," Donna Sue said.

Dwayne finished off the last French fry on his plate. He held up the manila envelope. "I got to go across the street and talk with Longshot and Ollie."

"See you later," Donna Sue said.

Dwayne left the restaurant and crossed Douglas to the OK Barbershop. It was too early for most of the barbers to be there, but Ernie Bascombe was putting change in the cash register for the day's activities. "Hey, Dwayne. Where you been?"

"All over the place," Dwayne answered, heading for the back. He found both Longshot and Ollie in their usual chairs, listening to the shortwave radio to get the day's morning lines on several eastern tracks. Dwayne presented the manila envelope to Longshot.

The bookie was puzzled. "What the hell is this?"

"It's my report on Stubb's murder," Dwayne replied. "It's solved and the killer is in jail with a witness waiting to testify against him."

"You're shitting me," Longshot said.

"Nope," Dwayne replied confidently. "But on account of special circumstances I can't reveal names for a few days. If you want a general confirmation on what I told you, you can contact Sergeant Ben Forester—I should say soon-to-be *Lieutenant* Ben Forester—of the Wichita Police Department."

"Hey, yeah!" Ollie said. "I seen where his boss in homicide killed hisself. What the hell is that all about? It didn't say much in the papers."

"That's part of what's being kept under wraps for awhile longer," Dwayne explained.

Longshot opened the envelope and pulled out some typing. "What's this?"

"My report for you guys," Dwayne said. "There's two carbons. They're for Ollie and Rory Talbert. You can keep the original. I'll get you guys another when I can get the names inserted into the report. Donna Sue is my secretary now. Well, at least part time for awhile." He paused. "By the way, you guys owe me another seventy-five bucks. I actually worked on the Stubb caper longer'n that, but there was other aspects to the case that I laid off on other clients. You can pay me later when all the information is released by the F.B.I."

Ollie's mouth opened in surprise before he spoke. "The Federal Bureau of Investigation?"

"Yeah," Dwayne said. "I told you guys this was a big deal."

"We'll pay you now, Dwayne," Longshot said. "And we won't bother getting ahold of Ben. If nothing else, you're an honest guy that don't lie." He reached into his pocket and pulled out his wallet. After counting out seventy-five dollars, he handed the bills to Dwayne. "You want to bet any of it?"

Dwayne shook his head. "No way. I got some big deals in the works, and I need the cash to help finance things."

"Okay," Longshot said a bit disappointed. "I'll read the report more careful when I get the chance. But what I seen tells me we got our money's worth."

"I'll see you guys later," Dwayne said. "I got to get over to my office and pay next month's rent."

As he headed for the door, Longshot separated out one of the carbon copies of the report and handed it to Ollie.

Chapter 22

An entire week passed before Agent Steve Williams decided that the time was appropriate to hold an official F.B.I. news conference at the Wichita Police Department briefing room. The *Wichita Eagle* and *Wichita Beacon* newspapers sent their crime journalists, and the local radio stations also assigned reporters to the event. Along with those half dozen representatives of the media were members of the city council and other civic leaders, including clergymen, the president of the Chamber of Commerce, and two ladies from the local chapter of the Women's Christian Temperance Union.

A total of two dozen people sat on folding chairs to get the official word on a situation that so far had been nothing but unconfirmed rumors and conjecture. Everyone present was aware of the attempt of an insidious encroachment on the community by out-of-town criminals, and they were still disturbed by the possible consequences had the bad guys succeeded.

The audience knew that the recently announced suicide of Lieutenant Buford Cordell was tied in with the unusual occurrences, and they waited eagerly for the expected disclosures to dispel misinformation. All conversation abruptly ceased when F.B.I. Agent Steve Williams entered the room and went to the podium at the front.

After thanking everyone for attending, Williams went straight to the meat of his discourse. "As you all are aware of by now, for the past month or so, a criminal organization from outside the city has been making an attempt to take over certain illegal activities in Wichita. I am speaking of bookmaking, bootlegging and prostitution. I am now happy to announce that this underhanded effort has been completely nipped in the bud. The F.B.I. originally became aware of the situation through informers, and immediately launched a campaign to squelch the scheme by sending in undercover agents to dig out information on the conspirators. Federal law enforcement was necessary because the plot crossed state lines. And I can now reveal the names of two very essential people in this plan who were trusted members of the Wichita Police Department. I am referring to Detective Lieutenant Benjamin Forester and Detective Sergeant Albert Gallagher. These officers were successful in convincing the mobsters they were willing to go on the take and would participate with them in their goals. They gathered some very useful information and solid evidence. Thus the people of Wichita can take great pride in the integrity and dedication of these two local law enforcement officers who risked their lives in the performance of these dangerous duties.

"I am sorry to say that one member of the force—Detective Lieutenant Buford Cordell—took payoffs to cooperate with the conspirators. The news of his suicide has already been released. Also, one of Wichita's leading citizens, Harry Denton, was also part of the criminal plot. This man, in fact, was a complete imposter by the name of

Daniel Meyers, and had an extensive criminal record going back to nineteen twenty-four. He was not in the real estate business as he represented himself, but a narcotics smuggler who participated in the import of dope from the docks of New Orleans for distribution into the central section of the country. We have gathered solid information on his duplicity through a Miss Phyllis Barkin who had been posing as his wife and is now cooperating with law enforcement. She was granted immunity from prosecution for her collaboration. Unfortunately, her former companion Mr. Meyers is currently a fugitive with a Federal warrant out for his arrest. Also wanted are R.K. Schomp and Billy Joe Clayton, both residents of Kansas City, Missouri who were the ringleaders. Other minor players in this affair have been arrested and are in custody in that city. Here in Wichita, a local bookmaker by the name of Arlo Merriwell has been jailed and charged with the first degree murder of Stubb Durham another bookmaker. Merriwell has struck a deal with the Kansas Attorney General through the F.B.I. for a plea bargain through his willingness to testify against the other conspirators. Rather than facing execution by hanging for first degree murder, Merriwell will be sentenced to life in prison without the possibility of parole.

"There is a strong possibility that an organized crime organization from back east had forced the Kansas City gang out of that community. We have no proof positive of this, but further investigation may substantiate these suspicions. They are believed to be a Mafia organization from Chicago or Philadelphia.

"Now I am pleased to bring to your attention a Wichita private investigator by the name of Dwayne Wheeler. Mr. Wheeler had been hired by interested parties to investigate the aforementioned murder of Stubb

Durham, the man shot dead by Arlo Merriwell. The out-of-state criminals attempted to recruit Mr. Durham into their organization, but he refused to cooperate with them. For that, he lost his life. I am pleased to inform you that Mr. Wheeler solved the case by discovering a surprise witness during his investigation. This individual, who is now being held as a material witness, will remain anonymous until the Kansas authorities complete their investigation into the matter. At any rate, it is Mr. Wheeler's methodical detective work that enabled the F.B.I. access to Arlo Merriwell. Without him, this case would still be open.

"This concludes my briefing, ladies and gentlemen. Due to the fact that prosecutors are solidifying their cases for future trials, I cannot answer any questions at this time, and certain important information is still being kept under wraps. There will be press conferences scheduled in the future as soon as circumstances permit. Thank you."

A young female radio journalist shouted out, "Have you rid the city of the crime and vice these mobsters wanted to take over?"

Williams strode from the room without answering.

THE NEXT DAY, AFTER THE NEWSPAPERS AND radio stations had spread the news, the population of Wichita, Kansas was collectively shocked. Most people had little knowledge of bookmakers or prostitutes unless they dealt with them. Buying liquor from a bootlegger or a bootlegger's agent was common, however, and many Wichita homes had bottles of liquor in the backs of kitchen cabinets and closets, or down in the corners of their basements. The idea of gangsters moving into their city disturbed the population's sense of safety and comfort, and many local churches held services of thanksgiving that the streets did not end up controlled by hoodlums.

Bud Terwilliger wrote a particularly flattering article about Dwayne Wheeler that ran on the front page of the *Wichita Eagle*. The private detective was portrayed as a daring investigator who risked his life to uncover the murderer of Stubb Durham. A photo of Dwayne was featured in which he was seated on his desk in his shirtsleeves, the shoulder holster holding the .45 semi-automatic pistol in plain view. He displayed a grim expression of determination and looked the part of the hardboiled shamus with his fedora hat tipped to a jaunty angle like a *film noir* private eye in popular crime movies.

The one thing that Dwayne would not talk about and didn't even want to *think* about was Mack Crofton's demise. In spite of learning of Mack being slated for death during Arlo Merriwell's interrogation, deep in Dwayne's heart of hearts he felt responsible for the little bootlegger's death. Dwayne had exaggerated having strong backup to Mack to keep the little guy spying for him. It did turn out that the F.B.I. along with Ben Forester and Al Gallagher were actually working against the Kansas City mob, but Dwayne didn't know about it at that time.

The revelations of the Dentons, now known by their real names, shocked the upper echelons of local society. The Prairie Wind Golf and Tennis Club along with local civic organizations and charities got together to arrange vigorous public relations campaigns to distance themselves as far from the imposters as possible; particularly because they had obviously benefited from donations given to them by the charlatans. This was money earned through the illegal smuggling of narcotics.

THREE DAYS LATER, A FARMER NEAR RICHMOND, Missouri went out to repair a windmill used to pump up water for his cattle on the far edges of his property. He was shocked to find three corpses with their hands tied behind their backs in a nearby ditch. When the local law began its investigation, they were baffled and turned to the State Police for assistance. The higher law enforcement agency recognized the incident as a gangland killing and called in the F.B.I. Consequently, the victims were identified as R.K. Schomp, Billy Joe Clayton, and Daniel Meyers AKA Harry Denton. It appeared elements of the Mafia had become disenchanted with the dead men's failure to make a graceful exit out of Kansas City, and the unfortunate trio paid a terrible price for their fiasco. Cuts, abrasions and cigarette burns on the corpses showed the last hours of their lives had been grim and agonizing.

AS THINGS GRADUALLY SETTLED BACK TO normal, Donna Sue Connors went to a secretarial school and obtained a typing certificate of 75 words a minute. Later that week, Dwayne picked her up at the Jayhawker Restaurant and gave her a ride to the Wichita Board of Education building to take a test that would earn her a high school equivalency necessary for entrance into a business college. He waited out in the hall while she and three other people were taken to a room for the examination. An hour and a half later, they reappeared to wait for the results of their efforts. Donna Sue sat close to Dwayne, nervously gripping his hand.

Within a half hour the grading was done and the

examinees were called in one at a time to get the results. Donna Sue was last after the other three came out with wide grins of pleasure at now being recognized as high school graduates. When she emerged from the room Dwayne could see from the expression on her face that she had failed.

"I didn't do good a'tall," Donna Sue said. "In fact, I did awful. The man in there said I'd have to go to adult night school and study for the test."

Dwayne tried to put a good face on the situation. "Well, sweetie, you just do that and before you know it, you'll be in that business college."

Donna Sue shook her head. "No, Dwayne, it's too much. I'd have to attend classes Monday, Wednesday and Friday evenings from seven to ten p.m. I think I'll just put it on hold for awhile."

"Just do whatever you think is best," he told her.

They left the building and went to the car. As they drove off, she said, "Right now I feel those same old frustrations I had when I got laid off from Boeing. God! If I could only have kept that job!"

"I guess you'd have been better off," Dwayne allowed. "But if you had, we'd never have met."

"I know," she said, reaching out and putting her hand on his. "Or maybe we would have somehow...no, prob'ly not." She leaned back in the car seat. "Life just ain't fair. All that extra effort for a diploma would pay off for a man. He could get a hell of a better job than a woman."

Dwayne looked at her with a smile. "How about if we go to Western Danceland Saturday night?"

Donna Sue didn't answer; she just sat and stared out the windshield.

"Did I tell you about Tommy Brady?" Dwayne asked.

"Just that you stayed out at his farm a few days."

"Well, Tommy and his wife Margie was real good to me and my mom," Dwayne said. Then he launched into the full story of the Bradys, the Salvation Army and how Tommy had ended up on the farm in Augusta.

"It's too bad he's by himself in the world," Donna Sue commented.

"So is Missus Durham," Dwayne said. "When Stubb was murdered, she ended up alone in her old family home."

"I'll say it again," Donna Sue said softly. "Life ain't fair."

———

DWAYNE CAME OUT OF THE CAPER WITH AN extra three hundred and fifty dollars left over from what he'd earned from the bookmakers and Mrs. Davies. This pool of money increased when Agent Steve Williams sent him a check for two hundred dollars in payment for his part in knocking down the Kansas City mob. This wasn't normally done, but Dwayne as a licensed private investigator had rendered a professional service to the F.B.I. which was above and beyond what the average citizen could have done. By accepting the fee, Dwayne could make no further financial demands of the United States Government.

———

ON THE NEXT SATURDAY NIGHT, HOWEVER, Dwayne and Donna Sue did not go to Western Danceland. Instead, they did something entirely different. Donna Sue thought it would be nice to take Tommy Brady and Mrs. Durham out to a nice restaurant. Even if

Mrs. Durham was only recently widowed, the couple might form a relationship that would eventually deepen into a romance since both had lost beloved spouses. At least they might become good enough friends to offer comfort and companionship to each other.

"Let's go to the Stockyards Hotel Restaurant," Dwayne suggested. "Folks say there's no better place in the world to get a first rate steak dinner. And it's kind of fancy, too."

"Yes!" Donna Sue said. "We can make a real night of it."

Dwayne sat everything up and borrowed a four-door Chevrolet sedan from Elmer Pettibone for the evening. Elmer did the favor out of gratitude to Dwayne for his part in foiling the K.C. mob.

Dwayne and Donna Sue picked up Tommy at his farm, then went to Mrs. Durham's house in northeast Wichita. When they got out of the car and walked up to the porch, Dwayne noted that Stubb's bloodstains were now barely visible on the sidewalk. Mrs. Durham answered the doorbell, and the three went inside the house where Dwayne introduced the older couple. Donna Sue had been a bit nervous about their initial reaction to each other but was pleased to note that Tommy and Mrs. Durham were perfectly at ease, and both seemed pleased to be going out. Tommy, with his friendly outgoing personality, quickly learned her first name was Alice, and it was "Tommy" and "Alice" from that point onward.

Dwayne drove out to Twenty-First Street just east of Broadway where the restaurant was located. They all went inside and were taken to a table in a corner of the dining room. Cloth napkins, a linen tablecloth, silverware and a centerpiece of flowers made for a nice atmosphere.

After everyone was seated, Alice Durham pointed to

the floral arrangement. "That reminds me of the nice bouquet you brought me, Dwayne. It certainly brightened up my dining room. And my life, too."

"I'm glad you liked it, Missus Durham."

Donna Sue gave Dwayne a slight smile. He had never given her flowers, and she knew the gift to Alice must have been sincere and compassionate on his part.

During dinner, Dwayne and Donna Sue were almost ignored by the older couple. Tommy spoke of Margie and their Salvation Army days while Alice was candid about her husband, telling how the church she had belonged to since early childhood had snubbed them because he was a bookmaker.

"I haven't attended worship in over twenty years," Alice said. "The nearest I've been to church was during the memorial services for Stubb at the mortuary chapel. The next door neighbors were the only others besides me who attended."

"That's a real shame, Alice," Tommy said. "I attend services at the Salvation Army Mission. Anyone wanting to be there is welcome." He was thoughtful for a moment. "Would you care to go with me tomorrow morning?"

"I would love to, Tommy!"

"Fine," he said. "I'll pick you up at seven-thirty."

Dwayne winked at Donna Sue across the table, and she smiled back. The dinner continued with Tommy and Alice completely lost in each other. Dwayne and Donna Sue quietly ate their steaks, letting the older folks enjoy the evening.

The outing ended with a trip to Armstrong's Ice Cream Parlor across from Roosevelt Junior High School. Dwayne amazed everyone by completely consuming a double banana split.

As more time passed, Dwayne faced his own disappointments. After incidentals and normal expenses, his capital had dwindled to four hundred dollars. It was time to expand his private eye business, and he determined he would need another three hundred dollars to get a new office, furniture, advertising, and a salary for both himself and Donna Sue during the preliminary stages.

Dwayne made an appointment with a loan officer of the Wichita Merchants and Farmers Bank to arrange for the financing. He met with a rather severe banker and presented character references from Lieutenant Ben Forester and the bail bondsman A.J. Kessler, and a letter of appreciation from the Federal Bureau of Investigation. He had also put the clipping from the *Wichita Eagle*'s article on him in the presentation.

The banker perused it all, then set it aside. He looked coldly across the desk at Dwayne. "Where is your residence, Mr. Wheeler?"

"I live in a rooming house on Estelle Avenue just north of Douglas."

"Mmm, I see," the banker said. "And where is your present office located?"

"In the Snodgrass Building on West Douglas."

The banker took a deep breath. "Did you say the *Snodgrass* Building?"

"Yes, sir," Dwayne replied.

"Do you have a bank account?"

Dwayne shook his head. "No, sir."

"What about collateral for a business loan?"

"I own a nineteen thirty-five Pontiac coupe," Dwayne answered brightly. "And it's all paid off."

The banker cleared his throat. "While your participation in the attempted takeover by Kansas City criminals is most impressive, it cannot be considered indication of you being a sound businessman. Your local credit record is less than desirable with the undeniable confirmation of your being habitually behind in rents and other bills."

The loan officer then summed up the refusal of the request for money with a statement that Dwayne's reputation in the city was only slightly better than that of a bankrupt indigent.

Not only did the first bank turn him down, but so did four others. Dwayne was completely stymied, reaching the conclusion that the best way for him to score some big cash was to make it betting on the horses. In desperation, he reverted back to his old habits, and purchased a copy of the *Racing Form*. However, on this occasion, he felt the situation demanded a more meticulous and detailed approach to choosing his bets. Instead of quickly picking promising horses, he decided to come up with a completely new method of logically and methodically choosing entries with the most potential for winning their races.

Consequently, that same night, he made a careful study of the horses available for the next Sunday's racing and ended up designing a complex system of comparisons as he burned the midnight oil in his room. He took former winning horses who had been running out of the money for awhile, and bet on them, figuring they were due to begin coming in first again. It took him a long time to research not only that copy of the horseracing publication, but he also made an extra effort by looking up race results in back issues. He noted each individual steed's best times, the other horses they had beaten in the past, the condition of the tracks, and the distances to be run on the next races. He also made sure the jockeys were among the best available.

Dwayne's precise listings took up an entire notebook. Dawn was breaking by the time he had all the information down with painstaking assessments and probabilities worked out. From all that data he ended up with a list of what he had determined to be the best wagers.

With that done, Dwayne went out to the hall phone, and called Longshot Jackson. He placed wagers on six races, betting all his choices on the nose. Dwayne figured that if at least three of these came in, he would have more than enough cash money to open the new Wheeler Private Detective Agency in the prestigious Schweiter Building at the corner of Main and West Douglas.

Chapter 23

On Monday morning, Dwayne Wheeler carefully combed his hair as he looked at his reflection in the mirror above the sink in his room. He finished the job and winked at himself. "Here we go again, ol' buddy."

With that done, he got his hat and jacket, and fetched the battered old valise from under the bed. Now, dressed and ready to meet the world, he left his room, heading toward the door at the end of the hall. He descended the back steps to the sidewalk leading to the gate and continued on his way to the street where the old Pontiac was parked.

After switching on the ignition, he stepped on the starter and pulled out the choke. As soon as he pushed it back in, the engine caught. An instant later he was rolling down Estelle Avenue toward Douglas. From there he made a westward turn that would take him to his first stop at the OK Barbershop.

Dwayne, with his valise, strode quickly past the row of barbers, responding to their greetings with only the briefest of nods. He did the same to Longshot Jackson and Ollie Krask who were comfortably settled at their positions by the bookie telephones. They watched Dwayne as he went straight into the shower room.

"It looks like he's in a hurry," Ollie observed as he nibbled on a Butterfinger.

"Yeah," agreed Longshot. "Things have been going really good for ol' Dwayne. He's prob'ly got some big doings to tend to today."

"Yeah," Ollie agreed.

Inside the shower room Dwayne quickly stripped down and got under the water. The washing down was quick but thorough, and he emerged from the stall to vigorously towel himself dry. A ritual of a neat close shave, a careful combing of his hair after an application of Wildroot Hair Cream, and an energetic brushing of his teeth, finished the session.

After donning a starched, freshly laundered shirt and carefully knotting his tie, he dressed in his gray suit recently retrieved from the dry cleaners. The last item to put on was his fedora, and he grabbed the valise and went back through the barber shop with the same speed he had entered.

Ollie, now chomping on a Hershey Bar with almonds, watched him go through the front door. "I wonder if he's got another one of them big capers going on."

Longshot nodded. "I wouldn't be a bit surprised.

When the valise was deposited in the trunk of his old coupe, he walked rapidly across Douglas to the

Jayhawker Restaurant. His entrance elicited a frown from Maisie and a happy wave from Donna Sue. Dwayne took a seat at the counter.

"Hi, honey," Donna Sue said brightly, pouring him a cup of coffee. "I bet I know what you want for breakfast."

"This coffee will be fine," he said.

Donna Sue's smile faded and was replaced by a suspicious frown. "If you tell me you ain't hungry because you ate yesterday, I'm gonna pour this coffee on your head."

"I ain't hungry 'cause I've had some disappointments," Dwayne said. "I couldn't get a business loan, sweetheart. I must've tried a dozen banks. They all turned me down."

"Oh, sweetie!" Donna Sue exclaimed. "I'm so sorry! No wonder you don't have an appetite."

"Yeah," he said. "I'm pretty blue."

"What're you gonna do?"

"Well, I came up with an investment idea that could triple my capital," Dwayne said. "I really worked hard on it."

"Honey bunch!" Donna said. "How'd it go?"

"It didn't pay off too good," he replied. After a pause, he added. "In fact, it didn't pay off at all.'"

"You lost ever' penny of that four hunnerd dollars?"

He nodded sadly. "Yeah." Then he sighed courageously. "I did my best. I chose a course of action I figgered was a winner. I did some research on the thing and worked all the angles." He shrugged. "I got to tell you that it seemed there was no way I could lose."

"Oh, sweetie, that's too bad! What did you invest in?" she asked. "Some stocks and bonds?"

Dwayne cleared his throat, then spoke in a low monotone. "Well...I figgered out a system where good horses that hadn't won lately could maybe—"

Donna Sue's voice was a shriek. "*You lost all that money on the horses?*"

"Well...yeah."

"You could have held on to it in a savings account and added to it later or—" She stopped speaking for a moment. "Oh, never mind!"

Dwayne suddenly remembered something he had read in one of the books he'd gotten in the army. It was a line by the English poet Robert Browning who wrote: *It all comes to the same thing at the end*.

Dwayne Wheeler couldn't have agreed more.

A Look At Book 2:
Wichita Manhunt

1940s Wichita, Kansas

Local shamus Dwayne Wheeler is in the middle of the freewheeling no-holds-barred postwar underworld. Enjoying steady work as a bounty hunter for a local bail bondsman, he can often be found tracking down and apprehending fugitives in a fair routine.

But when a rather eccentric bail jumper by the name of Fritz Harrigan drops out of sight under mysterious circumstances, Dwayne's care-free life takes on a lethal twist. He quickly discovers that Harrigan has some powerful protectors whose best interests would be served if he remains out of jail.

Before Dwayne can turn manhunter and get his man, though, he must first discover the secret of the fugitive's shadowy patronage. And as he begins closing in on his quarry, the stakes become higher...and deadlier.

Wichita Manhunt is book two in a historical private eye series that follows Dwayne Wheeler—a tough and hardboiled detective.

AVAILABLE SEPTEMBER 2022

About the Author

Patrick Andrews was born an Army Brat on January 14, 1936—his sister's arrival just two years later. His father was a paratrooper in the 82nd Airborne Division during World War II. His mother was a good army officer's wife, who, like several of her lady cousins, wrote short-stories and poems.

After the war, Patrick's father transferred into the Army Reserves, and they moved to Wichita, Kansas—where Patrick caught the scribbling bug. When Patrick got a job as a copy boy at the *Wichita Eagle* newspaper, he was ecstatic.

A few years later, Patrick got a yen to be a paratrooper. He enlisted in the Army and took basic training in Camp Chaffee, Arkansas, soon after being transferred to the 82nd Airborne Division in Fort Bragg. His career with the 82nd was rewarding—being promoted to sergeant and tasked with training cadets in West Point before retiring.

When Patrick read James Jones' *From Here to Eternity*, he appreciated the pride and struggling of soldiers. Soon after, he moved to San Diego, California and began writing and mailing manuscripts while working at a union typesetting company. He married and had one child, named William Patrick.

One pivotal night, Patrick was with a couple of his writing buddies, drinking scotch whiskey and playing at writing the *Sixgun Samurai* series. The next day, they drove up to Pinnacle Books in Los Angeles, where they walked out with a book deal. Patrick and his friends went on to write the series' twelve novels—which were also printed in the U.K. by Star Books, the paperback division of W.H. Allen & Co.

From then on, Patrick started writing and selling western, men's adventure, and military fiction. Years passed, and he had 24 published e-books with Piccadilly Publishing in the U.K.

Today, all six of Patrick's Wichita Detective books are getting another chance to see the light of day—with Rough Edges Press—and find refuge on a cozy shelf in Ocean Hills, California where Patrick and his beloved wife, Julie, live.

Made in the USA
Middletown, DE
28 September 2022